KEEPERS
OF THE
SEA CLIFFS

THE WINDBORNE SERIES

BOOKS BY LAUREL WANROW

The Windborne Series ~ for young adults

Double Rescue (prequel novella)

The Witch of the Meadows

Guardian of the Pines

Lost Whisperer of the Seas

Keepers of the Sea Cliffs

Solstice Gifts (holiday short story)

The Luminated Threads Series ~ for ages 15 & up

The Unraveling, Volume One

The Twisting, Volume Two

The Binding, Volume Three

The Luminated Threads Volumes 1-3 Box Set

Science Fiction Romance ~ for adults

Passages

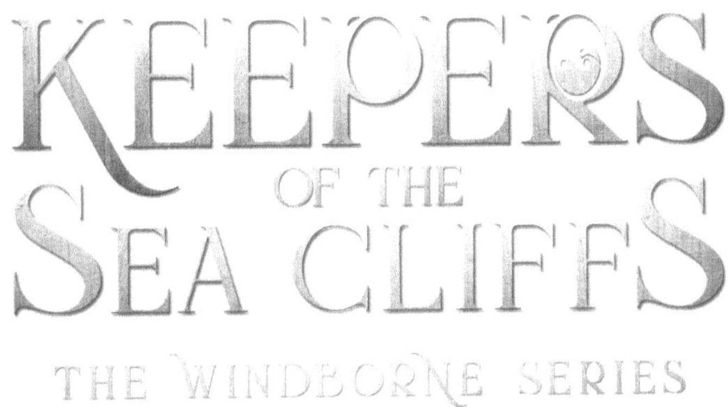

KEEPERS OF THE SEA CLIFFS

THE WINDBORNE SERIES

LAUREL WANROW

Sprouting Star Press

Laurel Wanrow/Sprouting Star Press
P. O. Box 2311
Reston, VA 20195
www.laurelwanrow.com

Copy Edit by Joyce Lamb
Cover Design by Deranged Doctor Design
Created with Vellum

Wanrow, Laurel

Keepers of the Sea Cliffs / Laurel Wanrow. ~ 1st ed.
ISBN 978-1-943469-20-8

First Edition: January 2020

For family.

1

IF EVERYTHING WERE PERFECT

North of the Windborne enclave of Tern Bay, on the Irish Sea
Early September, three weeks before the Autumnal Equinox Festival

A morning mist shrouded the Scottish coast, something Salm of the Seas liked to think of as his doing, a cover for him on his rounds. Truth was, it had nothing to do with magic, only the nights getting cooler as autumn came on.

The fog was, nonetheless, appreciated. If it hid Salm, or his arrival at *this* fishing boat for this surprise inspection, all the better. Honestly, he'd considered mutiny when Pop had assigned him to check out these sailors alone.

His only partners in this—backup, safety net or whatever he should call them on any given day—swam beneath the waves. The dolphins' torpedo-shaped bodies broke the surface at intervals, leading his flight through the damp fog.

See-low, the pod leader, sent him a message. *Close.* A distant splash against a boat's hull confirmed how close.

Stay underwater, Salm thought-spoke through his magic. *Position around the boat.* At his command, his trained dolphins could haul a rope, rock the hull or cause some distraction if he needed help.

The animals dispersed, and Salm flew cautiously forward. Most of the Windborne fishing boats the Seas family monitored abided by the conservation practices that they set out on the cooperative fishing waters. He and his father, Dolph, suspected that these witches did not.

After Salm's visit two weeks ago to collect their daily catch report—which had been brow-raisingly lower than any of the other boats working in the same area—they'd decided a surprise inspection a day early might reveal more. Pop was making his own inspection of another questionable fisherman, accompanied by another of their pods.

More sounds carried from the boat: the whine of the lobster creel hauler and then the *thunk* of a trap hitting a worktable. Salm slowed to the barest flutter of his feathered wings so he wouldn't blunder into their craft. The fog might as well have been his mother's chowder. Aye, it would hide his arrival, but then again, it might affect his ability to see what the witches were doing.

Pop had assigned him the smaller craft with fewer people on board. Captain Penny was new to their waters last season, though she'd come from a fishing family. Using the boat inherited from her father, she'd been friendly and agreeable as she set about teaching her daughters the business. On Mondays, she had another job. Without her on the boat, this could be a trickier confrontation.

The younger sister, Maeve, flirted awfully and hadn't stopped despite Salm telling her outright that he was seeing another lass. Even if he hadn't been, courting Maeve wasn't an option for him. Over a year ago, he and Maeve had tried merging their magic, but neither got along. She was willing to overlook that. He wasn't.

Those months had been a low point in his search for a partner. His ornery blue magic hadn't merged with anyone's…until he'd tried with Luna. His relief had soared with the gulls. Throughout the gray of winter, trapped with his parents and sister on the schooner, he'd come to fear his magic wouldn't cooperate with anyone's, he'd never have a special someone, he'd never have a family. Maybe at eighteenth year he shouldn't be thinking of those things, but after he'd checked the magic of more than a dozen witches, it'd begun to weigh on his mind that his older sisters had made courting look easy.

The gray silhouette of the boat emerged. Silently, he flapped higher and sent his family his status: *Arrived.*

From their family's schooner, Ma answered and so did his younger sister, Coral. *We've also sighted the boat we're to inspect,* she sent. Coral was tailing Pop, learning the ropes to approaching wily fishermen.

Salm hovered above the deckhouse. Below, the witches sorted through a trap's catch, tossing some overboard—likely crabs and undersize lobsters—and placing the keepers in a crate. He didn't see a gauge being used, but some folks did their measuring after the complete fleet of traps were hauled up, when the boat turned and the line of traps sank again to the seabed.

Maeve re-baited the trap, secured its hatches and handed it off to her older sister, Pauly, who stacked it with the others in the stern. Under the whine of the creel hauler that Maeve had started again, Salm lowered lightly to the roof of the deckhouse and folded his wings over the back of his rain slicker. *Hope they don't look up.*

The rope pulled up another dripping trap. Maeve leaned over the hull and manhandled the bulky D-shaped thing to the worktable.

Same thing again, Maeve dinnae inspect the bigger lobsters for eggs and none of them were returned. Salm watched for a third trap. Naught large released. Maeve finished filling the crate, moved it to midship and covered it. Not good. Odds were that out of three traps, at least one of those lobsters was a berried hen.

Aye, with the lobster season peaking, folks were busy. No time for recordkeeping, but apparently plenty of time to sneak around the rules that prohibited keeping the females with eggs carried on their undersides that would soon be ready to spawn.

Had he ever looked through their crates before? The top crates, but likely not the others. The Seas tended to trust their fishermen to follow the rules. When he'd seen the discrepancy in the catch reports, Salm's gut had clenched. The data from dozens of boats over decades of lobstering didn't lie. He should have been conducting more thorough inspections, rather than being in a hurry to escape Maeve's flirting.

Had it been a ruse to distract him?

Salm scrubbed his fingers through the beard he was growing. Last year, he'd been quite distractible when it came to lasses. He'd joked with them and laughed at their flirting. Today, he had to convince them he meant business.

As the creel hauler whined again, he lifted off the roof and let the boat drift out from under him. *Might be collecting berried hens,* he sent to his family. *I'm gonna go down and check.*

Blast, those greedy folks, Coral answered first. *What right do they think they have to compromise our fisheries?*

They've only been at fishing a year, Ma sent. *They probably don't realize how important the rules are.*

Coral grumbled something in return. Pop didn't answer.

Salm dropped lower to come in at boat level and flew up to the craft, calling, "Ahoy!"

The older sister looked up, met his gaze and dropped the trap she was carrying onto the others. He winced. The old-style wooden ones didn't take that kind of abuse without damage.

"Have a care, Pauly," Maeve shouted above the noise of the hauler without turning.

"Hoy, Salm," Pauly called loudly, as if issuing a warning—ha.

The whine cut off, and Maeve swung around, leaving the next trap tilted over the gunwale. Both lasses had the wide eyes of a tuna being run down by a dolphin.

He and Pop had been right. Now he just had to get his hands on an illegal berried hen.

Pauly darted a glance back to Maeve, then planted her fists on her hips. "Aren't you a day early?"

Salm landed next to the covered lobster crate before either could block him. "Aye, I suppose. We're busy this time of year and need the catch numbers to make a decision," he said politely, not daring to look down at the crate. "I can wait while you fill in the form. Just need through yesterday."

Pauly eyed him, then turned for the deckhouse. "Hold on."

Quickly, Salm lifted the cover off the lobster crate. All were dorsal side up, and he didn't want to start an argument by flipping and looking for eggs on spinnerets if he was wrong. "One or two look borderline small," he said and felt in his slicker pocket for his gauge.

"See here," Pauly said. "We do our sorting after. Makes the hauling go faster. Right, Maeve?"

Then Maeve was there, gripping his arm and leaning into him.

"Fine." Salm brushed off her hand. "But let's have a look, part of our checks. It's in the fishing agreement you signed."

Pauly stormed up. "Did you lay a hand on my sister?"

"What? No!" *Blessed Orb*. The accusation flustered him, but only for a moment. "I'm here to do my job. You can either let me inspect this catch here, or we'll head in and do it on the dock in Tern Bay."

"I—uh..." Pauly met Maeve's gaze—unmistakably thought-speaking with her—and a flash of light erupted.

Their magic hurled Salm over the gunwales and into the sea. The cold water stunned him. Then the life jacket he wore under his slicker tugged him upward, and a familiar prodding hit his shoulder.

Help? See-low asked.

Bilge-sucking catfish. Salm surfaced, spitting salt water. Blimey, he'd been caught unaware.

Splat. Splat. Lobsters were raining down.

Retrieve! Retrieve! he ordered the dolphins, and the water churned, excited squeaks filling Salm's head.

"Wizard overboard," Maeve crowed, and a life buoy landed near his chest.

He stared at it. *I dinnae want to give her* more *satisfaction.* But he felt like a drowned bird with his wings sopping like this. After shielding himself from Maeve's and Pauly's magic, he grabbed the ring, not making eye contact, because without a doubt he'd say something he'd regret. He didn't kick a single stroke, making the scallywags pull him in. At the side of the boat, he used magic to dry his wings, drew in their energy and dissolved them before he climbed on board.

He checked the lobsters in the now-half-empty crate before accepting the catch record that Pauly shoved at him.

"Anything else?" She smirked.

Aye, they thought they'd keelhauled him in this. *See-low?* he asked.

Retrieved.

"May I borrow a bucket?" Salm answered, and once they gave him one, he flew out twenty feet. He drew in his wings and dropped into the water again, calling, *Bring here.*

The dolphins filled the bucket with lobsters, and he had to magically net an additional three, each lobster a female with thousands of eggs under her tail. Those larvae represented the future of their fisheries. Once they hatched in the sea, some would provide feed for dozens of marine species, and in seven years or so, the rest would become lobsters big enough to harvest.

Salm belly-crawled onto See-low to get his back out of the water, magicked out his wings and dried himself *again* before lifting airborne. "These came from your boat," he shouted back to Maeve and Pauly. "Finish your haul of this line of traps and meet me on the dock."

"You can't prove those lobsters came from our boat," Maeve cried.

"She means," Pauly said, "that your dolphins brought those from the seabed!"

"It's my word against yours, and that's good enough to put you on probation for thirty days." Which wouldn't be nearly long enough after this insult—

Orb curse it! Beyond them duping him, this was a strike against him. He hadn't checked all the crates every time he'd been aboard this boat, an inexcusable loss to their fisheries that might have been caught months ago.

Taking one last look at the boat and the angry lasses, Salm knew he *had* to tell Pop. He'd go through the embarrassing explanation and take the public blame before the Tern Bay and Isle of Giuthas councils, because maybe Pop would have other ideas on how to snare these two for a stronger punishment.

Teach them to knock me overboard!

2

TACKING TOWARD PERFECT

Salm called his family during the flight into town. Pop met him at the dock. Before the council and an aerated tank of seawater holding nine berried hens, Salm sat with Pop through the sisters' harsh arguments. Then, upon their mother's arrival, the claim that her girls didn't lie.

This was going exactly as he'd feared.

It worsened when Pop asked for the town clerk to read back Salm's statement, and he dragged his fingertips through his beard, listening again to the humiliating tale of the dunking.

"Please send for Pete Smith," Pop said. "He's my second cousin once removed. Have someone go with him to our mooring on North Dock and call up our dolphins for their statement. Pete should understand enough of it."

Keenan, one of the council elders, did as Pop asked, wrote out Mr. Smith's translation of See-low's version of the boat inspection and brought the statement to the town hall. The newcomers hadn't realized that the word of a dolphin would hold in this enclave. The council suspended the sisters from their waters for this season and the next, which meant their mother could fish only with another crew.

Salm collected the lobsters while Pop signed the papers for the enclaves. At least he wouldn't be running into Maeve anytime soon. *If only Luna would agree to become my partner.* His work would be easier. His days would be freer. *I'd have someone to confide in, someone who knows me and would help me stand up for what's right.*

He and Pop walked down to the dock to direct the dolphins before they flew back to *The Peaceful Seas.*

"How was your inspection?" Salm asked. "Didn't interrupt it, did I?"

"We'd just finished. The fellow had sprained his ankle and coerced his twin brother to collect his catches for those weeks to keep up their income."

The brother hadn't understood that he wouldn't be penalized for good hauls and had lied on the report. They laughed over that. The fisherman swore everything else had been done according to their practices and submitted the true report. "He checked out fine today," Pop added.

"That leaves only one family out of sorts." Salm rolled his eyes. "In these lasses' eyes, I've pillaged their take and forced them to seek other work. I wouldn't put it past Maeve to tell the entire town she tossed me overboard."

North Dock was fairly empty of boats when they reached their usual mooring spot. With no one to overhear, Pop said, "A dunking isn't the worst that could have happened to you, though it certainly doesn't represent us well."

"I ken," Salm muttered. "But they'd never have blasted me if I'd had someone else with me."

"I glean you don't mean your sister. A partner, like your sister Wind now has in Bass?"

Salm nodded glumly. "I need time off to convince Luna to bond with me." When he'd confided his dream of owning and living aboard a schooner like his parents, Luna had protested that she couldn't leave her sisters. She didn't explain why. Luna didn't explain much about her family life.

"I don't understand why Luna can't leave home. The youngest sister is eleventh year, and their father works from home. It's not like we'd be moving to Ireland. Luna could see her family every week or so. She loves me, I know she does. But I haven't even formally met her father."

"How does Luna feel about your work?" Pop had met Luna when Salm'd shown her the schooner.

Salm couldn't answer.

"This work isn't easy," Pop said quietly. "'Tis a way of life you embrace like your one sister has, or leave like your other sister did. Have you told Luna about these less glamorous bits of our work?"

Salm *didn't* answer. Some, but probably not enough.

"I'm sure I do nae need to remind you to dress for town when you go calling," Pop said. "And a trim of your beard wouldn't hurt either."

"I ken," Salm growled. He didn't need these reminders at eighteenth year.

"She's certainly willing to spend a day with you." Pop nudged his side. "See if the lass will expand that. Your ma and I aren't working the week of Fest, so you could have off, too. Suggest to Luna that you spend it together and see what she says."

Salm grinned. "I'll do that." But his happiness lasted only moments before he sobered. "I should have been checking all of Captain Penny's crates, every visit."

"Are you doing so aboard every other craft?"

Salm kicked a pebble off the deckwalk. "The easier folks, I do. Several..." He counted. "*Five* captains give me a hard time. Another reason I'd like the backup."

"Our habitat canna maintain its productivity if hundreds of berried hens are taken each season."

Salm knew that *and* what he had to do to right this. "I have five more surprise inspections to conduct today."

Pop clapped him on the back. "Aye, mate. For my part, I will vary up our schedule so none know when to expect a visit in the future. If a bit more work is needed to run the figures differently, then I'll do it not to have folks dodge our policies." Pop lifted his chin toward the lighthouse. "After, see the lass if you can."

Aye, that was a plan. Seeing Luna would put the wretched morning with Maeve and Pauly from his mind. While they rewarded the dolphins with baitfish magicked from their supplies, Salm listed the captains of the boats he had yet to inspect, and his father suggested a few no-nonsense phrases to use.

"Until the end of the season," Pop said, "I expect you to conduct full inspections and submit a written report for each."

Orb curse it. His sixteenth-year sister had to make written reports. He hadn't made them since seventeenth year, when he'd passed his trial. Salm opened his mouth and closed it. The end of the season was in December. This was Pop's version of probation. If Salm couldn't enforce their conservation policies, it wouldn't matter that he'd grown up learning these ropes and wanted a life on the sea. As the Seas habitat manager, his father would deny Salm permission to work from his own boat until he had a better reputation among the fishermen.

"I ken," Salm muttered, and with a wave, Pop left.

Salm lay on the dock and gave himself a few minutes of petting the dolphins to clear his head before he contacted Luna. His close-knit family hadn't learned all of his secrets, like how it was the blessing of fair winds that he and Luna had easily mastered thought-speaking. That was one of the benefits that'd come with merging their energy so bloody well that he'd wanted to announce the magical achievement to every wizard he knew.

But he didn't dare. Luna might set his magic looping his

channels, but she hadn't agreed to live with him on board a boat *or* bond. Both were naggingly significant details. Despite his nineteenth birthday approaching, he couldn't get his own craft until he and his partner trained with his family and proved they could sail together in the worst of weather. Meanwhile, if either of them slipped up and let anyone suspect the depth of their merging outside a sanctioned Windborne bonding agreement—especially if her father caught wind—that would end the best thing to ever happen to him.

Luna?

Hmm, Salm?

Asleep?

Just drowsing. I've had hours of sleep because Papa took over watching the beacon for me last night. I have a job in town midday.

He could imagine her white-blond curls against the pillowcase and had to shake the image away. *I'm free later,* he sent her. *Meet me? I'll get Manta's boat if you'd like a sail.*

I'd like that, she replied, and they made the arrangements.

It took some hustling, but the pending meeting with Luna made him more efficient in approaching and inspecting the fishermen. Before the appointed time, he had his maps magicked from his cabin and his sister Manta's Sunfish sailboat rigged. Luna arrived at North Dock looking a dream, her fluffy hair captured beneath a broad sunhat and the lacy hem of her gauzy blue top fluttering around her linen trousers.

Spells, she looks so good. Even cocooned in a life jacket.

She flashed him a smile, her gray eyes hidden behind sunglasses, but her cheeks lifted, her head tilted impishly—

Orb take it, had he pushed that thought to her?

Aye, he had. He grinned back and stopped short of kissing her when she boarded the boat. He'd learned that lesson a year ago after hailing her in town. It was months before she'd acknowledged him again and weeks before he learned that she felt her pale skin and hair garnered enough extra attention without drawing more.

They set sail. Out on the open ocean, she leaned toward him on a long tack and chastely kissed his cheek before turning her face into the wind and sighing.

Enjoying yourself? he asked.

Quite.

They jibed southward against the wind so the return trip would be faster and were a cove past Kittiwake Point and the lighthouse before she turned to him again.

"I appreciate the opportunity to get out. Papa has been most difficult the last week."

"Because of me?"

"I've mentioned you, but..." She shrugged. "He's on us all about tidying up, which isn't an awful goal, except it's coming as I've had folks asking me to do home repairs in town. I need my own income, which Papa hasn't been able to argue down. Independence from him will allow me to build a life separate from Kittiwake Point. With Fest upcoming, I've had more inquiries."

"Maybe 'tis his way of preparing so he can enjoy the festivities," Salm murmured. This was as good an opening as any to ask her. "I have the week off at Fest. Would you like to spend time with me?"

Luna rolled her eyes. "If Papa doesn't find some errand or task he insists needs doing."

That was a *yes, but* answer. If he was going to succeed at convincing Luna they should bond, then he needed to draw her away from this town—for surely she'd take any opportunities for work that came up that week if they didn't leave. Besides, he wanted to feel like they were permanently together, and here, in Tern Bay, they couldn't act like they were. Folks knew they weren't. They'd draw looks. Possibly be reported. Depending on the individuals, wizards merging their magic could produce powerful energy. Thus, local authorities demanded the licensing records to track who was with whom in case of unexplained spells. To not be formally licensed was viewed as sneaking around.

Feeling as if a school of fish swam through his gut, Salm asked, "How about you go away with me?"

Luna eyed him.

Blessed Orb, she was going to say no. His stomach fish scattered.

"Where?" she asked.

Salm loosened the lines and let the sails go limp so they were drifting in the water. He retrieved his map case, unrolled the local map between them and pointed to several Windborne enclaves up the coast of Scotland or down to England that they might sail to.

Though her shoulder was against his now, she laced her fingers and rubbed her thumb over an old shiny scar on her wrist, half hidden by a woven rope bracelet that he'd made for her. "If we are on a boat, I feel you may spend our time pushing for me to come aboard your parents' schooner."

Aye, it might be hard not to. "Then…" He scanned over the map at the inland enclaves. "Bonterra is so big no one will know us. Or Loch Galloway is closer, though smaller."

"Loch Galloway." She nodded. "I've always wanted to see it. And we can rent a boat and do a day sail there, which should also satisfy you."

She'd agreed. Salm thrust the map aside and pulled her into his arms—as close as their life jackets allowed—and gave her the kiss he'd wanted to bestow upon her earlier. His energy swirled up, blue and strong and eager. Luna didn't disappoint him. Her silver magic frolicked over. They merged, magic combining in sparks and sizzles—all from his energy.

"Sorry," he muttered. "I'm the luckiest scallywag alive and can't wait to have you to myself."

"We're fairly to ourselves here," she whispered back.

They kissed, so deeply Salm's mind careened into the waves...

Then Luna was shaking herself free. "The shore," she choked out.

Hoy, the sound he'd thought was their energy was the surf and the gulls crying along the shoals. Salm snatched up the lines and the tiller and steered them seaward once more. Thank the Orb Manta's craft wasn't a keelboat. "How did you realize that?" he asked.

Luna laughed. "The birdcalls. These are your boating skills that you want me to put my life into?"

"Mine are beyond adequate when I'm nae distracted." He side-glanced at her. "Maybe for the first month or so, we'll stay at anchor in some hidden cove. Fishing for our dinner and only going to town when we run out of cornmeal and eggs."

"Sounds delightful." She scooted along the hull to sit beside him again, her arm around his back. "I'll get the time off at Fest, but you have to look respectable meeting Papa."

Salm's stomach lurched again. "Meet him... Are you sure?"

"I-I hope." She stroked a hand over his jaw. "Maybe shave?"

Well... It would be a small price to pay if Luna was agreeing. Salm cupped his hand over hers and kissed her palm. Shivers of her energy tickled at his lips. He grinned. "I can do that."

3

AGREEING TO THE IMPOSSIBLE

Windborne enclave of Tern Bay, on the coast of Scotland
Mid-September, the week leading up to the Autumnal Equinox Festival

Luna twisted her screwdriver clockwise, tightening the setscrew on the sink handle. She tested it, then cranked the cutoff valve.

"That's it?" demanded Lady Anemone, who'd been hovering in the doorway since she'd ushered Luna to the leaky loo sink.

"Should be." Luna turned on the faucet. The cold water sputtered a moment, then ran. She turned it off. Then on again. Off and on. It stopped clean each time. She washed her hands and dried them on the towel she kept in the pocket of her coveralls.

Lady Anemone uncrossed her arms. "Well, I'll be. Scallop was right. You are as quick as lightning with a repair."

Luna smiled, but inside gave a little sigh as she wrote the bill for the washer replacement on her receipt pad. Older folks in town had trouble accepting a woman who was handy around the house with things other than cooking and cleaning. She handed over the bill, and while Lady Anemone got her trade card, Luna packed away her tools.

After the exchange notes were magically credited and Luna's card was tucked into her tool bag, Lady Anemone eyed her speculatively.

Luna knew that look. "Let me know if there's anything else I can help you with."

"Do you have an extra few minutes?"

This was common, too—and a little annoying. Folks tested whether she could do one repair before revealing the list of everything they actually needed her to do. Besides being a woman, she was too young, they thought, at nineteenth year to be this skilled. She couldn't pass up a chance to completely win over Lady Anemone—being the town healer, the woman was a conduit for gossip in Tern Bay. If Luna pleased her, then word would definitely get around.

"Of course," Luna answered, careful to use her most pleasant tone.

"Come along." At the back door, Lady Anemone picked up her shawl, and Luna pushed her sunhat over the puffy ponytail tethering her curls.

She followed Lady Anemone across the back garden and down the alley. A few clucking chickens followed along for several houses until Lady Anemone shooed them away and opened the gate at the last one. The pale green house and bright yellow outbuildings in the enormous garden belonged to Mr. Smith. Luna knew who he was, same as she knew everyone in town, though she had never formally met the older man.

Lady Anemone climbed the back stoop and rapped sharply on the door. "Pete?" she called, then in a lower voice added, "A recent patient. Stumbled down the stairs."

Waiting, Luna surveyed the sea beyond the bay for signs of the Seas' schooner. Guillemots, cormorants and kittiwakes, but no sails. She'd hoped to see Salm before she headed home, even though he'd told her they'd dock near dusk, and that was hours away.

A robust man with his arm in a sling and his wrist wrapped came to the door.

Lady Anemone beamed proudly. "I've found your help."

"Keeper Jonah's lass?"

Luna froze her smile, though she wished someone, *anyone*, in town would acknowledge her by her name. They certainly remembered it, since she was *Jonah's lass* with skin and hair as white as the full moon.

"Dinnae let that trick your mind. She's capable, and everyone else in town is busy setting up for Fest, and I will nae come for tea again today and listen to you complain about that flat nae being ready to let out again." She pointed. "Or that garden spigot. You canna be wrestling with your slipshod backup with that wrist sprain."

Luna craned to see what was slipshod—oh. Water dripped into an overflowing bucket sinking into the muddy ground.

Pete Smith eyed her, the way most folks assessed her ability to do their repairs. Even Lady Anemone. He turned back to the older woman. "Ye could skip tea, if ye like."

Lady Anemone huffed. "I will not. The spigot will be my treat. Luna?"

Mr. Smith grimaced.

Oh, this exchange was too funny. She forced herself *not* to smile. "Where is your cutoff? In the cellar?"

"Upon the Orb, I'll have no peace. Fine, you seem to know what you're about. 'Tis below." He led the way to the sloping cellar door at the side of the house, but when he reached for the handle, Lady Anemone caught his good arm.

"Don't you dare. I don't need you repeating your antics. This lass can do it."

Wrestling loose, Mr. Smith put up a finger. "No magic?" he asked Luna.

"No magic," Luna confirmed. It was Tern Bay's town policy, but it didn't hurt for both of them to be up front. "All my repairs are true physical. Anything I work on can be manipulated by anyone else." Magical repairs often were jury-rigged things that another repair wizard wouldn't touch.

Luna found the cutoff and replaced the washer, thoroughly muddying the knees of her coveralls and likely her trousers beneath. It was worth it for the entertainment of Lady Anemone badgering her neighbor in the lovely, sunny garden. The older woman didn't hesitate to speak her mind, so unlike what Luna herself would do.

With the water on again, she confirmed the spigot was free of leaks, then emptied the bucket of water onto a row of late spinach.

When she returned, Mr. Smith had a key in his hand, and Lady Anemone waved her to follow them to the cart shed at the back corner of the garden. On one side, a sturdy wooden staircase took them to a newer upper level that overlooked North Dock, and Luna scanned the northern horizon again while Mr. Smith unlocked the door. Inside, the sunlight streamed through the many windows, falling brightly over furniture pulled to the center and covered with paint cloths in a combination sitting room and kitchen.

Luna removed her hat and looked around. "What a sweet little place."

"It should be," Mr. Smith grumbled. "However, my tenant moved out a week ago, leaving me with a list of repairs he never wanted to bother me with. Of course, now I canna do them and will miss my chance to at least rent the place during Fest and possibly even attract a new permanent tenant." He jiggled another doorknob across the room. The glass-paned door onto a small porch flew open. "This one latches only half the time. Don't know if ye can replace the knob, but I've got one there."

She plucked it out of a box on the counter. "Looks doable. And the other items?" She pulled out a showerhead and a tube of caulk.

He handed her a paper from his sling. "Replace that and the tub caulking, closet door is stuck open, drawer knobs are loose. The place could use a new coat of paint, but I..." He glanced at Lady Anemone.

"Not for two months."

Mr. Smith looked at the ceiling. "If ye could handle the other repairs today, and I'm nae able to let it immediately, perhaps ye could paint? How much would each be?"

She tested the drawers and closet door. "Let me have a peek in the loo." Heading down the hall, she added up the time it'd take. He had all the materials, which made the entire job easier. In the bathroom, she studied the tub. Because of the trip with Salm, she couldn't offer to paint. When she'd asked for this week off from monitoring the lighthouse, she hadn't told Papa she planned to spend it with Salm. Neither did Papa know they were going to Loch Galloway, but he would...right before they left.

As much as she wanted to go, she'd been dreading the conversation with Papa. She had to have it at the right time, when Papa wasn't drinking. He'd started keeping whiskey at home this summer, just when she'd gotten serious with Salm. Luna hadn't asked her father directly if that was the reason, and none of her sideways questioning had gotten him to confess what was bothering him. She hadn't dared to bring it up with her younger sisters.

"Is it that bad, dear?" Lady Anemone called from the hall.

"Aye," she muttered. "Who will care for Stella if I leave home for good?" Her youngest sister would be without her for five days while she was gone with Salm... If only Papa hadn't started drinking. *That* was another conversation—

Lady Anemone poked her head around the doorjamb. "Are you all right?"

Luna startled. The caulking—she really looked at it now.

"Uh, fine, thanks." She ran a fingernail along the tattered edge. "It looks half out already. No water damage below, is there?"

On the ground level, they checked the cart shed with a torch and found no signs of water. Mr. Smith seemed suitably impressed that she'd thought of this and agreed to her fee for the repairs. "Could you also do the painting?"

"I might be able to," Luna said, surprising herself. Why had she said that when she was to go away with Salm? She was looking forward to the trip...she thought. Five days with Salm also meant he'd have time to pressure her for an answer. She liked Salm. A lot. She just wasn't sure his plans for the future were right for her. Leaving her sisters, living on a schooner...

She hadn't seen him in two weeks, but now that work was coming her way, she hated to pass it up. She plastered on a smile for Mr. Smith and said, "I'll check my lighthouse schedule."

There. That would give her time to sort through her own confused thoughts about Salm and whether she truly should go away with him.

4

HOME SWEET...

Luna loved it when no one hung over her work, and this little flat felt cheery. Taking advantage of the fair autumn day, she left the porch door open after replacing the knob. The sea breezes cleared the stuffiness, and the cries of the gulls over the fishing boats kept her company like they did up on the point. The unobstructed view also made tracking the growing dot of a schooner easier. After caulking, she completed the other minor items, also tightening the drawer tracks and a few loose hinges. It was taking a little longer than her proposed time, but she wouldn't charge more for her lingering.

With the sun nearing the horizon, the air developed a nip. She went to close the door, but stepped onto the porch instead. *I'll just check the exterior...* The wind whipped at the loose material of her coveralls as she watched *The Peaceful Seas'* filled sheets propelling it southward. The schooner was still miles out, but she'd know it anywhere.

I could tell him I see him. She wasn't sure why she didn't.

Salm was...Salm. Sometimes, his exuberance overwhelmed her. He said and did unpredictable things. Sometimes, he made her laugh, but other times his antics embarrassed her. People already talked about her and her family and their nocturnal habits. When he wasn't being goofy, Salm worked hard and was considerate. But she couldn't shake the feeling that if they were together, she'd have to mind him like she did her sisters. And now, Papa.

Hugging herself, Luna scanned the door and window frames, both with what looked like a coat of fresh paint the color of marigolds. They looked fine. The place was cute, and a twinge of regret hit her as she packed her bag and locked the doors. What would it be like to call a place like this her own?

Being able to afford the rent fees to move out on her own had been Luna's goal in taking repair work. Following a few months of courting Salm, then breaking off with him last spring, she felt restless. Papa ordering her about like a child had become unbearable. She itched to do things her way. At nineteenth year, she was indeed free to do just that—except financially. Then she'd seen a plea to retrieve a ring from a sink trap three months ago and turned up with a thrown-together tool bag. Word of the ring's quick recovery had gotten around fast. It took longer for additional calls to come in, but her meager savings were growing.

She thanked Mr. Smith, pocketed her payment and let herself out of the garden. She'd just make it to dinner on time. Luckily, it was Nebula's turn to cook and hers to wash up. Folks crowded the boardwalks that fronted the shops and homes built up the cliffside. Many were strangers to Tern Bay, but then, setup for Fest would begin tomorrow. Luna ducked her head, letting the sunhat shield her face.

Beyond the last business on the southern edge of town, the ramp and beach were deserted, thank the Golden Orb. Tern Bay's rules prohibited flying only in town, but Luna often walked to the next cove if folks were about. Tonight, she didn't want to tarry. Stopping past Fintail's tavern, she put away her sunhat, unzipped her coveralls and shook her arms from the sleeves. Those she tied around her waist and then flipped her tool bag's leather harness over her shoulders and clipped it to hang at her middle.

Strolling onto the beach below the looming headland, Luna loosened her silver energy. It swirled over her back and formed white-feathered wings nearly her height. Spreading them, she checked the breeze off the water to prepare for flight.

A burst of conversation sounded on the tavern decking behind her.

"Wow," called the high voice of an awestruck kid, followed by a second, younger child's high-pitched calling of, "Mum! Mum! Mum!"

Curses. Another minute and she'd have been airborne and not as noticeable.

"*Shh,*" the mother hushed them. "She's a wizard, the same as you."

Aye, but pure-white feathers were rare among Windborne and always attracted attention. Luna's magic spread throughout her channels to buoy her body for flight, and she flapped hard, drawing additional squeals of delight, and rose with the wind. She circled with a warm thermal, letting it lift her alongside the headland known as Kittiwake Point. The family on Fintail's deck continued to watch, their eyes shaded against light reflected off the whitewashed cliff—a natural whitewash from the colonies of seabirds nesting here: guillemots, razorbills and the point's namesake, kittiwakes.

As she rose, their evening calls became distinguishable from the surf pounding the rocks below. Hundreds of birds swirled into the air, flying out and back again. Spotting her, they spun to circle her, wings everywhere, bills open in cries that merged into one piercing shriek. She flew straight through, letting them worry about missing her larger body and wings. Though she shouldn't really take the time, Luna reached out with spread fingers.

It was their game.

Their cries growing frenzied, the birds dove, racing each other for a dip below her hand and a pet of their head feathers. Still she rose, moving the target, always amazed at their skill in making contact, her heart swelling with each brush of feathered silk.

At the cliff top, the rocks greened with clinging grasses and shrubs. The land flattened out, topped by the gray stone tower of Kittiwake Point Lighthouse. The wide promontory was half again taller than the headland on Tern Bay's northern end, and the lighthouse raised its warning beacon another hundred feet. Since 1789, the light shone eighteen miles across the Irish Sea—strictly within their Windborne enclave—warning of the rocky shoals extending from the cliff's base.

Luna looked seaward once more. *The Peaceful Seas* was near enough that they'd begun lowering the sails. She'd asked Salm to wait until midnight to come calling at the lighthouse. By then, the routine of her family's night would be underway, and Papa would be settled after several mugs of tea. She glided over the undulating shadows of the moorland brush and landed within the stone-fenced yard surrounding the lighthouse and its attached keeper's quarters, her family home. Kitchen gardens lay to one side, a chicken coop and other stone sheds in the back, while the lighthouse sat squarely on the seaward side, a mere hundred feet from the edge of the three-hundred-foot bluff.

Inside, she dumped her tool bag among the wellies and fallen slickers at the back door.

Papa poked his head around from the kitchen. "A ball bearing needs replaced on the beacon's turntable."

Her lovely thoughts of meeting up with Salm dissolved, and Luna missed the hook to hang her sunhat. It fell to the floor. She used the time retrieving it to compose herself, because disassembling and reassembling the turntable mechanism to replace a cursed ball bearing had to be done during daylight hours. *Just when I'd planned to leave!* She slowly turned. "That didn't just go bad today."

"It got worse today."

"It'll last the week."

He opened his mouth, but Stella shoved under his arm. "Breakfast and I'm starved. *Come on!*" Her youngest sister stomped through the kitchen as only an eleventh-year witch could.

Papa turned, saying over his shoulder, "I want things in order for the week."

And I want to be free to set my own schedule. Luna smothered a scream before following. At least Papa didn't smell of whiskey. *I'll tell him about going away.* Immediately, her stomach clenched.

She squeezed past the stacked produce crates and bags of chicken feed they couldn't keep in the shed because of mice and skirted the slop pail someone had left instead of emptying. Pots and pans no one wanted to wash filled the kitchen sink, so she darted past the table for the washroom, her sisters' cries following.

"I have to wash up. Start without me!" She had to evict a cat sleeping in a sweater nest in the sink, but washing calmed her a bit, and finally Luna slid into her chair at the dining table. "Thank the Orb and you, Nebs! These potatoes smell heavenly." Luna had two bites of eggs and potatoes—the breakfast-type evening meal her father insisted the nocturnal family share—before realizing that no one had answered. She lowered her fork. "Sorry I'm late."

Her sister Nebula glared, nearly carrying off an adult version of a miffed cook in the floral apron she wore over a fancy blouse with lacy edgings. She'd paired it with too-short dungarees and striped socks that matched the ribbons woven through her blond braids, making her look younger than sixteenth year.

Luna glanced from Nebs to her father, pacifying words

already spilling. "I garnered an extra job, one I didn't want to pass up since people always find more that needs fixing during Fest. Word of my work should get around faster now."

Papa stirred his tea without looking up, the spoon dinging irritably with each turn of his large hand. He'd nicked himself shaving, and his blond hair stood up in back—he'd forgotten to brush it—and his skin was redder than his usual ruddy complexion. He didn't chastise her for being late, something he never let go of even after agreeing that she should earn her own income with her mechanical talents. *After all, I trained you for the skills to be put to use, not forgotten,* was his favorite line.

Filling the fourth side of the square table, Stella stood instead of sat, spreading butter on her bread like she was laying on mortar. Her braids also sported ribbons, green ones. She must have convinced Nebula to do her hair as well. The matching socks had to have been her idea, but where had those tattered dungarees come from? Nebula's? Oh. Papa also wore old work clothes—his painting clothes.

He added milk and a teaspoon of sugar to his tea. *Another* spoonful of sugar, she realized. The tea was practically colorless, the liquid to the brim, too full to even lift.

A feeling of dread stole over her, and Luna shivered in the warm kitchen. "What is it? Someone hasn't died?"

"We mixed whitewash for the shutters," Stella said. "Oh, and I saw a cormorant with plastic wrapped around his neck. Nebs doesn't believe me."

"That's not it." Nebula glared at Luna accusingly. "Papa's been waiting for you so he can tell us his news."

"What?" Luna asked again.

Papa glanced at her, then around the room, not directly at any one of them. He pulled a wrinkled sheet of paper from his pocket and unfolded it. The enclave's familiar flying tern logo graced the top.

"Is that the Fest schedule?" Nebula asked. "Let me see." She snatched at it, but Papa held it out of reach.

Was there something at the Autumnal Festival he wanted them to attend as a family? "Listen, Papa," she said carefully, "Salm is at anchor this week. We cleared my schedule because he's free."

Her father frowned.

"Surely you have nae forgotten?" Now did not look like a good time to bring up that she and Salm wanted to speak with him.

"This, ah, happened before, mostly." He smoothed the worn paper on the table—a schedule he'd obviously had for a while. Odd, because the only people who had the draft were on the town council. Papa wasn't. Oh, and the folks who had offered their services for the Fest this week. Her heartbeat sped up as a new worry rose beyond the problem of Papa stealing away her time with Salm.

"I, ah—" Papa cleared his throat. "Apparently, I agreed to hold tours of the lighthouse during Fest." He shoved the paper toward Luna.

Her breath caught. Indeed, tours of Kittiwake Point Lighthouse were listed. Three times on three different days. That explained the whitewashing. They'd need to clean the stairway. The tower windows. The yard. *Bullsharks.*

She read it again. *For the first time in a dozen years, Kittiwake Point Lighthouse and Quarters—*

"What? The keeper's quarters? Our home will be part of the tour?"

Stella squeaked, "Not *my* room!"

Nebula slammed down her fist. "You've got to be kidding."

"And quarters," Luna repeated. "No, Papa," she moaned and looked around.

The cutting board was the only cleared surface on the counter. The cupboards were so stuffed with books, old school papers, hairbrushes and lost mittens that they no longer closed. In the living room, overflowing end tables stood beside lumpy chairs upholstered in clean laundry and more cats. Wide windowsills were jumbled with shells, float balls and fish skulls found washed up on the beach. Swirls of dust along the baseboards led to a narrow path up the staircase between books, dishes and...*more things*. It was home, and it was a mess.

Luna put her head in her hands. Salm...their trip...but Fest was... "How will we clean...*this* in less than a week?"

5

PRESSING MATTERS

Eyes closed, Luna tried to push aside the arguments her sisters determinedly dredged up. Did she dare magically shut off her hearing to avoid the voices around the table?

"I've been asking you lasses what things of your mother's you want," her father was saying. "What we should store? What could go?"

Luna heard the sadness in Papa's voice. Logically, she saw his point.

"My old toys," Stella said. "My favorite books. That's what you asked me about. Not cleaning up so snoopy old witches can prowl through our home."

"We don't want to get rid of anything," Nebula ground out. "Especially not Mam's things. Not her boots that I wear when I canna find my good ones!"

"No!" Stella shrieked, and Luna wanted to shout with her. Nebs did anyway, and Luna understood perfectly. Those boots leaked, just like Mam's sweater was frayed, but Luna wouldn't ever give up the memories it brought her when everyone else had gone to bed.

"We dinnae need the broken teacups, the outdated spices,"

Papa said gently. "Even I have come to realize that when the things we use daily have no place. It's…hard. I have nae wanted to let go of Celeste myself."

Yet, when things Mam used were gone, would Luna's memories of her also fade? The last time she remembered the lighthouse being open for tours was a dozen years ago. While Mam was still alive. Mam had loved giving tours and showing off their home and work.

"No one likes to clean," he whispered. "Sometimes, it just has to be done. Aside from the excuse of the tours."

The tours and the people. Luna didn't like attention. She wanted quiet…the complete opposite of Salm. *Then, do I want to be with him?* That sense of not knowing what she wanted chewed through her again. *I need this week with Salm. I need to know how we would be together for more than a few stolen hours over too few days.* If she couldn't make up her mind soon, she would lose Salm. And now Papa and his cursed promise threatened to take the choice out of her hands.

Opening her eyes, Luna lifted her head. "When did you agree to put the lighthouse on tour?" An edge had crept into her voice. "And why?" she added, trying to keep her voice as quiet as his.

Papa pushed back from the table and crossed his arms. "It weren't my idea, you ken? Old Pete suggested it at the planning meeting a year ago. I said no. Then about every other meeting, Elder Bentha would bring it up. Good publicity, she'd say. Help us draw more folks to Tern Bay's turn at Fest. Pridelike kinda talk. We have so few public buildings for visitors to moon over. No one would let it go. Then they cornered me-like, in the tavern."

Nebula's eyes narrowed. "You mean it was a dare?"

"No. Well…" He eyed them. "Something like that."

"Over a pint?"

Papa frowned.

Meaning it was.

"You know Bentha and her partner. Said I was trying to drag us in the hole for this year. Said we weren't proud of our place. I let that so-and-so know we have never, in the twenty-one years the Ness family has run the Kittiwake Point Lighthouse, had our flame dark."

He'd been shamed into it, then. Certain folks in town were good at that. Resigned, Luna said, "It's done. Not a dare, but it's agreed to. On the schedule. It'll be harder now to get out of it than to do it."

"Are you sure?" Nebula asked sarcastically.

Luna didn't need to look around more to verify Nebs wasn't exaggerating. She'd lost her appetite. Luna stood, got a bowl to cover her plate and put it in the refrigerator. At the sink, she ran hot water into the cooking pots. Then she returned to the table to collect the serving dishes. Her sisters were still sitting there. She hadn't heard Papa go upstairs, but dusk had fallen.

"Luna?" asked Stella. "When will we do this?"

"*How* will we clean it in a week?" Nebula repeated Luna's earlier question.

With a sigh, Luna perched on the edge of her chair. "Starting tonight, of course. We have"—she counted to make sure—"six more days, not counting today, until the celebrations and tours begin. We'll do the best we can. With magic."

Stella sucked a breath, her face lighting up.

"Papa won't like that," Nebula said, yet she was smiling, too.

"Papa is the one who got us into this mess. He won't say anything." She moved a few dirty dishes. "Mam wouldn't have liked it either, and that's what's really bothering him. The house never looked like this while Mam was alive. We don't have her…"

"What? Determination? Training?" asked Nebula. "Don't say it's because she died and didn't finish teaching us—that's what Frannie says."

Aye, Nebs' critical friend would say that. "Don't let him see you using magic until I can talk to him."

Nebula crossed her arms. "He'll say we don't have the energy to spare."

They didn't. Working with mechanical equipment didn't generate magic. Windborne wizards created their energy through interactions with the land, its plants and animals. Luckily, running the lighthouse covered their family's contribution to the Tern Bay enclave's shielding, as well as earning Papa pay in trade credit. "Gardening and outdoor chores will create a bit of magic. See if we have any garlic bulbs to put out. Pet the chickens and herd them to the corners of the yard to search out bugs instead of just scattering feed. I'd contact Mr. Grouse and see if he has any rescue birds in need of care, but I dare say we don't have the time."

Stella huffed. "Then we can't use magic? Wait, we can go after that bird I saw!"

Luna glanced at the clock, its hands showing half past six. "Salm is due here in five and a half hours. It's been two weeks since I've seen him, and I'm not missing my time with him."

Nebula snorted.

"Luna and Salm," Stella began singing, "sitting in a tree, K-I-S-S-I-N—"

Luna pointed a glowing finger. Stella ducked.

"Remember, I might not have much, but the magic I do have is lightning hot." Any mention of lightning sent Stella scurrying for her covers. She hated storms. Luna stood, removed her hair band and fluffed her hair. "Start by returning all your belongings to your rooms. Carry them up. We'll have to save our magic for larger jobs. Kitchen, living room, stairs, anything on this level goes up. Or out." She started to flick her finger, then stopped, physically went and fetched two empty crates to the front door. "Put anything you don't want anymore in these. We'll donate to the Fest's flea market."

Stella groaned. "Taking all this stuff up will just mess up our rooms, and then they'll see that."

"Our rooms are all alike. Showing one is enough."

"Papa's?" Nebula asked, too gleefully.

Probably not, but they'd deal with it tomorrow. "I'm going up to see about that bearing. If he'll talk, I'll get more information from Papa. In the meantime, you two start." She poured tea in Papa's giant mug. One of them took it up to him each night.

As she'd expected, Papa had the beacon already turning when she climbed to the top of the lighthouse. The lower casement windows were open to the balmy evening, but the grating sound coming from the light's base canceled any sense of peace that should have descended with the sun. Her father made a halfhearted gesture toward the turntable and continued washing the windows, a frown furrowing his lined face.

Oh stormy nights. The rumbling indicated the bearing had worsened, and she couldn't replace it at night. The lighthouse had to stay operational until dawn. She set aside the mug, picked up an oilcan from the ledge and dropped to her knees beside the rotating mechanism.

Papa already had it well oiled, but she added more anyway, charting her course for the morning as soon as he shut off the beam. She'd remove the cover to get at the ball bearings, clean the pieces, replace them and—barring any trouble—reassemble it. Therein lay the uncertainty: Would she find anything else wrong? Would the two-hour job extend to four, or the entire day? She had to keep the day available, just in case, because come nightfall, that beam had to be operational.

That meant she and Salm couldn't leave tomorrow.

Luna straightened. Papa didn't look around. She stood there, debating whether to tell him that her plans for her week off had included going away with Salm, then pivoted. Nothing she said would be civil yet. She'd find the replacement ball bearings. Get her tools up here. Maybe she'd feel calmer after another trip up and down the six-story stairwell.

She didn't.

Now Papa was out on the catwalk, cleaning the outside of the windows. How would he react to what she wanted to tell him? She set out the tools she'd need on the floor, then rearranged them. How was Salm going to react when she told him she couldn't leave tomorrow? Luna wrinkled her nose. Salm was a hard worker and easygoing. He'd understand that work to keep the lighthouse operational came first.

She hoped.

Luna picked up Papa's forgotten mug, magically heated the cooled tea and slipped outside with it. The tide was going out, the rhythm of the waves just background noise in the still night. Papa's arm swept mechanically, without enthusiasm, and in the rotation of the beam, his face looked more lined, the skin below his eyes dark and sagging.

"Papa? When will you admit that running the lighthouse alone is too much for you? The schedule might say Nebula and I are assigned two nights, but you're up here for part of each one."

He accepted the mug. "I canna sleep nights after decades of a nocturnal schedule."

"Uncle Rigel wrote at summer solstice that he'd slowed his business, only partially to spend time with Cousin River before she goes to academy. Last year when we visited, he admitted he napped every day—at fifty-second year. You're the same age. You can admit you need help, just as I can admit that I don't want to be your full-time replacement."

Papa sipped his tea and stared down at the sea.

Mentioning Mam's brother brought another idea to her. "Ask Uncle Rigel to come watch the lighthouse again." Her uncle had done it when they went for a trip to the States. He'd required minimal training because he and their mother had grown up in a lighthouse-keeper family. "It's been years since we got away for more than a day. Please. Take a real break so you can sleep."

Her father didn't respond.

Papa had said nothing about her canceling her week off. Should she tell him about the planned trip? She and Salm might still be able to leave in the evening, if the repair came off. Luna bit her lip, thinking. Better to talk to him tonight, then tell her father tomorrow, after she'd garnered his good graces with the repair. She paced the catwalk to the door, but hesitated, looking back toward her father. He met her gaze this time.

"You've been upset about preparing for visitors," she said kindly. "Is that why you're drinking more?"

"What I do in my off-hours are nae a concern of yours," he snapped.

Luna gripped the railing. She'd guessed correctly. "Papa, I won't always be here to take care of things. Stella needs—"

"Have you gotten the lasses going on cleaning?"

Exasperated, Luna fled down the stairs. If she went away with Salm and left preparing for the tours to Papa, would he drink more? Could Nebs and Stella manage…

Downstairs, the disarray in the kitchen hadn't changed. The living room looked worse. Nebs was gone. One of the crates had a cat in it, the other a sock. Luna plucked out the sock and tossed it at Stella. "That wasn't for laundry."

Stella held up a book. "Oh, Luna, look what I found!"

"If you're keeping it, take it to your room." She toed the collection of books around Stella into a pile. "With these. Go." Stella yammered something back, but Luna stomped to the kitchen and banged through washing the pots and pans so she couldn't hear anything.

No, her sisters couldn't manage the cleaning. *I'm not sure I can.* Luna lifted her gaze to the deep windowsill above the sink, one cluttered with knickknacks and ripening tomatoes. In the back sat a framed photo of Mam holding her and baby Nebs.

I know I promised, Mam, but this is terribly hard. How am I to start my own life?

After the dishes, Luna cleared the table and began on the counters, staying out of the way of Nebs and Stella drifting through the downstairs rooms. Stuff was definitely moving, but the crates remained empty. Papa had a point about throwing out old spices...and maybe sorting the pantry? If the baking tins fit in, then they'd have the counters cleared. She'd emptied half the pantry's contents onto the counter and the rest into the compost bucket and was wiping down the shelves when two raps came at the door, followed by two more.

Luna's gaze shot to the clock. Midnight.

Salm.

6

FISHING FOR HOPE

Shouts leaked from behind the closed door of the keeper's quarters. Salm cocked his head—no, he shouldn't eavesdrop. He backed off several steps. Had Luna told her father already? Then he should knock louder and divert Keeper Jonah's anger. Salm stepped to the door again and put his ear to the crack.

Nay, 'twas witches yelling.

"Why do you get to go out, and we have to work?" the youngest shrieked.

"I'll do my part when I come home," answered Luna.

"Then we can wait until—"

"I'm the oldest," she ground out. "You're to do what I say. Papa says."

Salm smiled. He liked that about Luna, how she knew precisely what to do and just took charge. Sailors needed that upon the seas. One never knew—

The door opened. He stumbled back and caught a glimpse of Luna…in time for the door to close again. She wore her coveralls, dirtier tonight than he'd seen them. Her hair had sprung loose, and something smudged her face on one side.

Blow me down. His smile faded. His fingers twitched over his leather waistcoat, tugging it down over his clean trousers. Clean shirt, too, cuffs even buttoned, his best clothes. Did this mean she didn't want to see him? Then what about their plans—

The door opened again, and Luna squeezed through a crack before slamming it closed. His hopes rose at the sight of her in fresh clothes, and he started to smile again, started to say what he'd planned—"I'm happy to see you"—but her pale-eyed gaze glanced off him like a gull wheeling from the bow, and instead he asked, "What's wrong?"

He regretted it before she even had time to mutter, "Nothing."

That was always her answer. He'd known Luna four years, maybe more if he really thought about it. But not until he'd turned fifteen did he start to notice the witches in different ports and come to know Luna better. Her short answer was Luna through and through: sweet and strong, ready for any adventure he proposed. But she didn't talk about herself. And never about her family.

In the dark, a dusting of silver magic sparkled on Luna's skirt and in her fluffed curls—oh, he wanted to dive his fingers into them. More shed from her hands as she wrapped her arms around herself, hugging the sweater covering her shoulders, though it wasn't cold.

She wasn't inviting him in, that was for sure. Which meant they weren't speaking with her father—oh, hoy. "You told your father that we planned to go to Loch Galloway?"

She walked a few steps from the house, shaking her head.

Blimey. He didn't blame her. Speaking with a lass' father was as scary as walking the plank, but to ask to take one away for the week had made him feel like shark bait. So...they still needed to break the news together. Following Luna, Salm checked his good clothes again, then flicked his fingertips. His energy sparked, taking the edge off his nerves. This caught him broadside. Luna was often quiet when they met after weeks apart, but this time, he'd thought their plans were firm: He'd arrive, they'd talk to Keeper Jonah and be off for the week together.

She hadn't told him *not* to come up. This was awkward. Usually, they met on the dock and flew to the moor or walked on the beach. And kissed.

Kissed a lot.

Clearly, she wasn't in *that* mood tonight. In that way, she was like their dolphins, having to be cajoled into the right frame of mind to work with him. Maybe all lasses were. He'd gotten only close enough to Luna to learn that sometimes he had to wait— and still he didn't get it right every time. But he was trying.

He angled around her frozen form and brushed aside the fluff of curls from her downward-tilted head. Her round face was bunched in creases, her lashes lowered, gaze not meeting his.

Ah, blast it all to the bottom of the sea. He wrapped her in a hug and kissed what was available—her forehead. She might have changed her mind about the trip, but he wasn't about to let her forget what they had. He let his magic loose. Blue strands swam from his fingertips and flushed over her. In answer, Luna's silver magic stirred, then flushed, brightening her skin for a nanosecond, then retreating but leaving her hair whiter than it already was.

She leaned into him, arms still crossed and stiff. "Can we go somewhere else?" she whispered.

He clasped her elbow and steered her away from the cliff where the lighthouse perched, past the sheds and through the gate in the stone wall surrounding the keeper's yard. With the wind to their backs, they walked inland across the moor. "Let's fly," he murmured in her ear.

She nodded and unfolded her arms, letting her warm hand slide into his.

He threaded their fingers, and then they unfurled their

wings, his dark brown like his hair, her feathers pale like her hair. They had to move to arm's length so their primary feathers wouldn't hit each other, but she squeezed her fingers tighter around his. He gave an answering squeeze, and they began to trot.

A salty draft coming up and over the cliff caught under their feathers. Two flaps, three, four, and they arced their wings and glided. The wind rushed over them, making conversation difficult, which was the plan behind his suggestion. Salm took a slight lead, breaking way with Luna in his lee. When he flapped higher, she did, too. When he turned, so did she. They skirted the edge of the cliff, letting the ocean breeze take them southward away from the lighthouse. It would have been nice to just keep going, but Kittiwake Point was near the boundary of the enclave's magical shielding, so they soon circled and headed inland.

Much later and farther away—on the northern side of Tern Bay—he chose a sheltered spot among some boulders and out of sight of the harbor, where *The Peaceful Seas* was docked. They'd sat here on his previous visits to port, talking and kissing. Tonight, he wouldn't say anything about ships or sailing with him. Whatever the reason for why they weren't talking to her father, he wanted her to bring it up.

He drew a breath and steeled himself. First night back in each other's company—he had no right to assume they'd be kissing either. Tomorrow. Tomorrow would be soon enough for kissing.

"That was fun," he started. "It's great to see you again." Somehow, his arm went around her shoulders.

She turned, her face inches away, and she smiled. "You, too."

Might as well get the question off his chest. "No trip to Loch Galloway, then?"

Some emotion rippled across her face. "We have a repair to make on the beacon turntable." She described the problem and that it'd take both her and her father to dismantle the mechanism.

"Why Tern Bay still uses this old-fashioned device when solar power is available is a mystery to me," Salm said. "You should consider it."

"They've been round and round about it," she retorted. "The council didn't think our weather would reliably support it. It's not like going without your evening reading lights if we had a run of cloudy days." Luna crossed her arms.

Sink your own ship, mate. "No offense," he said quickly, but he didn't quite understand why she was so upset. "If we can't leave tonight, then after the repair is completed?"

"There's the bearing and...other things. Papa...I canna ask right now."

He stopped himself from blowing out a breath. "I ken you dinnae want to cross your father, but at nineteenth year, 'tis nae a matter of *asking*. You simply need to *tell* him—"

"Trust me, Salm, I know what I need to do," she huffed. "It was a nice idea," she said a minute later and more softly. "And I'd like to someday, but right now it doesn't feel right to go off together...not bonded."

Salm had offered to bond with her—prebond in their case, since both of them were under twentieth year—to make things right in her father's eyes. *She* was the one refusing. Question was, when would Luna confront Jonah Ness?

I dinnae want to fight with her.

Apparently, Luna didn't want to fight either. She kissed him, light and quick, before nestling into his side. He hugged her tight and pressed another kiss to the top of her head. They stared seaward, the closer waves glinting in the few lights of Tern Bay. Seventeen miles across the Irish Sea, the two mountain peaks of his home island, the Isle of Giuthas, were dark silhouettes against a starry sky.

"How have you spent your days?" she asked quietly.

He described the trips inspecting the Windborne fishing boats, and a bit of guilt pinged at him. He still hadn't told Luna how difficult some of the Seas work could be, like his confrontation with Maeve and Pauly. *This week...* "We've had a few new folks move to the isle," he said instead. "We're still chasing ocean rips, but with their energy, they'll be easier to repair."

"Good," she murmured.

He'd rather get on with making new plans. "I canna believe we both wrangled a free week before Fest."

"And the dolphins?" she asked.

He frowned. "Ah, there's a funny thing. One pod has ranged farther than usual, and we've lost touch with them. Hope they'll turn up, or we'll have to look for them. Would you like to sail with me to do that?"

"Perhaps later in the week." Her answer was light, but her body stiffened against his.

He'd talked long enough. "How are things in town? You've had a lot of work?"

"With Fest coming, aye. Smaller projects townsfolk have put off too long."

"Like?"

"Beyond the boring stuff? Shutter repairs on the rooms facing the main deckwalks. Ensuring gates will latch before the Fest hordes descend on us."

"Aye." He laughed. "Far more interesting than hemming sails and replacing lines, my most common repairs."

"How's your family?"

"Scattered like autumn's leaves for the week. What do you say we watch the sunrise one day, the sunset another, then spend high noon on a secluded beach and midnight on the moor?"

"But Manta and Piper are still in town?"

It finally sank in. "Luna," he said in exasperation. "Are you avoiding making any plans with me?"

"I, um, I'm not sure I can." She turned away.

He tugged at her hand until she looked at him. "You can't, or you don't want to? Have I *completely* put you off, asking you to come aboard *The Peaceful*?"

"No, it's not...maybe, but that's not..." She drew a deep breath. "It's not you. It's my family."

Argh. This was an answer he'd heard before. If they didn't begin to share their problems, how could they hope to live together? "Anything I can help with?"

She shook her head, managing to look away again.

He cupped a hand around her neck and drew her lips to his. At first, Luna responded halfheartedly. He deepened the kiss, stroking the line of her jaw with his finger, trailing a bead of blue energy. She shuddered, and her lips moved with a fierceness that he welcomed. They clung together, as close as clothes allowed, heat rising, mouths crushing each other, but when he moved to correct the obstacles standing in their way—obstacles he had corrected before—she clasped his hand. They broke apart, breathing heavily into each other's faces.

"That was sneaky," she panted.

"'Twas either sneaky, or we'd lose our time together tonight."

"Tonight has already been lost." She let out a long sigh. "Papa let some pushy old barnacles on the Fest planning committee persuade him to put the lighthouse on the tour."

"That'll be fun to see. I haven't been up those circling stairs since I was small."

"Exactly." A gloomy edge clung to that one word, and before he could reason why, she added, "And our home."

What was the problem *exactly*? "I suppose it's a historical building? Folks like those on the Fest tours." But she didn't answer. "Does this have anything to do with why I've never been invited in?"

She crossed her arms. "Our place is a mess. Now we must spend the *days* beforehand cleaning."

Ah, that was the problem. She felt she couldn't do anything else but help her family. Salm flexed his shoulders, releasing their tension. "I'm a fair hand at that. Let me help."

She shook her head again, and it felt like the current had ahold of him and would drag him under. He didn't understand why she didn't want his help, and clearly more questioning wouldn't get her to explain.

"Answer me this," he said carefully. "Do you still want to be seeing me? I do nae mean this week. I mean, at all?"

Her head swung around. "Aye," she said firmly.

His breath released. "Thank the Blessed Orb. I have to assume that's not our magic talking, since neither of us had it out this time." He captured her hand again. "I want to see you, too. It's a precious chance to get to know each other better." He moved in, but she leaned back.

"This is not how I want you seeing me, amid my family's horrible inability to maintain a home. You'll only come away knowing what the rest of the town already believes—that Jonah didn't do right by raising his daughters on his own."

Salm laughed. "Be assured, I have absolutely no issues with this daughter."

She gave him a light shove with a bit of spark in it, and he laughed harder.

"This isn't a joke. You haven't seen it." Luna rose, brushing her skirt like she was about to go. "We could spend the week just emptying the house."

He scrambled to his feet. "At least we've gotten to the bottom of your problem. And it's not me." Thank the Golden Orb. "I can help batten down your hatches."

Luna threaded her arms around his waist and pulled him close. "No, it's not you. I'm so sorry—"

"Nothing to apologize for." His lips trailed over hers in

another kiss. After a few minutes, they were sitting again. His head was muddling, his energy humming, and yet earlier she'd indicated *no more*. Made it clear she had to get home. Salm pulled back, his arm still around her shoulders, but with some space between them so the ocean breezes cooled things off.

He'd gotten an agreeable answer: She still wanted to see him. Yet the way they'd been seeing each other, a few stolen days every month, was too slow for him. Too little. He rested his forehead to hers. "Then we will not be talking to your father about going away for a week. But can we talk to him about *us*?"

Luna sighed. "Not tonight. I must go back and fix things."

"Tomorrow?"

"We will be cleaning."

"Luna. I won't pressure you about coming on board *The Peaceful*, but there must be some midway step that we can take. At least making your father aware that we have a *serious* interest in each other and plan on setting a course for our future."

She stood up. "Later this week."

He snatched her hand. "I said I'd help. I meant it. What time tomorrow?"

"No, we couldn't ask you—"

He put a finger to her lips. "If it's the only way I can see you this week, I want to."

She brushed off his hand, her fingers landing inadvertently on his bicep to hold him away. With a grin, he flexed the muscle.

"Maybe..." She shifted her shoulders. "We *could* use help carrying things to the sheds. Outside the house only. Give me time to organize things. Midafternoon."

It wasn't a week away in Loch Galloway, but it was a week together with lines out to hook the loveliest witch he'd ever met. He bent in and kissed her. "I'll be there."

7

ALL HANDS ON DECK

Daylight crept through the clouds, propelling a yawning Luna up the lighthouse tower. As soon as Papa halted the turntable's rotation and extinguished the beacon's flame, she fitted a wrench to the first bolt on the cover for the ball bearings. She'd sleep better after this was completed and she had a firmer idea when she'd be able to meet up with Salm for something fun.

Last night, she'd made splendid progress putting the kitchen back together, though the main room had only gotten worse. While Nebula watched the beacon for a few hours, Papa had continued cleaning the lighthouse tower. He'd dusted, swept down the 156 steps and five landings, then polished the brass handrail and half the spindles. He'd finish tonight and start on the office. Stella had disappeared, claiming to be cleaning her room.

The quarters were large, designed for a family and difficult to keep up. *Nothing like that sweet flat at Mr. Smith's.* Or a boat.

Luna put the thought from her head—this was at least a start!—and pulled on the last bolt head. It was stuck. She added oil and tried again.

"Let me," Papa said behind her. It didn't budge. "Was it nae threaded right during the last...oh."

She glanced at him, puzzled. Then, as her father pointed a finger to the bolt and applied a dose of his blue-green magic, she understood.

"I thought we agreed—" she started at the same time he said, "I ken we agreed—"

He glanced at her sheepishly. "The bolt threads are too worn. This was meant to hold it until a replacement bolt arrived, but..."

"You never ordered the replacement."

"Believe me, I will nae forget again."

"This is something for the logbook," she reminded him gently.

"I dinnae doubt it's there," he huffed.

And it was, the notation made during a week months ago when he'd worked seven straight nights and neither of them had reviewed the entries. By midmorning, she and Papa had replaced the bad ball bearing, jury-rigged the bolt with epoxy and magic and put the mechanism back together.

"If the last held for months," she said, "this will make it a week."

Papa shook his head. "Canna risk it. I'll be at town hall myself when they open, place my order and request the council send someone for it today."

Oh. They had the elders send someone for parts only if it was urgent. "Fest?" she said.

Her father scowled.

"It doesn't have to be perfect. Just operational—"

"On my watch, it does." He pivoted and descended the spiral stairs.

She lifted her hands helplessly. Spells. And she'd missed her chance to broach the subject of getting away with Salm. She set aside the tools they'd need again tomorrow morning and took herself to bed.

At noon, she forced herself downstairs. Papa's bedroom door was closed. In the kitchen, she couldn't find a note. Would the bolt be here today or not? She didn't dare wake him. Papa's breakfast dishes were in the sink. With a glance toward the stairs, she picked up his mug and sniffed.

Whiskey.

Argh. If she'd found the bottle last night, she would have gotten rid of it. She woke Nebs and Stella, half thinking to ask them to look for the whiskey, too, but thought better of it. That confrontation had to be private. She didn't want to involve her younger siblings in Papa's drinking.

"'Tis a nice day," Luna announced as she spooned porridge into three bowls. "We'll move things to the shed. Clean the yard, too, I think."

Hours later, she wasn't sure they'd ever get outside, except to carry crates to the shed. Luna stood in their front doorway and surveyed the main room of the keeper's quarters. They'd cleared the corners, the tables and the shelves. Hidden among their things, they'd uncovered the brass compasses, altimeter and spotting scope that had been passed down by prior lighthouse keepers.

Nebula set the altimeter on the coffee table. "People will like looking at these," she said. "The maps, too." The framed, historic coastline maps had been stacked in a cupboard.

They would, except... "If we have more than three visitors in here, they won't be able to get around each other." Fingers raking back her curls, Luna scanned the room again. "Some furniture has to go. Nebs, help me carry the armchair to the shed."

Stella pouted. "But Miss Kitty loves that—"

"It'll come back in after the tour," Luna said impatiently. "Bring that crate."

They managed to wrestle the chair to the slates outside the front door before Nebs pointed out that the shed had no more room.

"Then we sort it next. Let's get the dresser out, too." The oak dresser easily slid to the doorway on rags, but once Luna and her sisters lifted it over the threshold, it was too heavy to carry farther. "Leave it," Luna said. "We'll have to wait until Papa wakes up for work this evening." Or if Salm was sincere, for his arrival.

"Thank the Orb." Nebula flopped into the cat-scratched armchair.

Indeed. Yawning, Luna folded her aching arms on the dresser top and closed her eyes.

Bam!

Luna jerked upright.

Stella had dropped another crate beside them. "I'm not carrying stuff if you lot have quit."

Stormy nights. Luna fell against the furniture again, fixing her sister with her *I'm in charge* look. Four hours of shifting through stuff—as well as shifting Nebs and Stella—sent her thoughts toward bed again.

Stella glared back just as hard. A shadow crossed overhead, and they both looked up. Squealing, Stella ducked.

Luna opened her arms and caught the small gull as it flew to her. "Rissa." She sighed. "Still here?" Every time the young black-legged kittiwake came around, she expected it'd be the last. His colony that nested on the point would be migrating to the open sea any day now.

"How come he never flies to me?"

"You shriek too much."

"So does he," Stella muttered. "If I could find my cormorant, he'd be nicer after I helped him." Though Nebs had said she hadn't seen plastic on any of the birds that had flown over the yard, Stella insisted that she had.

They ought to search, even if it was to appease Stella, but they couldn't afford the time…at least this week.

"They're wild birds, not pets. Some birds never appear to be grateful for our help," Luna tried to gently remind her. "If you see the cormorant again, you call me while you keep track of him." She petted Rissa's gray back, then hefted him. He was a good weight for migrating. The black collar of a first-year juvenile still streaked his neck, a little fainter than when Mr. Grouse, a Windborne ornithologist, dropped the thin orphan chick by for them to rear. Rissa, named for his genus, *Rissa tridactyla*, flapped heartily when she tossed him into the air. He circled right back around, jeering at them.

Luna ignored him, not because she wanted to, but because she had to if he was to leave with the rest of his colony. "Is that the last of the crates?" she asked Stella.

"No."

"Then let's fetch them." She gestured toward the house.

Nebs propped her feet on the crate, and Stella climbed onto her lap.

Luna stomped through the doorway and leaned against the inside wall. After she took a few breaths, calm returned, and she could open her eyes. Removing the furniture had cleared the front room, except for a small table that also had no proper place.

She picked up the table and carried it outside. "Bring a dresser drawer each," she said as she walked past her sisters.

Stella whined.

"I'll make us second breakfast," Nebs offered.

"After you bring the drawers," Luna called over her shoulder.

They brought the drawers and left them outside as she tried to make room for the table. Biting back the urge to yell for Stella, she returned for the crate her sister had left. It'd be simpler to do the shuffling in the shed by herself.

"Ahoy!"

Startled, Luna looked up. It was Salm, carrying his family's dog, Skipper. The black-furred Schipperke wiggled enthusiastically as Salm landed and strode over, his wings magicking away.

Flights! He'd come…aye, of course. He had said he'd help. "You're here," she said somewhat stupidly in her happiness at having him so close.

"Glad to see me?"

"Who wouldn't be?" She petted Skipper behind his ears.

"Hope you don't mind him coming. I'm on dog duty this week, and he needs a run."

"The chickens…"

"He won't chase them. Granny broke him of that." Salm put Skipper down. The dog trotted to the stone wall outlining their yard and tracked along it in the opposite direction of the chickens. Salm took the crate from her and leaned in. She backed away, her gaze flicking toward the quarters.

"Oops." He grinned. "Spies?"

"As good as." She jerked her chin toward the shed, and he followed her inside. After adding the crate to the stack, she pulled him out of view of the door and kissed him.

A sly smile slid over Salm's face. "Better than the one I'd planned. How'd I rate that?"

"For being so wonderful. For not complaining that this has taken over our week. For being you."

"High tides. Anytime."

"I owe you."

Salm clasped her shoulders. "Oh? Now let me think on that." He lowered his lips to hers.

Kissing him, tasting his familiar tang of salt and lemon, she wanted nothing more than to disappear onto the moor and continue this. Darn Papa for giving in to those people. Salm's hands moved confidently over her back, molding her body to his and to his humming skin. By the Orb, no! If she allowed him to flush his brilliant energy over her, she'd be lost to it.

She'd promised herself she wouldn't again fall blindly into a muddled haze of thinking that she could have a life with Salm of the Seas. It wasn't so simple as Salm thought. Joining him on a sailboat would take her away from Tern Bay. How would Papa manage everything, and with drinking? Nebs and Stella thought they knew everything, but neither did.

Luna gently pushed Salm back. "We could be interrupted at any point."

"Aye, like by someone bringing you lunch."

They whirled around. Stella held out a plate with a sandwich and potato salad—and smirked. "Shall I fetch another? You could keep kissing, then."

Luna groaned, but Salm smacked his lips. "Looks tasty. I've eaten, but potato salad, please."

Stella flounced back to the house, but she'd be back in a trice —to see Salm.

At Salm's urging, Luna took her sandwich and ate as they followed. A gray and white ball of feathers dove from nowhere. Luna ducked, and Salm threw his arms up, waving Rissa off. She shoved her food into Salm's hands and caught Rissa, tucked the gull under her arm and took back her sandwich.

Salm laughed, and she had to grin. "Just another day at Kittiwake Point. Could you help move the furniture? Once I'm in the shed, Rissa will leave us alone."

Hands on his hips, Salm looked over the dresser and chair. "I am allowed to use magic, am I not?"

"Sure." She had little left, but that didn't need to be said. "The dresser first, please?"

He streamed blue magic, lifting the dresser and floating it over the ground as if it were surfing.

A low whistle sounded. "Impressive," Nebula cooed from the doorway, and beside her, Stella clapped.

"Thank you, ladies. For my next stunt..." He waved his other hand, and the armchair rose.

The dresser tilted, and Luna yelped, "Salm!"

He whipped both hands to it, letting the armchair fall. Nebs and Stella broke into laughter, and Skipper came running to see what the excitement was about. Stella fell to her knees and called the dog.

Frowning, Luna tossed Rissa airborne and rescued Salm's plate that Nebs was accidentally lowering to Skipper's curious nose. At least he didn't bark. "Did you two want a break? Or can you carry—"

"Break!" They tumbled inside and closed the door.

With Rissa circling, Luna ran for the shed, close on the heels of Skipper, who appeared to be afraid of the gull. Salm and his strong magic more than replaced her sisters for these tasks. He lowered the dresser before the shed, accepted his potato salad, and they went inside. While Salm ate and Skipper poked in corners for mice, Luna checked for Rissa. Gone. She went out to fetch the table. If they put a cloth on top, they could stack crates on it.

Salm's exclamation reached her as she returned.

"I told Papa the shed was stuffed full," she called.

"You aren't kidding. But Skipper has found..." A long *creeeak* sounded.

Rusty hinges, her brain automatically identified. *They need oil—* oh. Oh no.

"Wow." The exclamation came from deep inside.

Luna stumbled into the shed and set down the table. "Salm?"

He wasn't among the jumble of crates, but she already knew that. Her gaze darted to the wide wooden staircase, most of the treads taken over by a canner and jars. The hatch to the upper level was open, for the first time in over a decade.

8

A PLACE OF MEMORIES

Stomach roiling, Luna blinked back unexpected tears. A blue glow flared and filled the rectangular opening to the upper level of the shed.

"This is incredible." Salm's hushed words carried from above.

She pulled the shed door shut before she crept up the stairs. She didn't cross the threshold. That was forbidden. "Salm," she called under her breath.

"C'mere." He waved her in. "Plenty of room in here to store the dresser and anything else you desire."

Oh, if Papa woke and discovered they'd opened the hatch… or realized something about it was amiss! Or if Stella found them. She wouldn't be able to keep this secret.

"Salm," she said a mite louder. In the dim light of Salm's glowing fingers and the sunlight around the edges of a sagging curtain, she made out the familiar, shrouded shapes. Her heart wrenched.

"Just need to move aside—" He tugged off a sheet. "Hoy, a telescope, a nice refractor." He flashed a grin to her. "Did you…" A frown formed. "What's wrong?"

Looking over her shoulder, she beckoned him, and he came to the doorway. "We're not allowed," she whispered. "How did you get in here?"

"It wasn't locked. The lock was hanging on the hasp, unlatched, if you're thinking I magicked it. I suspect someone was afraid the old thing wouldn't open again. It needs some graphite. Your dad doesn't want Stella in here?"

"He doesn't want *any* of us in here. This was my mother's room, her studio." Yet, even with the threat of her father's ire, Luna couldn't resist looking.

The brass had tarnished on the refractor's tube, but the memory of its shine called to her. She glanced around. Sheets covered every telescope and piece of furniture, but she knew them by heart. A second, larger refractor and Mam's Dobsonian reflector, the cabinet for her eyepieces and smaller equipment. Her desk, her chair, the daybed she sometimes napped on— where Luna had napped with her. A tear rolled down her check. She brushed it away.

Salm heaved a sigh. "Darned shame. That's a mighty fine instrument. Can I at least have a look at the others?"

They shouldn't...but she was so tired of Papa keeping her from memories of Mam. "The table came from here anyway." She pointed to the spot Skipper was sniffing. "To the side of the desk. You get it while I open the drapes." She stepped into the room, her breath catching, another wave of sadness overcoming her.

Salm clasped her arm and searched her face, holding up his glowing fingers to see better. She tried to summon a smile, but he brushed a callused thumb over her damp cheek, and she couldn't. She leaned her forehead against his shoulder, and when he hugged her, she huddled against his bony frame.

"Not allowed?" he asked. "How long?"

"Since she died. Eleven years."

"That's...long. A long time to mourn."

His statement still held a question. "She...it happened during childbirth. Stella's."

"Oh."

He held her, not moving, while the memories she'd pushed off for so long came flooding back. Mam's face twisting at the first contractions, blood puddling on the floor, her screams. Papa magicking the contents of the linen closet and thrusting a towel to try to staunch the bleeding, yelling for Luna to hold the towel and putting more into her hand before leaving for help because he hadn't dared to move Mam. Nebula crying as Luna did, too, and switching out towel after towel, all of them soaking red, not knowing what to do, or how to help when the baby's head appeared. Mam weakly telling her, "Wrap the babe, keep it warm. Take care of it for me," before she passed out. The healer arriving. The confusion of the baby coming, it—she—crying while Luna held her in one of the sweet quilts they'd made for their new baby, while a roomful of people worked over her mother, who never made another sound.

When her tears subsided, Luna wiped her face on a handker-chief that Salm handed her and stared into the room.

"We can go," Salm said. "'Tis too much."

She didn't want to go. She wanted to look while she had the chance, while Salm was here to deflect Papa's anger if he turned up. "We'll make it short." She crossed the room and opened the draperies covering the entire southern wall. Dirt streaked the windows and the glass-paned door, which was wide enough to wheel out the instruments. Weeds had overgrown the slate patio carved into an upper bank behind the shed, but the view was still just as beautiful, a vista overlooking the blue sea and the cliffs of Britain in the distance.

"Flights." Salm's low exclamation drew her attention back to the room. He'd removed the sheets from both the other tele-scopes and was admiring one.

Luna crossed to the squat tube in its rotating wooden base.

"Her Dobsonian was her favorite. Mine, too, because she let me use it. It's easy to point."

"And the art?" Salm ran his fingers over the pen-and-ink illustrations of several mythological constellation figures on the white tube.

"She drew them mainly for me to learn the patterns for star-hopping to find the fainter nebulae." Luna pointed to another group of stars with wisps depicted between them. "I could find the Orion Nebula by the time I was three. When Nebs was born, I wanted to name her that, but my parents made me settle for just Nebula."

"We could still call her Orion. Ori, for short."

"Don't you dare! We're on good terms these days." She turned the scope on its stand. It moved smoothly. "Papa refinished the wood to show off her work when Mam completed the drawings. I'm glad he didn't burn it, too, after she died."

"Burn it?" Salm choked out. "Why would he do a dunder-headed thing like that?"

She shrugged and shook her head. "One afternoon, I woke to the smell of smoke, a larger fire than we usually had to burn rubbish. He was tossing in all her work, frames and all."

"The burn on your wrist." Salm caught her hand and stroked the shiny spot.

"Aye, it happened when I tried to pull out a drawing. Papa stopped me, dressed the burn and sent me to my room, where I watched Mam's pictures go up in flames and bawled." She started to pull away, and Salm kissed the scar before letting her go. She glanced around. "I have a chance to look at Mam's things without Papa knowing." Her gaze landed on him again. "Do you mind?"

He went to fetch the table, while she uncovered the desk. It was locked. The daybed was still made up with sheets and the star-patterned quilt Mam had sewn for it. She pressed the fabric to her nose, but it no longer held her perfume. She pushed it away as Salm returned. As he set the table in place, she refused to look to the empty shelves where Mother's sketch pads and completed drawings had been stored. Instead, she drifted to the equipment cabinet. It didn't lock, and everything was inside, the best she could recall.

"The eyepieces are here. We could still use the telescopes," she murmured.

"That'd be brilliant," Salm said in the same hushed voice. "I admit, the brass of the big ones appeals to me, but you said this little one is easier to use?"

She selected an eyepiece and inserted it, turning the setscrew. "Let's spy down the coast."

He struggled to unlock the door, while she rolled the scope closer, removed the end cover and tilted the tube horizontal.

A *swoosh* sounded from inside.

"That's not right." She grimaced. "Hope it's not a mouse nest. Mam had sealed the studio against them."

"Skipper has left, so I suspect that magic has held." Salm righted the tube, and together they peered inside. "Paper." He fitted his hand between the supports. "*Sheets* of paper. Must have been rolled tight to get them in there."

Luna clapped a hand to her mouth, tears welling as a long-forgotten afternoon flashed to mind. "They were," she choked out, and he paused in trying to reach them. "It's several of Mam's drawings I hid while playing a hide-and-seek game with her."

9

COMING TO LIGHT

Salm stepped away from the telescope and the papers that were clearly important to Luna. *What is the right step here?* "You should magic them out," he offered.

"Magic shouldn't be used on these," she whispered, her tears twisting his gut.

Witches and their sentiments—three sisters meant he had too much experience with this. "Is there a way to open the tube?"

The mechanical problem brought Luna around. She showed him how to disconnect the braces that held the secondary mirror in place. He fetched a screwdriver from the workshop below and set to work.

Once the braces were out, Luna reverently removed the drawings. She separated the thick papers, curved from their years of hiding, by delicately sliding one from the other without scraping them against each other.

He gasped when she unrolled the first.

Kittiwake Lighthouse loomed over a cliff he well recognized, viewed from the north from the moor above Tern Bay. The second view was from the sea, due south, and for the third,

Luna's mother had zeroed in on the headland itself. The lighthouse and keeper's cottage were as accurately depicted as if she had taken a photograph while flying directly level with them. Every undulation in the cliff face stood out, their tiny ledges pockmarked with uninked spots to indicate the whitewash from the nesting colonies. Beneath them, boulders trailed out into a shoal.

"Your ma drew these?" he asked, despite the signature reading *Celeste Ness* at the bottom. "The detail here is incredible. Low tide," he murmured. "That last rock is only visible at low tide."

Luna smiled up at him. "You know your landmarks, Salm of the Seas."

"I bloody well have to, or I'd get myself dashed into toothpicks sailing up to woo you."

She chuckled at that, happiness lighting her eyes. "Right now, what is the tide?"

"It's turning," he said without having to think. "In thirty minutes, the sea will submerge that rock."

"Indeed, it will. On this drawing as well."

The words took a moment to register. He tore his gaze from the drawing. She was still smiling, but also watching him curiously. "You don't mean—"

Luna carried the drawings to the windows and held one out to him. By the Orb, if this was what he thought, she certainly did trust him. He took it gingerly and tilted it to fully catch the light. The change was slow, subtle in the inked lines, but the waves gently lapped at the rock, as they did only at the point of low tide. Then a flock of gulls rose from the cliff and whirled out over the water.

"Flights!" It took a moment to get more out. "Your mother magicked her artwork."

"Only places like this and objects. Never people or individual animals. Flocks of a certain size appear arriving and leaving."

"The regular tides I can understand, but birds?" He stared at Luna. "That had to be more difficult."

"And anything upon the sea, in real time. If a flock of seagulls is rafting on the waves, boats sailing by, a pod of your dolphins swimming through. We could have searched the drawings for your lost pod, but Papa burned the others."

Hoy, really? "Her beautiful drawings, the spellwork..." He raked his fingers through his hair. "She had *talent*. How could he?"

She shook her head. "Mam had completed views of our enclave borders and many of this side of the Isle of Giuthas. Most of your fisheries area would have been among them. Of course, it would take hours of viewing the images to see them come and go, so..." She shrugged.

"Hardly more productive than me being on the water looking for them."

"Though you could have lined up the drawings and watched many areas at once. That's what Papa never liked, how we would stare at the drawings for hours, instead of being outside, soaking up life, as he said." Luna wiped a tear forming in one eye. "These were a part of her. I wasn't even sure the magic would still work after she passed."

He lifted the paper and studied it more fully. Trees in the yard swayed with the wind, the heather shrubs shuddered and clouds built on the horizon.

"At dusk, the ink will fade, and the page will darken, though the drawing doesn't go black as night. The lighthouse beacon comes on. We used to have a drawing in the dining room that Nebs and I watched after we rose for the night. Mam finally moved it to the loo and made us brush our teeth and wash up while we stared." Luna's smile was wistful.

Salm wanted to lean over and kiss her. Instead, he soaked in the feelings coming from Luna. *She's opening up, sharing with me!* He slid his hand into hers. "What a wonderful memory."

She sighed. "It was. Then she died, and Papa destroyed every piece of her art."

Aw, blast. Her family memories were such a mixed catch, and he had no idea what to say to make it better. If anything could. Reluctantly, he handed back the drawing. "These are precious, then. Do you want to return them to their hiding place?"

She bit her lip, staring at the curled papers for a moment. "I want them out to remember her, but I best keep them hidden. The question is where?"

Salm lifted a finger. "I have just the thing." He closed his eyes and imagined the salon aboard *The Peaceful Seas* and the edged counter where he kept his map case. His fingers tingled with magic, and he sent the stream to wrap the case and magicked it to him. The leather case appeared in his hand.

"Waterproof," he said, "though it'd be best to sandwich your drawings between my maps." He tipped them out and separated them into four groups.

She inserted the drawings, and they put everything back into the case. Luna held it for a moment, then handed it to him. "Could you store it aboard *The Peaceful* for me? Just until these tours are over and I know it won't get misplaced?"

"Of course." He magicked it back to the schooner.

While he put the telescope together again, one of the lasses called Luna's name from outside. His heart leaped, freezing the screwdriver in his hand.

Luna dashed for the hatch, and he cranked the screw deeper. A few scuffs on the steps sounded, but enough time seemed to pass before Stella asked, "Where is Salm?"

That lass is a keen one. He'd never throw her off like he had Maeve and Pauly.

"Where is Skipper?" Luna asked in return, and their garbled conversation moved outside.

Salm closed up and hung the padlock back as it'd been.

Outside, her sisters ran up with Skipper in tow, and Luna smiled behind them. He grinned back, thankful they'd been spared dredging up an explanation.

As the afternoon wore on, Salm hauled while Luna sorted and packed and directed Nebs and Stella in helping. They managed to fit everything Luna wanted to store into the shed.

"You have my undying thanks for coming today," Luna whispered as her sisters headed for the quarters. "I've never had them stick to a task for this long. You're much more entertaining than I can be. I-I don't think I've seen you put that to use with work before."

"Oh?" He waggled his brows at her. "Have I impressed you?"

"Salm of the Seas, you are one of the hardest workers I know and one of the most considerate, helping clean a mess that isn't yours. Now don't let that go to your head."

"Duly noted. I'm grateful I won't have to walk my sister's dog after this run Stella's given him." He winked. "Kidding. I'm happy to be here with you." Salm ran a hand through his hair and brushed off his trousers. He wasn't dressed as well as he was last night, but that couldn't be helped. He'd shaved again today. "Time to meet your father?"

"I...erm, not sure he's up yet. And..." Several emotions washed over her face.

Salm watched, holding his tongue, because she seemed distraught above all else.

"I'm sorry, but this isn't the best time to meet him."

So...no reason? *This is so like her to secret...* No, Luna had told him more about her family today than she ever had. He had to be patient, let her do this in her time. "Tomorrow, then?"

She rose on tiptoes and brushed her lips to his. "Tomorrow. Thank you."

"Yay!" Stella called and, when they looked up, waved at them from the window.

Luna groaned. "You better scoot or prepare for lightning,"

she yelled, spunky as ever. He laughed as she flashed a magical warning and stormed inside.

When Salm flew up the next day, he spotted Luna first thing—at the top of a ladder. Hair pulled into a single puffy ponytail and wearing her coveralls, Luna was sweeping cobwebs off the second-story windows. Below, Stella sat on a lower rung with a pail of chicken feed, tossing bits to the hens and the swooping Rissa, while Nebula planted something in the garden.

He hovered beside Luna. "High rigging work today, then?" He gestured to her broom. "I can do crew chores."

"Is that what we are now?" Stella asked. "A ship's crew? I like it. Give us our orders, Captain."

"Ahoy!" Salm boomed. "Gather those hands to clear the decks." He pointed to the chickens.

With a giggle, Stella ran off, chasing them to the far corners.

"No." Luna frowned. "She's supposed to be weighing down the ladder for me."

"I can take care of that." With the toss of his hand, Salm magicked a coil of thick rope to drape across the vacated rung.

Luna's frown deepened.

"What?"

"Luna won't let us use magic unnecessarily," Stella announced, once again at the bottom of the ladder and staring at the rope. She had a feed pan in her hand, and the chickens clustered around her feet. "Not for things we can do by hand. We're short on energy." She sighed dramatically. "We're *always* short."

Oh. *Oh blast.* That wasn't something Windborne cared to admit. Salm dared a glance at Luna. Her mouth was set and her cheeks a bright red.

"Stella," she bit out. "See to the hens, and after we'll tidy the yard. That might garner you enough power to escape my anger once we're alone."

Her announcement was met with a wail. "We'd build more energy if we forgot about those tours and hunted for the bird I saw whose neck was trapped in plastic!" Stella complained. "The cormorant *limping* by…" she railed on.

"If we see him, we'll catch him," Salm called down. This was his fault for stepping in and contradicting Luna's directions. *Ah, hell, I've opened my big mouth and inserted a whale,* Salm sent to her.

Luna's eyes widened. *Don't let them know we can thought-speak. One inkling and they'll be teasing, and Papa will learn of it.*

"I didn't mean—look, forget I suggested anything." Salm landed and gave Stella an awkward pat on the shoulder. "Better to have Luna captaining these quarters and rousting the hands." He leaned back and called up to Luna, "Just tell me what I can do to help you."

Above Stella's whining, Luna appraised him, lips pursed. Then she brushed back a curl that had escaped her ponytail and descended the ladder. "Please finish removing the cobwebs and wash the windows so we may whitewash. Stella, the chickens. Then you can rake up beneath where I'm trimming the wisteria."

Luna marched to the shed, and Salm escaped up the ladder. He kept an eye on her comings and goings as he moved from the quarters to the lighthouse to wash those tower windows while on the wing. After Luna had carried two armloads of wisteria back to a burn pile alone, and he was fairly sure Stella would be busy raking and Nebula was still planting garlic bulbs, Salm swooped down behind the house. He collected an armload of branches and intercepted Luna at their back wall.

"We got off on the wrong foot," he said.

"I have a lot to think about today," she murmured and turned for the quarters.

He ducked around and blocked her. "I won't thought-speak to you here or whatever else." She shook her head, but he wasn't going to let that be it. "Tell me, please. I want to fix things between us."

Luna leaned against the wall, looking across the moor. "I love the feelings you give me..."

Finally, he quietly said, "I love the ones you give me."

"I need the other parts of us being together to be right for me, too."

"Like me not ordering you around. Or taking your place doing that with your sisters."

"Aye."

"I'll work on it, I promise. But you're gonna have to help me out here, Luna. I'm a fellow. I can be kinda wrapped in my own ideas, according to my sisters. I'll do my best, if you give me a chance."

She turned and ran her gaze over him, almost like it was the first time she'd really looked at him. "I appreciate that you aren't treating this like a joke. You're really listening." Sighing like she'd come to a decision, she narrowed the space between them. "I want to try."

He smiled, even more when she traced his jaw with her fingertip. "As long as we're talking, we can work this out."

After the windows and yard were completed, she did invite him into the keeper's quarters because Luna *had* decided to swab the decks. They moved the front-room furniture to the kitchen and began attacking every surface with dustcloths and rags tied to the ends of brooms. He would have magicked the dust away, but after his first mistake, he kept his mouth closed. It wasn't his house.

By the time they'd mopped and remopped the floor slates, even he couldn't distract Stella from whining.

"Go take a nap," Luna told her and pointed to Nebula. "Five more minutes. We just need the furniture put back."

"May I?" Salm asked, and when Nebula pleaded, "Please," and Luna nodded her agreement, he spread his fingers at the floor and flushed blue magic beneath the sofa. It rose on a layer of wave-like energy and glided across the room.

With a squeal of laughter, Stella flung herself onto it as if she rode a surfboard. Luna caught the sofa by the back and guided it into place. Nebula steadied the coffee table and then had a ride herself in the armchair.

When they were done, Nebula looped her arms around him in a quick hug. "Thank the Orb you like Luna so much. Come for dinner some night I'm cooking—"

"Nebs," Luna snapped. "I'll issue any meal invitations."

She wrinkled her nose. "Then I'll make him cookies after I've had a decent nap. Come on, Stella. Best to get away while we have a witness. She won't dare be mean." They clambered up the stairs.

Salm went to Luna and rubbed her shoulders, his fingers combing up into her hair and catching in her curls. "Of course, I'll wait for you to decide, but I'd love to come sometime. I like your family."

She leaned her head to his. "After Fest."

A minute passed, then he offered, "We should take a break, too. Want to go for a flight before we start on the kitchen floor?"

"Hmm," she murmured, which sounded like a nay. She lifted her head. "If you wish to look through the scopes, there isn't a better time. Papa sleeps his heaviest now."

In her mother's studio, they uncovered the Dobsonian.

"Outside?" Salm asked, and she nodded. The door to the slate patio took a bit of urging, but at last it swung inward. Salm yanked a circle of weeds from the patio, and they moved the telescope out onto it. At midday, the only thing to look at was the cliffs and birds. He swung the Dobsonian generally in that direction and stepped back, gesturing to Luna. "You do the honors."

"First light in eleven years." The smile she tried for didn't reach her eyes. "Though Mam reserved that phrase for starlight."

"Then so shall we," Salm said. "Tonight."

She ducked her head to the spotting scope mounted on the telescope's side and twisted the focusing knob before gently pulling the telescope tube to point it. The Dobsonian swung easily, and she tracked back and forth, then settled on one spot. She smiled, genuinely this time.

He poked her ribs. "I don't even have to look to know what you see."

She stepped back. "Look anyway."

Peering down the eyepiece, he saw a nest clinging to the rock face, three gray-backed birds jostling for purchase in it. As he watched, pieces of seaweed sloughed off, and one bird tumbled, caught itself and hung on arched wings, beating at its fellows to shove between them. Salm laughed. "Kittiwakes."

Luna ducked her head. "Another week and we might not have this view. Depending on the weather, these parents will be urging their young to migrate."

"Rissa, too?"

She bit her lip. "It would be best for him to go."

He rubbed a hand up her arm and across her shoulders. "You're gonna miss that little freeloader. We could sail out to the rafts on the other side of the isle."

She shook her head. "To the Atlantic, you mean. Nova Scotia. That's a kittiwake's destination."

"Blow me down. That's...how far?"

"Three thousand miles."

"No wonder you're worried about him."

Her shoulders lifted in a shrug. "It's his life. I may have raised him, but I have to let him lead it."

Brave words, but that didn't make Rissa's impending departure any easier.

"Let's try for something else." She shifted the scope downward, toward a far beach.

Even without the scope, he could make out large flapping wings. "Cormorants," he shouted.

Luna snorted. "At least look, to pretend you're identifying... Oh. I, uh..."

"What's wrong?"

She didn't give over the scope for him to look. "One doesn't look right. He's dropping fish rather than swallowing them. Blessed Orb! *This* is the bird Stella told us about."

"Should we—"

"Aye," Luna replied, already abandoning the telescope.

10

CLIFFSIDE CHASE

Keeping an eye on the injured cormorant was trickier than Salm had imagined. The seabird dove underwater twice while he hovered at the edge of the cliff, waiting for Luna to collect supplies. *I canna lose Stella's bird.*

He had it isolated when Luna glided up and tossed him a buoy-edged net like the one she also carried.

"Where did it go?" she asked, and he was relieved to be able to answer. Tucking her wings to avoid the uplifting winds, Luna dove over the edge of the cliff.

He followed. They picked up speed, the wind blowing in his ears louder than the waves.

Spells. He didn't do this as much as she did and never close to the jagged rock face. With a slight adjustment of wingtips, he rose a yard. The turbulence increased. That's why she flew so close to the cliff. But the proximity must have unnerved even Luna, for she whimpered. She repeated the plaintive cry, high pitched and whiny, something he'd expect from Stella. It didn't make sense.

Then answering whines rose around them.

It'd been a call? Aye. The kittiwakes turned their heads, then rose into the air. Within seconds, a cloud of white-tinged gray surrounded Luna.

He lost her.

Come on, she called. *Stay with us to hide our approach.*

He snorted. Her idea of camouflage was incredible.

The flock swerved out to sea, and he chased after, managing to blend into the group, trusting the gulls to get out of his way. Kittiwakes to the left, to the right, above and below. Damn if they didn't seem to know the exact spread of his wingbeats. He didn't hit a single one, and neither did their sharp bills peck at him in annoyance. They paid no attention to him as they tracked Luna. If a stranger had come this close to his dolphins, they'd have surrounded the person in curiosity.

They made a wide arc, gracefully circling the diving seabirds while descending as if to land on the sea beyond them.

Brilliant camouflage, he told Luna.

Thank you. As soon as I'm behind him, I'll move in. You'll be at the side for a second chance.

Salm scanned the cormorants on the water. Blimey. Now he had to admit... *Uh, which bird is it?*

The one on the left.

I'll take your word for—oh, aye, there's the plastic bound around his neck.

It won't affect his flying. You ready for a chase?

I'll do my best.

They lowered with the gulls, bellies nearly skimming the wave tops. Good thing he did *this* on a regular basis. Flying had to be on autopilot to keep both the proper floating bird and Luna in sight. It was easy to tell from this angle that the poor thing was suffering. He pecked at the debris around his neck and listed to one side as he floated.

Ach, I feel awful to have put off looking after Stella told us, Luna echoed his thoughts. *We could have had him cared for days ago.*

When Luna pulled up, so did Salm. The net swung from her hands, nylon spreading, buoys dropping—

He copied her, seconds behind, his net neatly swinging to overlap a portion of hers—

A squawk sounded. The plastic-wrapped seabird startled, saw them and dove beneath the surface.

Curses.

Bullsharks, Luna spat. *I never miss.*

He laughed. *You bloody well do.*

She darted over the sea, hooked her net and lifted, shaking off the water. He retrieved his as well. *Keep an eye out. We'll have only seconds before he takes—*

A dark shape moved below the surface, a familiar thing to note when one worked with dolphins. Salm careened after it, shadows falling in his favor. Magic zinged to his fingertips as the cormorant bobbed to the surface.

He tossed. The net landed true.

He whooped. "I got him!"

Not yet, you don't. Luna swooped and dropped, arms wide, fingers splayed with loose magic stretched between them. She caught the bird—net and all—around the middle and rose. He squawked and twisted, thrashing in her grip. He slipped loose, and she lunged after him, her arm wrapping the bird's body as her wings disappeared. Luna fell into the sea.

Salm whirled to where she'd disappeared, watching her shadowed figure, about to dive to help when she popped to the surface. Aye! She had the wriggling bird under one arm. He snaked his head upward, the long neck reaching despite the fishing line entwining six-pack rings. The bird looked at Luna and darted—

"Watch the beak!" Salm streamed a magical shield between the bird's face and hers.

Your shirt, Luna called as she treaded water in the rolling waves and struggled to hold the bird at arm's length. *Covering his eyes will calm him.*

Automatically, Salm tugged, then remembered he was *flying*. He magicked off the shirt and rushed forward.

The bird twisted around, beak snapping—

"Ouch! Bugger off, mate." Finger bleeding, Salm hovered and hooded the bird, and Luna smoothed the wings with her energy, keeping them tight to the bird's body.

Their gazes met, and they broke into laughter.

"Right, I didn't have him," Salm admitted. "Jolly good pounce! You did Stella proud."

"I have, as long as ignoring her doesn't mean he's so far gone he won't make it. For all that plastic he's carrying, he's still agile." She tilted one arm, showing her own bloody scrape. "You fared well for a first-timer. And stayed dry, too."

"Lost me shirt, though."

"Thank the Orb." Luna grinned. "Can you carry him? Between him and my soaked clothes, I likely can't lift off."

"You could strip, too," he suggested, but opened his arms for the bird.

"Ach, you wish." She passed him the wrapped bundle and turned on her belly to magic out her wings. Up they rose.

"Pretty small for a cormorant," he called.

"This isn't a great cormorant," she said as they flew to shore. "He's smaller and has that green sheen to the feathers. He's a shag, a European shag, and he should be out to sea, not hugging the coast."

"The limits on his eating have done him in, then?"

"I expect. If you've got your knife, let's get to shore and remove this plastic."

He had it. No beach lined this shore, so they flew to the moor. The sound of the surf dropped off as soon as they were over the cliff top. They nestled into a patch of dry grass among the heather. On her knees, Luna murmured to the bird, "There,

there," and hummed while she tucked the shag's body under one arm and his head under the other. Salm unwrapped his shirt from the shag's neck. Fishing line wasn't just snarled around the long neck, it was embedded.

Salm whistled.

The bird squirmed at the sound, and Luna hummed with renewed vigor.

"Sorry, laddie boy, but this is quite the mess you've collected. I need wire cutters or something with a smallish nose and cutting action. Even nail clippers would be better than my knife."

"We have wire cutters, in a kitchen drawer," Luna said. "I've used so much energy already that I hate to magic them here."

Hadn't her work with the gull flock to make the capture generated replacement energy? Caring for the injured bird certainly would.

"I could go for them," he offered, "but wouldn't it be as fast to carry him there? The line is rather tight. We might need other tools. Let me hold the head while you do a better assessment." They traded positions, and he held the shag.

Still humming, Luna ran her fingers up and down the neck, poking her fingertips between the crisscrossed lines. She shook her head. "The feathers are damaged on the lower side, and— oops, what's this...no." She grimaced. "An abscess. It'll need to be lanced, and we have no more antibiotics on hand. Our healer, Lady Anemone, can get me more, but I need a dosage. Do you know where Mr. Grouse is this week?"

"Nay, but I can find out." His family connections for thought-speaking were stronger than with other acquaintances on the Isle of Giuthas. He reached his grandmother, and she called their enclave's wildlife wizard, Merlin. It took a few minutes for her to get back to them.

"He's on the mainland," Salm told Luna. "They're finding

out exactly where." In his arms, the shag strained toward the cliff edge. "He wants out there again."

Luna flashed a smile. "Do you blame him? The fresh sea breezes, the tides rolling in your dinner, warm sand to rest upon and the excitement of searching the rock crannies for the perfect nesting spot."

"Maybe the thrill of fighting off the other shags to win the perfect mate."

"Exactly!" Luna laughed.

"You've watched it all happen here."

"And more. Storms rolling through, massive flocks turning in unison, the cries of the hungry chicks rising at neap tide, the moor in bloom for miles in every direction, then an hour later, the perfect sunset coloring the ocean in the opposite direction. I can't imagine a place with more activity or wonder than the sea cliffs."

Salm grinned, but his heart sank. "It sounds impossible to compete with."

Luna stilled, her eyes showing surprise. She looked out over the cliff, then back to him. "You, Salm of the Seas, are giving it a fair run. And..." She licked her lips. "On a ship or on the shore, we would never leave the coast far behind."

He nodded, afraid to say more, and Luna bent her head to cutting off what plastic she could and continued her humming. After a few minutes, he realized the bird had become utterly still in his arms.

"Luna? He's not dead, is he? Too much shock?"

She put a hand to her lips, suppressing a laugh. *Asleep. Well, sedated. I managed to get him under a sleep spell.*

He raised his brows. No wonder she was using energy so rapidly. *New skill?*

Old one. I don't mention it to folks. Papa suggested I might not want to be known as the crazy bird girl.

He can do it, too?

Aye, but don't say anything. That's how he knew I'd garner name-calling, as he did as a child. If he had more daylight hours, he'd love to help Mr. Grouse with the trickier injuries. But he hasn't been able to since… She shrugged.

Your mother passed. I understand. It's hard to do everything.

Salm's grandmother sent word back that Mr. Grouse was only a half hour away and willing to come down. *Thank everyone for me, Granny,* Salm told her. *And thanks to you, too.*

When will I get to meet this lass? Granny asked.

Salm glanced at Luna and smiled. *Soon, I hope.*

With her needle-nose pliers and fine wire cutters at hand, Luna placed a towel over the dining table and gestured for Salm to set the shag upon it. "Keep a hold of him," she said as she got to work. The last thing she needed was to have to chase the bird down inside their newly cleaned home—or to wake Papa. Still, she was glad to have Stella's bird caught and to have accomplished it with Salm.

She sneaked a glance at him. He gently held the beak with bloodied fingers, because Salm had unquestioningly followed *her* orders. Maybe she was overthinking every little thing that happened between them.

Luna had removed most of the plastic by the time Mr. Grouse slipped through the back door without knocking.

"Rest of the household asleep?" he asked quietly.

"Aye."

The ornithologist had been here countless times and moved from that pleasantry to running his hands over the bird. Upon reaching the nasty red swelling on the neck, his tic of rapid blinking paused.

'Tis as bad as I suspected. Thank the Orb she'd had Salm call. Still, it gnawed at her that the infection might have been

avoided if she—or someone in the family—had listened to Stella.

Mr. Grouse checked the rest of the bird's body and readied cotton swabs and saline rinse, while Luna returned to trying to get the wire cutters under a stubborn bit of line. He stopped her.

He rummaged in the pockets of his sportsman's vest. He'd carried in a bag, but she knew from past work with him that this garment kept his frequently used tools at hand. He withdrew a leather case containing a nail kit. But instead of reaching for the nail clippers, he pulled out a three-inch-long plastic tube with tapered ends. It came apart to reveal a small, metal, hooked blade at one end.

"Seam ripper," he whispered.

"Ah, my ma has one of those in her sewing basket," Salm whispered.

"Hold the bird," Mr. Grouse said. "Just in case."

Luna laid her hands over the bird's head, and Salm cupped the wings. Mr. Grouse wiggled the hook with its balled end at a deeply embedded line, but couldn't get it under. He moved a few inches and tried again. The bird shifted.

Night, Luna thought to the bird. *Nothing to see.*

Mr. Grouse clasped the muscular neck. "Sorry, mate." Pushing firmly, he angled the ripper down, and with a twist, he caught the line in the hook. It cut through with a snap.

The shag lunged, beak opening amid a fury of squawks as they held him. In a trice, Mr. Grouse snatched up the needle-nose pliers, caught the end of the line and unwound it as the bird grappled.

"*Shh,*" she shushed. *Help,* she tried to communicate. *Fish.* She sent him the image of swallowing them.

The calls quieted some, but when Mr. Grouse lanced open the abscess, the shag gurgled a deep throaty cry.

"What's going on?" Stella stood in the doorway in her night-dress and carrying a doll.

This time, Luna shushed her sister and nodded for her to come closer.

Stella ducked to her side and slid her arm around Luna's waist. "You caught my bird?" She looked from Luna to Salm. "Or did Salm?"

Of course she'd assume her hero would have done it. Luna jostled her. "We did it together, silly girl. It's a shag, and they're a lot harder to catch than a kittiwake." Continuing to hold the shag, she pressed her forehead to Stella's. "I'm sorry we didn't search right off. I promise that next time I won't worry about chores and go sooner."

Stella hugged her. "Thanks."

The bird's calls continued as guttural whines under Mr. Grouse's treatment. The bird must have sensed that the wizard wouldn't hurt him. That made it easier to hold the head, but Luna continued her sleep spell. *Night, sleep. Sleeeeeep.* Aloud, she asked, "Salm? How are your fingers?"

"Just the one." He stretched out his index finger.

"I'll get a bandage." Stella dropped her doll on the table, fetched the first aid kit and returned. She cleaned and dressed Salm's hand while Mr. Grouse did the same with the bird's wound.

"Thank you," Salm said, admiring the bandaging from all sides. "This should last me through my chores on the ship and here."

"You're gonna do more chores with us?" Stella looked up at him with puppy-dog eyes. "Like whitewashing?"

"If I'm needed."

They both turned to her, and Luna couldn't help smiling. "That evolved in a rather cunning way." When they started to protest, she said, "We could use loads of help with whitewash-ing." Except, a thought pinged through her: *Instead of white-*

washing here, I could be painting Mr. Smith's flat and earning a decent trade credit.

Stella looked at Salm again, and he said, "I promise, I'll whitewash!"

He smiled at her, and as Stella put away the supplies, he smiled again over her head—at Luna.

The closeness of it felt right. Maybe being with Salm was the right thing to do.

Mr. Grouse washed his hands and then dispensed antibiotics and directions. "You can care for him the ten days?"

"I'll get a kennel ready." Stella turned toward the door.

"Oops." Luna caught her arm. "You're in your nightie and should be sleeping. What would Papa say?"

"Get dressed?" she asked hopefully.

Luna fixed her with a look.

Stella's shoulders sank. "Do I have to?"

"You may set out the baitfish to thaw and help with the first round of feeding."

Blinking, Mr. Grouse leaned down, putting his face level with hers. "Any chance you can thaw one fingerling so we can give him a little snack right now?"

Stella's face lit up. "You bet."

When she returned, Mr. Grouse had her put a pill in the baitfish's mouth and lent her much-too-big leather gloves to hold it with. "Regular meals can be slid into his cage in a pan of water. This is how I pill seabirds." He wet the fish in a bowl of warm salt water they'd mixed up, then pried open the enormous beak. "Head first," he said. "Same way a bird would eat it so the scales lie flat as it goes down."

Stella backed away, but Luna pushed her forward. "Are you helping or not?"

She made a face at Luna, scooted to the bird's mouth and poked in the fish, head first.

Mr. Grouse clamped the beak shut and lifted the shag's

head. He stroked the uninjured spot just below the beak, and the shag swallowed. The bird seemed surprised as the fish went down.

"He'll be interested in eating more now," Mr. Grouse said. Then he shook a finger at Stella. "No one's losing a finger. You wear those gloves and get your sister to do all the parts I did, you ken?"

"Aye, sir."

"Back to bed," Luna added. "You can check him before dinner and feed him…" She looked at Mr. Grouse.

"Five fish, then five more an hour later," Mr. Grouse said, his bag in hand as he made his way to the door. "Same for midnight and breakfast until we make sure he isn't regurgitating any. I'll check in tomorrow."

Stella let out a gleeful cry and ran up the stairs. "Let's call him Charlie!"

"Quiet," Luna hissed after her. "Flights." She shook her head.

"What's wrong?" Salm gathered the bird in his arms. "She did just what you said."

She led the way to their combination chicken coop and rescue-bird outbuilding. "Noisily for this house. The last thing I need is Papa waking up. Though he's the one behind us doing wildlife care, taking on a bird now is bad timing with the tours starting in four days."

Now Salm shook his head. "You sound just like my mother, always worrying. Lighten up a bit. Would it be the most awful thing if your father did wake up? He'd yell at her himself, and maybe next time she'd remember."

"He'd yell at me, too," she muttered. Undeservedly, which really grated now that she was older.

Salm huffed. "It's not your responsibility to raise your sister. Blow it off."

Where did Salm get off telling her what to do? Salm of the

Seas knew nothing about how things ran on Kittiwake Point. She frowned at him.

"Not to his face," Salm added. "Just to yourself. Or to me. You're welcome to rant to me anytime."

Those weren't the kind of interactions she wanted with Salm. Instead of answering, she pulled out the supplies they needed. They set up a kennel with toweling to protect the shag's feet, a wooden box for a hiding place and a tin tub that they filled with ocean water flown up in buckets. Salm teased her that she was babying the bird, but more than a few days in freshwater and the shag's salt glands would shut down. They talked and joked as they settled the bird, then returned to her mother's studio to put away the telescope. By the time she locked the patio door and closed the drapes, she wasn't mad any longer.

She hugged him in the dim studio. "Thank you, Salm of the Seas, for going on a wild shag chase with me."

"'Tis as lively fun as dolphin training. We make a good team. What's my reward?"

"Baitfish?"

He rolled his eyes. "Tha' is nae a treat for a sailor, lass."

Under his affected accent and teasing, she pretended to think about it, but he grasped her shoulders and kissed her, his lips firm and assured, warm and salty. Longing shot through her, and her magic rose. She pushed him back before he pulled down her defenses. "I've lost so much time—"

"You canna say rescuing the bird wasn't important. To the shag and to Stella. To you. To Mr. Grouse. We both earned elder points there. It was a fine adventure for me as well, and I'm sure your family will agree. Now sit with me, lass." He tugged her toward the daybed. "An hour. Three-quarters if you plead absolute guilt."

"But I—"

"But my reward!" He released her shoulders and dropped onto the bed with a pouted, "Save a drowning sailor. Please?"

She laughed and fell into him, pushing him over onto the bed. "You aren't drowning."

"Too much talk. 'Tis swallowing me, and only a kiss can save me."

She kissed him and rolled to his side. Salm snuggled her close, drawing the quilt over them and rubbing her shoulders. She should protest, but it felt so good, and an hour's break wouldn't hurt. As her mind became foggy, she had a drifting thought that this nap might last longer...

The call of her name pulled her back to consciousness. Then Papa's bellowed, "Luna!" snapped her from sleep.

The room was dark, but not hers. Where—

Oh Blessed Orb, no!

Arms, legs and the quilt tangled her efforts to rise. A bobbing lantern blinded her, then Papa's angry face appeared beside it, inches from her face—and Salm's.

11

TRULY REBELLING

Luna sat up on the daybed and, beside her, Salm did the same. Still, her father loomed over them.

"What in the name of all that is good are you about?" Papa's lips snarled back into his beard, his teeth and eyes glinting white in the lantern light. Then his magic rose. It swirled off his arms and shoulders until it outlined his upper half in blue-green, like a swampy will-o'-the-wisp come to life from childhood ghost tales.

Luna cringed. She hadn't seen him this furious since he'd burned Mam's drawings.

Papa must have realized it—or seen the fear in her eyes—because he backed up. His arm shot out, his finger pointed, not at her, but at Salm. "Not in my house. Not with my daughter. Out."

"No." Luna shoved her legs off the bed and stood. She repeated it louder, "No."

Salm rose behind her, the hard soles of his boots hitting the floor, the quilt sliding off his trouser-clad legs. "Sir, I'm sorry. We didn't mean to—"

"My lass with a man in my beloved wife's bed," Papa spat, his face twisted.

"We fell asleep, Papa."

"No lad is going to be with my daughter, in my house."

Why didn't he believe her? He hadn't been drinking—she'd smell it on his breath. "Papa, look at us. We're fully clothed. *We fell asleep.*"

Red-faced and temples bulging, her father glared.

Luna clenched her fists. He was shutting down, unwilling to listen. She cast a glance at Salm. He lifted his brows and darted his eyes toward the doorway. Aye, their escape was clear, but she had to at least try to reason with her father. "Besides cleaning, we caught a shag with an injury. Mr. Grouse has been by to see it. After that, we were tired. That's all."

"Ye got away with it this time, but not again." He reached for Luna, blue-green magic sparking around his fingers as he grasped her shoulder.

Bullsharks. Luna batted him away with a handful of silver energy. Salm ducked, a blue shield washing his skin. In a split second, she copied him—because her father had tried to quash her.

Her! How dare he think he could ground her magic?

"You canna...do this," Papa growled. "Not in my house."

Awash with silver magic, Luna gestured to herself. "Look at me, Papa. I'm no longer a wee lass. I'm a grown woman. I love you, but I won't lose Salm because you think you know what's best for me. I get to make those decisions."

He opened his mouth, ready to speak, and she waited, breath held.

"Salmon," he finally boomed. "Do nae ever set foot on Kittiwake Point again."

"He won't have to," Luna shouted. "*I'm* leaving and not coming back." She shoved past him. She heard Salm on her heels as she stormed down the stairs and burst from the shed.

Her unfurling wings hit Salm's. She moved off, but he caught her hand.

"Your sisters," he whispered.

Nebs and Stella peered around the door of the bird shed, both wide-eyed. "You aren't *really* leaving?" Stella called.

Stella's desperate cry...the looks on their faces... Luna's heart tore.

But to stay would mean surrendering to Papa's rule, and this time she wouldn't be able to live with herself if she did that. She darted back and kissed them both. Then she put her hand in Salm's and flew away.

A quarter hour later, Luna faced Mr. Smith at the doorway of his big green house. "I'm interested in leasing your flat. How much is the rent?"

The elderly man cocked his head. "Three hundred a month. We could have worked out an agreement with what needs fixing around this old place, but I'm sorry, it's rented."

Luna's hopes crashed as soon as he said *could have*. The price was high, but a work trade would have made the difference until her business increased. "The renters are here for just Fest?"

He shook his head. "And beyond. I'm sorry."

"I'm sorry, too," Luna mumbled, and she turned away as tears threatened to escape. *Stormy nights, what do I do now?* Salm had said he'd meet her on *The Peaceful Seas*, so she'd go there to think about how to apologize to her father.

The walk to the harbor cleared that idea. She wasn't going back home, not now that she'd made the break. Tern Bay's little family-run businesses and these folks' homes stirred her urges to have what they had. She could see herself traveling these deckwalks every day to work. She just had to build what she'd started.

Somehow.

A few fishermen were working on their fishing boats moored at North Dock. Most didn't look up, though a pair of girls stopped talking to stare as she passed. Luna vaguely recognized them, but didn't know their names, just that they weren't from Tern Bay.

Why was she nervous about being watched? *Because I know I might stay the night, though they do nae.*

At the Seas' gangway, Salm ushered her belowdecks, and she slumped against the booth seat in the schooner's salon. She was dressed in her rattiest work clothes, with only the satchel that she'd paused to magic from its hook at the back door. She clutched it to her middle, sorely missing the comfort of her mother's sweater to wrap herself in. She couldn't remember where it was and couldn't afford the magic it would take to search.

Salm set a plate of scrambled eggs alongside the mug of tea she hadn't touched and slid into the booth on the opposite side with his own plate.

She stared down at the fluffy mass, not as yellow as their eggs, nor flecked with herbs. Was Nebula fixing their eggs now? Surely they weren't waiting for her, but what had Papa told them? Her eyesight blurred. Her satchel held her extra brush, sunhat, hair bands and ribbons, notebook, two pencils, her wallet with her Windborne and human ID cards, a few exchange notes and her trade card and a multitool. No women's supplies, not a change of clothes or even a slicker.

"Luna?" Salm's hand was warm overtop of hers.

When had he stood up?

"You should eat before your food gets cold." He carried his now-empty plate to the sink, refilled his mug and topped off hers from the kettle before sitting again.

Right, because she had nothing, she'd best not pass up a meal. She released the satchel—her palm hurt where a metal ring had bitten into it—and picked up the fork.

"Maybe you should say something," she muttered. "'Tis strange to be with you and not have you talking."

He smiled halfheartedly, still holding the mug. "I canna believe you stood up to him. I think you meant it—"

"I did. I'm not going back home." The words came out more forcefully than she intended.

They stared at each other.

"Aye," he said after a moment. "I'm proud of you. I would like to help you, but I don't know if you want that from me after..."

Luna stared at her plate, then made herself take a bite of eggs and a sip of lukewarm tea. Days ago, she'd told him she couldn't go away with him. That hadn't changed. Moving on board with Salm's family wasn't the right solution either. Staying with Salm, even temporarily, was sure to put the idea of permanence into his head. *And start rumors if folks took note of it.* She cringed at the thought. But... She picked up the fork so she wouldn't have to look at him, then put it down again and made herself meet his gaze.

"Thank you. I would like to accept your help for now. I have trade credit enough to pay for my share of the food and a bit toward rent—"

"No rent."

"—until I—but I should, and 'tis just until I can find a place." She rubbed her arms.

He disappeared down the corridor and returned with a quilt that he wrapped around her shoulders. He planted a quick kiss on her head before dropping into his seat again. She hugged the material to her. It smelled wind-fresh and lemony, like him.

"I canna stand to see you hugging yourself without something, and I ken you do nae want me right now, as I'm the one who got you into this eddy."

She sighed. "It's as much my fault as yours. I knew he'd be

angry if he discovered us in Mam's studio. I just thought...he wouldn't."

"I meant, I didn't fall asleep." Salm gave her a crooked smile. "Maybe drowsed a bit, so I didn't hear him coming. Would've left if I had."

"You weren't asleep?"

"I wanted to take what time I could with you. And I already ken that you telling off your father and leaving home doesn't change your desires to build a business. You won't instantly decide to live on a boat because of this."

Was he upset they hadn't gone away? Or about her decision that she wasn't ready to live aboard a boat with him? He didn't look angry, but she was too flustered to read him right now. "Oh, Salm."

"Answer me this: Did telling your father you were leaving feel right?"

She bit her lip. "I should be a good daughter and say no. But aye, it did. I've been going behind his back for too long, knowing that what I want to do isn't what he wants for me. I can't live his way, so it's best I—" Her voice caught, and a tear rolled down her cheek.

"Set your own course," Salm finished. "I can see you doing that. You're a strong woman, Luna Ness. Obviously, if you're willing to put up with me."

Her tears flowed in earnest now.

"You are welcome to stay aboard *The Peaceful*." He lifted his hands. "No rent and no strings attached to that offer, until you chart this. What do you want to do?"

Fine, no rent. She couldn't afford to argue. She wiped her face. "I'm sorry to cut into our time together, but I must put out the word I'm available for repairs this week. I'll need the extra work that always comes up during Fest."

He nodded. "Then you should. Being together here, we'll see enough of each other."

Her stomach dropped. "Oh. Your parents... I can't disrespect them any more than my father believes we disrespected him."

Salm chewed his lip, confirming she'd guessed correctly. "I'll put it to Manta," he said finally. "She'll decide if we need to cut into their holiday with the news. She'll probably let me off the hook, because she won't want to do that."

Good. His older sister ran the bakery in town and had good instincts.

Mouth twisting, he raked a hand through his hair. "Aye, 'tis different being alone together on board as opposed to up on the moor, but we're both of age."

"Flights. They think we...?"

"I'm not the oldest, you ken? Wind, my oldest sister, kept her activities tame, but I've nae done anything Manta didn't. Well, except I've dueled a bit. My older sisters were always too busy with the lads for that."

Luna rolled her eyes. "And you trust her recommendations?"

"I do." He smiled across the table at her. "You'll have work, and since I'm in town, I've dolphin exercises to complete, and I also took on training my younger sister's friend Ty for the regatta during Fest." Salm explained that he'd joined Coral in giving the newcomer sailing lessons each afternoon. "But we still have the time together that we'd planned for this week." He looked at her hopefully—far too hopefully. "Perhaps a few nights snatched, you ken?"

In that one look, she was undone, a spike of warmth hitting her middle and staying. In Salm's arms, she could feel so loved, and she wanted that feeling now.

But I'm in so much trouble already. Luna shook her head, and Salm sighed.

"Your decision," he murmured. "Probably the right one."

Another tear rolled down her cheek. "Honestly, Salm of the Seas, you are the most impossible dreamer and the sweetest wizard in all of Tern Bay. Why do I keep saying no to you?" She stumbled to her feet, skirted the table and fell into his arms.

"I have no idea." His whisper was warm on her neck, his kiss long and lingering, magic-free. "I put all my lines in your direction in hopes that you would take the bait, but—" He shrugged. "I know that taking on the solitude of a sailor's life would be difficult for you. Ma warned me I couldn't be angry if you say no, and I'm not."

Luna leaned back to study Salm's face. This freedom to make her own decisions felt as right as telling Papa she was leaving. "I wouldn't say all your casting has failed yet. Leave a few lines in?"

Salm wiped her cheeks with his callused thumbs. "Done." He grinned at her, kissed her, started to clasp her neck, then stopped, shaking out the hand like he'd been burned. He pulled her down into the booth seat next to him. "Blast it, getting carried away again. Tell me your plans, or your hopes, if that's where you're at."

With a sigh, she leaned against him. "I wanted that little flat of Mr. Smith's with the view of the harbor and the lighthouse. I canna imagine a more perfect place. But it's taken, so I shall have to search around for another."

"Things will be tight during Fest," he warned.

She flashed a quick smile. "Aren't they always? Thanks for letting me stay. Which cabin can I have?"

"Take Manta's. The berth is wider, and the door locks." He gave her a wry grin. "Mine does, too, actually."

12

A FRESH START

Luna woke to the usual cries of gulls and a gentle rocking that wasn't usual, but was familiar.

Boat. Ship, she corrected, blinking her eyes open to take in the ceiling and pale blue walls of Manta's cabin. It'd taken her forever to fall asleep last night, out of her routine of a dawn bedtime. But morning meant work now that she was on her own. Funny, the berth didn't feel especially roomy. She rolled over, and what she'd thought was the wall moved.

"Salm," she hissed.

His dark curls shifted, his face turning toward her as he smiled. "Good morning, love."

"What are you doing here?" she demanded. "You said you'd sleep in your own room so you could answer truthfully that you had."

"I did." His grin broadened. "When I woke in the early morning, I discovered you hadn't locked your door and slipped in with you. It's lovely." He ducked his nose to her neck and drew in a long sniff. "Positively lovely. Half studio dust, half wet bird feathers." He kissed her there and up to her ear.

"Stop," she moaned in desperation. "We agreed..." She

pushed him away, though it definitely wasn't what she wanted to do.

He sighed, tipping his forehead to hers. "I ken the rules. No sex, especially not on the ship. But you dinnae say we couldn't touch, or kiss, or think about sex."

She shoved him back. "You-you're incorrigible!"

"I am," he said smugly. "And you love me for it."

"Aye." Half laughing, she pushed harder, driving him to the edge of the mattress. Blue magic flared over his body, and he rose above her, leaned down and pressed his tangy lips to hers.

He'd been out in the salty breezes already. She kissed him back a moment before saying, "I need a shower."

He lowered his feet to the floor and stood, withdrawing his magic. "Towels are in the cupboard in the head. We have the same on-demand water heater Windborne landlubber homes do, and our freshwater tanks are full, so take as long as you wish." He turned to go, and Luna's gaze followed him out to the passageway.

Clanking in the kitchen and running water meant he was filling the kettle. Tea. She hoped it'd be strong. She'd need it today.

Last winter, Manta had told Salm to encourage her to see Lady Anemone about birth control pills. Their energy had merged well, and they'd been getting...*closer*, but hadn't actually done anything at the time that he'd brought it up. His forwardness had stunned her, but the next time they'd seen each other, he'd asked again. "I'm nae trying to pressure you," he'd said. "But I will nae do more until we can be safe."

Windborne had all the information that humans did on safe sex. Lady Anemone conducted classes for the local youth and had visited—probably at Papa's request—when Luna had come of age and then again when Nebula had. Luna had pulled out her booklet and reread it. The pills were safer and available if she asked Lady Anemone for them.

But she didn't go to see Lady Anemone before Salm came into port again.

"Maybe I'm not the fellow you want to do this with," he said.

She did want to. Just not *talk* about...it. And she saw Salm only a few days every few weeks. He stopped asking, and between visits she tried not to think about it or him. They hadn't committed, so there wasn't a reason to change anything. For a time, they split, and he approached other witches. He'd told her that when he asked to see her again this summer.

It was wonderful to be back together, and their energies merged so well that they were able to thought-speak. It was a clear sign that Luna should do *something*, but she procrastinated. Then Nebula had asked her how a girl was supposed to know when the time was right.

She and Nebula went to see Lady Anemone together.

Luna had been a wreck, but once they'd begun discussing women's issues, Lady Anemone made it so matter-of-fact that Luna was grateful for an older woman's advice. Plus, the healer relieved her of advising her younger sister, when she herself didn't know what to do.

Afterward, she was better prepared and loved Salm even more for waiting and letting her decide. But today, after finding him in her bed, she had to make sure he didn't automatically assume that she was here to stay.

Luna is here, on the schooner. "Do nae mess it up, old mate," Salm muttered. He hadn't, not yet. But what could he serve for breakfast—or dinner, for her flipped schedule? A check through the refrigerator didn't yield many choices. Fish didn't seem right. He knew the Nesses ate eggs for their evening meals, not morning. A hunk of cheese would do for toasted cheese—but he had no bread.

Why hadn't he picked up any yesterday?

Because your fool head was caught up with her.

Her footfalls sounded in the passageway, and the door to the head shut.

He had time. After turning off the kettle, Salm raced up the companionway ladder, across the deck and down the gangway. In minutes, he was walking into One Good Bun, his sister's bakery.

No less than five customers and as many young'uns stood between him and the counter. Even the path around the end of the counter was blocked. His sister's partner, Piper, had a lady bending his ear about her Fest party order. Salm and Manta's youngest sister, Coral, was having to shout a new muffin's ingredients to old Sir Porbeagle, who could well afford to gain a few pounds but scrutinized every bite of food he ate.

Salm paced behind the customers, spotting the wheat loaf he wanted, but having no polite way of getting close enough to pluck it from the pile. Three minutes passed, then five. Flights, he wanted to get his bread and be out of here. Perhaps he should go around the row of shops and through the alleyway to the back entrance—

Piper looked over, and Salm dashed a hand up. "Can I just get a loaf of wheat?"

"None left." Piper indicated the woman he'd been helping, now leaving with her bulging tote bag. "Next batch'll be out in twenty minutes."

"Anything, then," Salm snapped. "Something to make Lu—" Hell, he'd nearly let that slip! "To make breakfast."

"For that lass who spent the night on your schooner?" The question came from a feminine voice Salm recognized, and choking, he spotted Maeve. Behind him.

Her chin lifted, and her eyes held a vengeful glare.

Oh Great Golden Orb. "For me—"

"Luna, isn't it?" Maeve asked. Loudly.

The room quieted.

"But I want chocolate chip," a little girl whined into the silence as two old ladies turned to stare over their shoulders. A young couple with a baby tried to keep straight faces, while others didn't bother.

Spells, if only he'd checked the room. Or seen Maeve first. After her anger at being suspended from fishing, he would have known to raise anchor and flee.

"Who's next?" Coral's voice broke the awkward pause. "I can help someone."

Piper grabbed a random loaf and leaned over a woman's shoulder to hold it out to Salm. "Settle up with your sister later."

Salm dipped a nod of thanks and pivoted. Folks stepped out of the way, all looking curious. One bloke winked.

Curses.

Smirking, Maeve held the door for him. He had half a mind to drag her out with him, but continuing any conversation with her on the deckwalk would only net him more trouble. She'd clearly come in after him. Had she followed him? Her family's boat was also moored at North Dock.

Flights. He was in for it now. He knew only half these people on sight. But they all knew Luna.

When he got back to the schooner, Luna wasn't in the salon, and he didn't go looking for her. He flipped on a burner and set butter to melting in the frypan. With the kettle heating again, he sliced the bread.

Should he tell her how he'd already blundered into letting the whole town know she was staying with him?

He dropped in two slices and pulled out the cheese.

Maybe no one would say anything?

Ha.

Maybe they could take that trip up north that they'd planned and give folks the excitement of Fest to forget.

By the time her door opened, he had the sandwiches covered and toasting, her tea steeping and no decision. She came up behind him and wrapped her arms around his middle.

"Smells wonderful."

He cleared his throat. "Good. Wasn't sure what you might like." He turned as she released him. He handed her the mug of tea.

Luna put her nose to it and sniffed. "Mmm. Not my usual, but smells good. Morning tea is a must," she said with a smile. "Beyond that, our meals are anything. It depends on who is cooking." Her smile faded, and she blew out a sigh. "It was my turn this morning. Kippers."

He hugged her, but it didn't feel right. "I've blown it," he admitted. "Worse than not sacrificing your line to save a sail."

She stroked his cheek. "Grilled cheese is fine. Substantial, actually, to hold me while I get a few signs printed and leave word with several businesses that I'm available to work during Fest. After, I must hunt for my tool bag. It's not in the regular spot beneath the coat pegs, and I canna magic something without knowing where it is."

Right, her work. They could nae leave Tern Bay. "Not the food. I had to get bread at the bakery, and when I, uh, nearly blabbed that I needed it so I could make you breakfast, one of a local fishing crew I am on the outs with picked up on it and announced you'd stayed aboard last night."

Her face lost its animation, and his misery multiplied.

She licked her lips. "But Piper and Manta, Coral even, they know we've been courting."

He shook his head. "It wasn't just family there."

"Oh," she said *very* quietly.

Blimey, he was sunk.

"Place was packed. She likely followed me from the dock for a confrontation and caught up there. Probably told everyone you were visiting only because she's mad I got her family suspended. Folks were... I'm sorry, Luna."

"They were interested, I'm sure." She carried her tea to the table.

He followed her and placed his hands on her shoulders. They were stiff. "I'm sorry. It never occurred to me anyone would take note of my ship's activities. I'd never intentionally embarrass you."

She blew out a breath. "I know that, but it doesn't change what's done. Why is the family suspended?"

He told the story of discovering Maeve and her sister collecting berried hens, including how they'd tried to hide it. Pop was right that Luna needed to know the less-savory parts of their work, because it had now affected her.

"I was going to suggest we go to Loch Galloway, but I know you need to work," he said.

Luna shrugged. "Maybe this will gain me customers—the gossipy ones."

He winced. "Is there anything I can do?"

Face set and avoiding his gaze, she looped her satchel strap over her shoulder. "You could sneak up to the point and fetch back my tool bag while my family is asleep. That will give me more time to line up customers and allow me to avoid my father."

"Aye, I can do that." Hopefully, Keeper Jonah wouldn't catch him.

"And you'd better do it *before* Papa hears I'm sleeping with the freshest lad across two Windborne districts." She picked up her sandwich and left, her shoulders squared, stoic as always.

13

SKULKING AROUND

It wasn't as if Salm had never snuck up the back way to Kittiwake Point before. Luna had shown him exactly which flight route over the moors was hidden from their quarters' windows. He'd met her enough times along it that the landmarks were as familiar as avoiding submerged shoals around the Isle of Giuthas. But with her father cleaning the lighthouse for Fest, Salm might be seen from the tower.

Just before the last rise to the point, he dropped from a low skim of the heather and ran in a crouch to the shrubs at the crest, withdrawing the magic from his wings. Once the tingling of the energy change ended, he pushed through the overgrown branches of the footpath. Craning upward, he studied the widow's walk and the windows within, looking for shadows or movement.

None, only gulls winging their spirals around the buildings. He put one foot up the slope, drew a breath and hiked toward the wall surrounding the keeper's yard. No shouts rang out. He could claim he was just out for a hike—ach, that would sound lame. Anyone's brow would raise at that after he lifted the latch of the back gate.

No one was in the yard.

How about *I'm checking on the shag for Mr. Grouse?* Aye, that would sound better. He veered toward the shed where they'd housed the bird. Didn't hurt that the path put him in the lee of the chicken house. Salm paused at the side, rechecked the yard for activity—just the chickens—then set out for the back door and Luna's tools.

A gull flew in his face, squawking.

Salm ducked. "Hoy!" The blasted thing bombed him again, its cries loud enough to cover his slip—and to rouse the entire colony. He scampered back to the cover of the shed. Circling for another go, the crazed bird rose—a kittiwake? Could it be... "Rissa?"

The gull gave a pitiful cry and swooped. This time, Salm opened his arms as he'd seen Luna do and caught Rissa to his chest.

"*Shh,*" he hushed, cupping Rissa's head and stroking him.

Blessed Orb, this bird recognizes me? It must. Since Luna had rescued the chick, Salm had seen him with her every visit he made, but he'd never caught the thing. The bird nuzzled into him, making little whimpering sounds. "Come now, what's yer problem?" he asked. "You miss her, too?"

Luna usually gave the bird a fish and sent him off. It was a sorry use of magic, but he'd set out a package of baitfish to thaw this morning for his dolphin work this afternoon. He magicked one to his hand.

Greedily, Rissa took it and flew off.

"You ungrateful ball of feathers," he muttered, but at least that was easily resolved—if he could get inside the house before the kittiwake returned. He peered around the side of the shed. All clear.

A surge of guilt coursed through him upon passing the crates stacked outside the back door. In a trice, he had the door carefully pushed in. He paused on the threshold to listen, scanning the entryway. Everything that had been on the floor was gone. Magic jumping, Salm skulked through the house. The tool bag wasn't in the kitchen. Or the dining room, or the living room. Luna's family had finished their work yesterday, removing all the extra stuff to…somewhere.

Spells, what an idiot I am. Salm pivoted and hurried outside. The tools weren't in the top crate. He set that one aside and bent to the next. Something poked him in the back.

Someone. He jerked upright.

"What are you doing?" Nebula asked.

Salm blew out his breath and grinned at her before bending to shuffle through the crate's contents.

She poked him again with the unused paintbrush she held. "You better be treating my sister better than I hear."

Blast it all. He straightened. "I'm here for her tools, you ken, so she can work. What did you hear?"

"You've kidnapped and sullied her. She's paying you to hide her from Papa. That the two of you are running off to live in the human world. Luna should string you up by the bollocks."

"All of which makes no sense, since I didn't deny she was aboard our ship after *Maeve* told everyone." He told Nebula why Maeve and her sister were angry. "'Twas a *near* slip on my part. I merely said I was making breakfast. A perfectly innocent comment that Maeve elaborated on, making my pure intentions to help—"

Nebs snorted. "You can't feed me that bait. Your intentions to help Luna are about as *pure* as the ones I sometimes fall for with Kelly."

Had she really just admitted that? Salm waited a beat, and indeed, her eyes widened. He grinned. "See how easy it is to let things slip? And does your father know just how much time you spend in Kelly's company? More than I manage with Luna, I'd wager."

"You say another word about that," Nebula snapped, "to me

or anyone, and I'll tell Papa you were trespassing. Get out of here before he catches you." She set aside the crate he'd been searching, grabbed Luna's tool bag from the bottom one and shoved it at him.

He took it and left.

Luna forced herself to go to the printshop first. She had to have flyers to use to solicit prospective clients. But as she mocked up her services on one of Ms. Tulip's computer templates, she bit her lip. Contact location?

She didn't live at Kittiwake Point Lighthouse any longer, and neither did she wish to put down *The Peaceful Seas*. She clicked *save*, closed her file and rose. "Be right back," she told Ms. Tulip.

Luna walked briskly along the main deckwalk toward the center of town. Out-of-town vendors were setting up booths, but so were the townsfolk, and those who weren't were running errands. After several double takes, smiles and a couple of people clustered together and eyeing her, Luna ducked her head.

Still, a woman stopped her. "I know it canna be true," said Mrs. Grouper, the proprietress of the fish stall Luna's family frequented. "But Salm of the Seas implied that you and he—"

"Mrs. Grouper, Salm and I *are* seeing each other. Do you still need the canopy for your booth repaired?"

Mrs. Grouper pressed her lips together, clearly warring with herself. "I'll see if the Fintail's boy can fix it."

Luna said, "Good day," and cut through a side alley to walk behind the businesses. Word was spreading. She didn't have that many friends her own age in town, keeping the hours she did, and now she hesitated to ask any of them for advice on the flyer. But Manta would know what to do, since she ran a business.

She rapped at the alley door of One Good Bun and let herself in when Manta called, "Hello."

Manta gestured for Luna to come closer to the mixer she was adding ingredients to and handed her a note from her apron pocket. "Lady Anemone called here, thinking either I or Salm could get the message to you."

The note said Mr. Smith had more work for her. Luna clenched her hands. "I hope you believe me that we only slept aboard the ship. I wouldn't—"

"I know. Just..." Manta rolled her eyes. "Try not to let anyone discuss it with you so they have nothing to repeat."

"It's harder than you think," she muttered. "I'm posting for work for Fest. I hope if people see me about, they'll know I'm busy, and the attention will die down. I'm also looking for a flat."

Manta searched her face. "Are you breaking up with Salm over this? I know he has a big mouth, but Piper said Maeve's tattle was what set the hook."

"Nay. But I canna commit to sailing with him. With this row with Papa, I don't feel... I need... I refuse to return home, but—"

"You need time." Manta hugged her, then brushed the flour from Luna's hair and shoulders, laughing. "I wish I'd taken a place of my own for a spell, but I loved Piper, and 'twas easier to bond with him and be out of my parents' sight. They insisted, in fact, which Jonah hasn't?"

"He might if he knew how tight we are. Or hears what people are saying."

"Rent that flat. Or take a room. Old Mrs. Crest is knocking around her big house alone. She might rent the upstairs. Elder Bentha is letting rooms for Fest. So is Lady Anemone." Manta knew of more folks than Luna did.

"Until I can, I have no contact information to put on my

flyers. And until I earn more credits, I hesitate to commit to a lease. Could I use One Good Bun as my contact until I do?"

Manta hugged her again. "Of course." She scrunched her nose. "Keenan rents rooms, did you know? I believe by the week. The docks aren't the nicest area of Tern Bay, but Keenan is a good man and honest."

"Thank you."

"Bring us a stack of your flyers," Manta called as Luna closed the screen door.

Luna completed her flyer and submitted the order for printing. Instead of waiting, she walked up one level to the green house on the corner and knocked on Mr. Smith's front door.

"Ach, that was timely," he said to her. "Trust Anemone to relay a message. The drooping gutter is around back."

Luna followed him around, flew up to the roof to check that gutter and the others. She didn't mean to look, but the flat over the shed was visible. Beach towels hung over the deck railings. Heart heavy, she descended. "Brackets will hold better than the nails. Do you want me to get you a price?"

Mr. Smith agreed, and without letting herself look again toward his back garden, Luna returned to the printshop, collected her flyers and spent a minute scribbling out a list of possible rentals.

Where are you? Salm's voice came into her mind. *I have your tools.*

I only have one job lined up. I'd like to pass out flyers and…such before I carry them about. From the looks people are giving me, I don't feel 'tis a good thing for us to be seen together in town.

Or you at The Peaceful, *I suppose. Shall I leave them with Manta? At the back door?*

Luna cringed. It was a good suggestion, right in the middle of town, though Manta might tell Salm of their earlier conversation. *Excellent. I'll be by within the hour. And Salm? I'm also looking for a flat. Staying on* The Peaceful *is going to be awkward.*

There was a pause before he said, *I suppose, but let's talk about it, you ken? I'm off to help some fellows clean up a problem in a local estuary.*

The questions from the townsfolk started as soon as Luna pointed out her new contact was One Good Bun. After an awkward first encounter, she had a firm answer for the second: "At nineteenth year, don't you think it's time I struck out on my own?" She didn't wait for more questions before steering the conversation back to business—or leaving—but at some point, people would find a way to ask again. That was the way of small enclaves.

She took out her list of rentals. After seeing the little flat she could have had to herself, Luna hated considering anything less. But she had to, either before Salm's parents returned or Papa found out where she was.

At the first, Mrs. Crest eyed her. "I could consider it. You can look at it now if you like, and while you're there, I have a stair railing that's come loose. Rumor has it Keeper Jonah's lass is handy."

Luna's hand tightened on the door handle. The way her lips pursed at the idea, Mrs. Crest wasn't really considering renting to her. Likely, this was a ploy to get a bit of free work while Luna "looked at the room." She needed the exchange notes.

"I can give you a price while I'm up there and fetch my tool bag if you think it's a fair one."

The rooms were well furnished and too well kept, with knickknacks filling every surface. The railing was a simple job. To her surprise, Mrs. Crest said yes to the price. Luna said she'd return in an hour and used the trip through town to stop at the other places on her list.

Regularly let rooms during Fest were already taken. Two basement flats had definite openings in a week. Though cheaper than Mr. Smith's, they were dark, dampish things she could see herself in only if desperate. She wasn't, not yet. Three others had vacationers booked, if she was willing to wait out the autumn season.

One matron eyed her up and down. "I have a firm no-overnight-visitors policy. I'll need your references."

The room shared a bath with two others. "I'll think about it," Luna replied.

While in the hardware store pricing Mr. Smith's brackets, she'd picked up another three jobs. She retrieved her tools, completed Mrs. Crest's work and accepted her exchange notes and the news that the woman's neighbor wanted to see her about a step.

The man showed her the job, and when she returned with the replacement boards, he had his primer and paint ready—and a chair that he settled into.

"So," Mr. Bass started, "I hear tell you've moved out of the lighthouse."

The day continued like that. Everyone had something they wanted repaired, mainly for the opportunity to question her. By the end of the day, she had a month's equivalent of Mr. Smith's rent on her trade card, a list of work for tomorrow and no place to rent.

She returned to *The Peaceful Seas* at dusk, not bothering to look around to see if anyone was watching. They all were.

Salm met her on the deck, took her tool bag and led the way below deck. Only then did he pull her into a hug. She sank against him.

"You're exhausted." He ran his fingers through her hair, and when they caught, he massaged her scalp. "Did anyone say anything?"

"Those that didn't have found more repairs they suddenly need done tomorrow. I've had to put a few townsfolk off to fit in two vendors that were directed to me this evening. A cart's side and a canopy."

Salm laughed. "Excellent."

"'Tis. I should have several months' rent by the end of Fest, though dodging questions has made me wearier than the actual labor of the repairs did. Maybe after tomorrow, the news will have lost its freshness."

"Oh no." He gave a half laugh and a sweeping bow. "If that happens, we shall hug on the bow and blow kisses to each other as you walk off the gangway. If gossip keeps up your business, we shall keep up the gossip!"

When he wrapped his arms around her to demonstrate, she pushed back. "You're crazy, Salm. What are you going to say after my father hears the gossip and shows up to confront you?"

He shrugged. "You're nineteenth year. An adult Windborne. What can he do?"

"Papa does nae see me as grown. Besides, age isn't the point. I didn't magically change. I still want to see my sisters."

The grin slid from Salm's face. "You think he would forbid that?"

A shrug kept her tears at bay.

"Nebula was preparing to paint this morning when I picked up your tools. The living room was spotless."

Nebs and Stella had actually buckled down without her? "The rest?"

"Fairly cleared out. I hate that you're estranged from your father, but also glad you're standing up for yourself."

Luna tightened her hold on him.

"Hoy, Rissa did a funny thing. Your feathered freeloader flew at me and begged *me* for a fish," Salm said, probably thinking it'd make her laugh.

It made her more homesick than ever.

14

UNABLE TO SETTLE

The next morning, Luna fully expected to find Salm in her bed again. He wasn't. A savory scent enticed her to dress quickly and step through the bulkhead. His cabin was empty and so was the salon, but he'd made tea, and fresh pasties were warm under the lid of a frypan.

Salm?

On the deck.

She poured herself a mug, wrapped a pasty in a napkin and climbed the ladder. He was sitting cross-legged in the sun on the deckhouse, where anyone could see. She hesitated and glanced around... Why bother? Everyone had heard by now anyway. Before she could magic out her wings, he dropped off the roof and gestured her to the sunny side. They sank to the deck and leaned shoulder to shoulder against the wall.

"You didn't come to my cabin this morning," she said.

"Figured I better bring myself to the point we don't have to lie."

"Thank you."

He kissed her cheek. "Not that I didn't want to watch you sleeping."

"Me, too."

Soon, he left to make fishing boat inspections with his dolphins. She'd finished the dishes and was about to leave when a soft voice called from above the hatch, "Luna? Are you there?"

Her sister knew better than to board someone's boat—ah. Nebula hadn't. She was hovering above it, Stella fluttering beside her. *Spells, what a wonderful sight they are!* Luna ascended the ladder, and they threw themselves at her.

"You've decided to move onto Salm's schooner?" Stella blurted.

"No." Luna smoothed her youngest sister's hair and kissed her forehead. "Not yet. How did you hear..." *Stormy nights.* She didn't need to ask when she was the talk of the town.

"Manta," Nebula said proudly. "Salm's sister had to know." She held out a canvas bag. "We brought your clothes from the laundry. Figured you wouldn't know where they were well enough to magic them to yourself."

True. And they'd moved so many things while cleaning up that it hadn't seemed worth the magic to try. "Thank you." Luna searched the bag. "You didn't happen to bring my sweater, did you?"

"Haven't seen it." Nebula fingered the pullover Luna was wearing, a loan from Salm. "You don't like this one better? I wear Kelly's cardigan when I can."

"Much as I love Salm, I miss my own things." And her hair looked washed out against the cream-colored yarn.

"Then why did you leave, Luna?" Stella whined. "Don't you love us anymore?"

She hugged her. "Of course I do." She brushed her fingers through Stella's curls, magicked a ribbon from her satchel and tied them back with a bow over one ear. "But I'm not coming back, so you'll need to learn to do these things for yourself."

"It's part of growing up," Nebula said with a nod. "Papa told you that." Yet she eyed Luna. "He skipped the real reason why you took off *now*. He was yelling?"

So Papa hadn't told them he'd found her and Salm together. "Telling me what I could and could not do." Luna sighed. "It's time I decide these things for myself."

"But you didn't say goodbye." Stella wiped her eye. "Rissa misses you, too."

"Ah, don't you pull that forlorn puppy-dog act on me," Luna said. "You know I'll start weeping myself. I suspect this is more about you having to take over my chores than anything else."

Stella tried to hide her smile but succeeded only in looking sweeter.

"Now how is the shag doing? Any sign of redness or swelling around the stitches?"

"Nay, but dried blood is still on his feathers since he's wearing the hood and can't clean them."

They answered her questions about his wound, eating, pill-taking and assured her, unprompted, that they were cleaning his kennel and pool.

"Though 'tis sodding mean of you to dump all that on us," Nebula grumbled. "On top of the cleaning."

"Salm's help made up for some of my part. And the rescues have always been a family activity," Luna answered. "I just *happened* to have done more with them than either of you."

"This bird likes me better than Nebs," Stella said smugly.

"You insist on giving him the fish," Nebula retorted, then with a glint in her eyes, demanded, "Show us Salm's room."

Luna shot her a warning look. "Don't you want to see the cabin I'm sleeping in instead? Or my place, once I rent one? You shall have to bring Rissa around when I do."

"I'd rather see the schooner," Stella said stubbornly.

They begged and teased for a few more minutes, but she didn't feel right inviting them in without Salm present. Finally, Nebula pulled a paper from her pocket.

"Papa said to give this to you, if we should *happen* to see you." She rolled her eyes. "And he sent us to town to sell eggs without even checking if we had any to sell."

"I was packing you these in secret." Stella took a cloth bundle from her small satchel and pulled up one edge. Inside was a clutch of cream and brown eggs.

"Oh, bless you." Luna took the eggs and hugged her sister. "It does nae feel right to wake up and not have fresh eggs for dinner."

"Now can we come in while you cook them?" Stella asked.

Ignoring her, Luna shifted the eggs to the crook of her arm and unfolded the note.

Daughter, I wish to speak with you together with your sisters. Is there a time in the next few nights when you could stop by? Your Papa.

Luna refolded the note. "What does he want to talk about?"

"If the shag can be released?" Stella asked.

"Too soon," Luna answered. "Count out the pills and you'll have how many more days. Then I need to check him first." She glanced at the eggs. "Is Papa trying to bribe me to come home?"

"*We're* trying to bribe you to come home," Nebula said in exasperation. "At least until after these cursed tours. Papa is insisting we uphold *his* agreement. If you aren't going to let us in, then we better get back."

Luna saw them off, watching as they flew over the harbor and flapped higher to the top of Kittiwake Point. Then she left for work.

Between jobs, whenever she saw a *Rent for Fest* sign, she knocked at the door. Everyone was full, or had no plans to rent after Fest. After six refusals and finding herself not far from Elder Bentha's at the very top of the cliff, she climbed on up to the cottage where a rental sign greeted her in the yard. It was the next-to-last place on her list. She knocked.

Elder Bentha's bonding partner, Mr. Douglas, answered. "We heard Jonah's lass was taking on repairs for the community. I play a little poker with Mr. Smith. He raved about your quick work."

Aye, that was before she'd become the talk of the town. But Luna smiled. "'Tis true, and I've also moved from the lighthouse and am looking for a place to rent. I see you're renting rooms," she finished as Elder Bentha came to the door as well.

"We still have Gill's old room free," he said. "Third floor and faces—"

"We'll not be letting that one," Elder Bentha said loudly, her cheeks flushed.

Mr. Douglas frowned. "I wish you had let me in on this change of plans."

"I think she means you're not letting that one *to me*," Luna said, her gaze on Elder Bentha. "Good day." She turned and walked down the steps, keeping her chin up, though her gut churned. How many of those other places she'd asked about had been "unavailable" only to her?

Without looking at the list, she knew the last item was Keenan's and his flats above Dockside Diner.

Too tired to approach him on an empty stomach, she stopped at a vendor to get a battered sausage on a stick for lunch.

"Make it two, and I'll pay," said Lady Anemone from behind her.

"No, you don't need—"

"I insist." Lady Anemone held up her hand. "Come sit with me. You look like you need the break. Add two frozen lemonades to that," she said to the vendor.

Stormy nights. She was in for a lecture. Luna accepted her sausage, coated it in mustard and slung her heavy tool bag over her shoulder again. She followed Lady Anemone to an empty bench. Settling down, Lady Anemone handed Luna one of the drinks and began eating her own food with no comment.

Luna ate, too. The sausage was filling, but the tart sweetness of the frozen lemonade pumped up her energy. After several spoonfuls, cold lodged in her chest, and she had to slow down.

"Feeling better?" Lady Anemone asked after several minutes of silence.

"I am, thank you."

"I always find the lemonade reviving. Those dark circles under your eyes said you needed it."

Luna nodded to that and then pulled her wad of notes from her pocket, preparing to extract herself.

"Repairs?" Lady Anemone asked.

"Quite a few. Enough to cover rent on a place of my own, which I'm sure you've heard I'm looking for."

"I have." Lady Anemone spooned up a frosty mound, but didn't eat it right away. "I'm not one to nose into others' business, and I've not hesitated to remind folks that they should do the same for our own."

A rush of gratitude flooded Luna. "Thanks," she said.

"Many are simply looking out for you, love."

That was the point. She was nineteenth year. Did she need looking out for?

"I'm not asking for details, but is everything all right with… your current arrangements?" The words were only slightly different than what anyone else had asked, but the empathy lacing the healer's voice threatened to crumble Luna's guard.

"As right as it can be leaving my sisters and home."

"And your father?"

Luna swallowed and took a breath before answering, "I miss him, too, but we need some distance and time."

Lady Anemone's eyes narrowed. "Leaving hasn't fixed things?"

"Nay." The word was out before she'd decided to speak. She pressed her lips together.

"I'm here if you need anything, lass. My rooms are all let for

Fest, but I can make up a cot in my parlor if you need it. That would be temporary, only for this week of Fest. I can only tolerate so much craziness."

"I appreciate the offer," Luna whispered.

Lady Anemone stood up. "Back at it, then. Your stack of work looks daunting even to me." Her own notes appeared in her hand. "Regular rounds, on top of four first aid stations to check. Please stay off my list, lass."

Luna laughed. "I'll try." She shuffled her work requests, but her thoughts continued on with settling a place to stay, and her eyes glazed over. She glanced northward. *No time like now.*

Dockside Diner was packed at the noon hour. Keenan's one server, his niece, rang up a customer, then turned to her. "Afraid there's a wait. Like, ten minutes?" the witch said.

"I'm not here to eat," Luna said. "I wanted to talk to Keenan about renting."

"All full for Fest," she got out just as Keenan called, "Table three!" and slid plates with steaming fish and chips onto the counter of the pass-through. His gaze met hers. "Luna? I need my railing fixed if you have the time." He gestured her back to the kitchen.

Thank the Orb, she could ask him in private about renting.

As luck would have it, the repair was on the balcony of one of the flats. Keenan unlocked it and waved her in. "I told the renters I'd need to be in today to replace the wobbly railing, but I didn't expect to be swamped in the diner."

"I can do it today," Luna replied. The room combined a tiny kitchen and living room overlooking the cliffside and several houses rather than the harbor—too bad—but as Keenan led the way to the French doors, she glimpsed the bedroom and a bathroom. "How much?" she asked.

"I hoped you might do it for twenty exchange notes."

That was low—oh. She laughed. "That's fair. But I meant

how much to rent one of your flats, and have you any available?"

He did, after Fest, and the rate was manageable. "The bayside ones all have permanent tenants, but if any come open…" He cast a glance at the door. "I've got to get back to the kitchen. It's noisier than you are used to, but I rent by the week or the month and ask for that length of notice. Look around. Let me know what you decide when we settle up on the railing." He left.

Luna stood, staring after him. Aye, Keenan was in a hurry, but he hadn't said anything about visitors. The entire town knew she was seeing Salm of the Seas. Surely Keenan had heard.

If he had, then unlike Elder Bentha, he didn't care. *But Keenan is also a Tern Bay elder. He should care, since he had to enforce the bonding licensing policies.*

Should she bring it up? Maybe he hadn't asked because he didn't want to know.

She looked around again. Then thought on it while she fetched the replacement bracket for the railing and completed the repair. The area was noisy. Despite the size and the view, the privacy of her own loo and kitchen would make up for that.

After packing away her tools, she took out her exchange-note pouch as she looked around. The paint was scuffed, the cupboards older and the mattress saggy. She blew out a breath. It wasn't bright and airy like Mr. Smith's flat, but she could afford it. No one would be monitoring her comings and goings. With the balcony on the back side of the building, fewer people could monitor Salm's. *I never thought there would be so much to consider when choosing a place.*

She counted out a week's rent in exchange notes, then another week's. *That gives me time to try it, then I can find another if I need to.*

In the diner's kitchen, Keenan paid her, and she paid him. "The place is all yours in a week," Keenan said and stepped back to the grill. He didn't ask about visitors, and she didn't volunteer anything. Quite quickly, she was pushing her way through the waiting customers and outside.

What will Salm think?

She could tell him now via thought-speaking. She could have asked his opinion at any point while she was working alone. She hadn't. And she knew why. She just didn't want to think about why.

Automatically, she took her work notes out of her pocket, but deciding which to do next seemed too difficult to manage. But she had to. She was paying for a place to live now, and with that one change, she felt different in a way she couldn't explain. Not happy, not sad, but…

Sneaky.

Did I make the right decision?

She shuffled the out-of-towner requests to the top and forced herself to do the first. She was on her way to the next when Salm contacted her.

Might your family's sailboat be available to borrow for an expanded sailing lesson I have in mind for Ty?

If she'd been living at the lighthouse still, the answer would have been a ready *aye*, but the question made Luna pause. *Papa hasn't* disowned *me*. She still had use of their family's things, including the *Midnight Marauder*. And since he'd sent the note, likely Papa still expected her to come home again.

Aye, she sent Salm.

And how about you? Can I borrow you as well, to sail it while I crew and keep an eye on Ty?

She went to the nearest railing and looked over the harbor. The waves were moderate, and wind blew steadily from the southwest. Luna yanked on the strings holding her hat and let it drop down her back. The breeze whipped back her curls. She ran her fingers through them. The sailing would be good, and she hadn't been out in days. *Aye.*

She still didn't tell him about her new flat.

Although they wouldn't sail for another few hours, Luna went to South Dock to ready the boat. She retrieved their equipment from their locker, rigged the two sails and wiped the seats. She settled into one with a book to have some time alone. To her surprise, Nebula arrived soon after, her friend Kelly in tow.

With a wave, Kelly continued on down the dock to his family's mooring.

"Another message from Papa?" she asked Nebula.

"Nay." Nebula grinned. "Salm turned up this morning. He remembered that Kelly and I competed in last year's Fest race and asked if we'd like a practice run. At first, I told him that I had to clean the back hall." She wrinkled her nose. "A little nastily, which I now regret. Salm pitched in and scrubbed the cupboards and floor. I cleaned the table and every spindle of the chairs. With the clearing out you did in the kitchen, everything is put away behind doors that close. They won't bear looking inside, but the room is spotless."

Luna blew out a breath. "That's wonderful."

"You're telling me. I'm thrilled to be outside, and with Kelly, too." She winked and tossed Luna a wave before heading down the dock.

Folks walking along cast her curious glances. Luna sank lower into her seat. No one stopped to talk to her, but she could hear the lively conversations Nebs engaged in. Soon, all the old folks who passed their afternoons fishing or sitting and talking in the community pavilion at the dock's end knew Salm was running a practice race.

Ugh. Luna wanted to tell Nebs to keep it to herself, but that would embarrass Nebs in front of Kelly, and Nebs would then do the opposite, like go up to the main deckwalk and make an announcement.

Salm and Ty sailed up in a 420, a dinghy-sized racing sailboat that they'd borrowed from someone in town. Newcomer Ty

Sterling took care navigating toward the dock, his silver-eyed gaze darting to judge the distance between boats more than anyone local would have. They tied up at her family mooring and immediately ran off to make the bakery's bread deliveries. A half hour later, Salm returned in high spirits with both Ty and Coral trailing him, their brown-haired heads together in conversation. He clambered into the *Midnight Marauder* and leaned in like he was about to kiss Luna.

"Don't," she hissed. "Everyone is watching."

"Ach, I forgot." He straightened and looked around. "I think people are disappointed."

Indeed, many in the crowd gathered under the pavilion had turned to watch them.

"Salm," she said under her breath. "Put on your life jacket." *Before something else happens.* Ducking around, Luna cast off and eased out the sheet. The sail luffed. After Salm had secured his life jacket, she handed him the jib sheet. "I assume with Coral crewing for Ty, we don't need to wait for him."

Out in the bay, their boat skimmed along to the buoy Salm had designated as their start line. The motions were automatic for her, as they were for Salm, so they didn't need to talk, and the tension in her shoulders began to ease. It was a beautiful day to be on the ocean. The autumn sun lit the colorful houses rising up the cliffsides, and Kittiwake Point Lighthouse stood proudly above the crashing waves. Maybe Salm was right. She should join him on a boat and leave behind the gossip in Tern Bay and every other port.

Salm put a hand on her knee, and she covered it with her own. She wanted to tell him about the room she'd rented, or thank him for helping Nebula clean, or even that she loved sailing with him. Instead, she said, "I want to be careful in public. I don't like the attention we are garnering."

Salm met her gaze. "I will try to remember. But I'm excited

to be sailing with you. Aren't you excited to be out on this gorgeous day?"

She was. Just as she could tell he was. They followed such similar courses in so many of their thoughts and feelings. So why were her emotions twisted up in these knots? Why didn't she want to make her decisions *with* Salm?

15

THE WINDS OF CHANGE

Salm plucked another bass fillet from the egg mixture, flopped it into the bread crumbs and dropped it into the frying pan. Beside him, Luna cut up scallions and herbs and told him about her day repairing canopy posts, portable tables and a loose railing at Keenan's diner.

He smiled at her. *This is all going so well.* They'd be looking for a ship of their own next week, he was sure of it.

"Keenan didn't have time to fix it himself, with the extra folks coming in." She cracked the eggs her sisters had brought her into a bowl to whip. "The best part is, one of those flats above his place will be available right after Fest. It'll be kind of noisy, but ironically, it's the most private of any I looked at, with its own loo and kitchenette. He called it a studio. I won't be in someone else's house."

No, she wouldn't—*what?* Salm jerked around to look at her. "What'd you just say?"

"It's my own place. No issues with you visiting."

By the Orb... "You took it?"

"Aye."

"In that..." *Wreck of a building,* he didn't say. "You a..."

Woman… Spells, he certainly couldn't say that. "You, uh, alone. On the end of town where the rougher blokes come and go."

She'd begun whipping the eggs, but now set down the bowl and crossed her arms. "You think they will bother me?"

He rolled his eyes.

"You think I canna protect myself?"

"I didn't say that."

"Think I'll fall in with the wrong people?"

He swiped off the burner and let the tongs clatter onto the counter. Argh! Everything he said came out wrong, because… because… He didn't know why. He felt angry, but for no good reason. How could he respond and not be an ass? He pressed his fingertips to his chin to stroke his beard that wasn't there anymore. Growling out a curse, he stormed across the salon. At the ladder, he mounted the first step…and stopped. He couldn't walk out on her. Walking out on her would be worse than saying it. *One, two, three…* He got to ten and turned.

Luna had remained in place, staring at him. His hands lifted automatically, and his feet carried him two steps before he realized he intended to stroke her arms, to make an attempt to pacify her. He didn't dare walk closer. His gut churned, but that might be due to the scent of the savory herbs and fried fish. Salm wasn't sure with his feelings so disheveled.

He let his hands fall to his sides. "I-I wish for you to have your freedom, but I also wish for you to be safe. That end of town is nae safe."

"Because?" she prompted.

"'Tis where blokes hang out to pick up lasses. For trysts." Salm threw his hands in the air. "It has nothing to do with Keenan or his building or business. He runs a tight ship." *Why do I have to be the one to explain this to her?* "'Tis the proximity to the docks. Folks coming in after a few days out on the water. Folks who are…lonely."

Luna laughed, but not humorously. "You think I don't know

what goes on over at Maisy's place? I do. It's a *block* from Dockside Diner. Everyone else landing in Tern Bay knows it, or finds out quick enough. What's the real issue here?"

Salm fisted his hands. "You are tearing me up inside, Luna. I want to protect you and take care of you, and yet you will nae let me. Ever."

"We agreed that independence is important. Or was that me stating it and you going along?"

"I didn't," he spat. "I want you to be independent. And I want my own damned independence, the possibility of which is a motorboat racing over the horizon. I just..." He was practically yelling. He threw his head back and stared at the ceiling until he could quietly say, "If I canna get a ship, I will be aboard *The Peaceful* forever."

"Stop being dramatic."

"'Tis nae drama. 'Tis fact."

"Why does it have to be a schooner? Can't it be a smaller craft?"

The snort was out before he thought twice. By her narrowed eyes, he knew he'd blown it. "I canna believe you are asking me this."

"Think about what *you're* asking me. Is it any different than what my father assumes I'll do? I move onto a sailboat, I do what you do, and then I lose myself. I want to do something *I'm* good at. And I want to support myself. It's not like I *want* to rent a flat from Keenan. But it's available, and it's what I can afford."

"Tha' is one good thing," he muttered.

"It's a compromise. I want a home of my own where I can come and go while building my repair business and not feel like my activities are monitored. I could join you sailing more often if I'm not worried about earning as many trade credits for housing." She drew a breath. "I want you to live with me."

"I want you to live *with me*. On a ship." He shook as he said the words.

She pressed her head into her hands. "I said that wrong. I want us to live together. To... Can we just start with I want us to *be together?*"

"I love the sea, sailing, the dolphins, my work. None of that is on land."

"I'm not asking you to give up those things. I also love the sea, sailing and the seabirds. It's *my* work I'm unsure of—what and where. I'm so cursed busy doing things for other people that I've not had a chance to do anything for myself. I want to be more than Keeper Jonah's lass."

That made sense. *It probably also means she wants to be more than the partner of Salm of the Seas.* He nodded glumly.

"I need...time." She collected her thoughts. "A year, Salm. I need a year to sort things with my family. For Stella to get used to the idea. For Papa and me to train Nebula reliably or find other help for him. For Papa to acknowledge that I'm growing up, that I'm capable. And for me. I'd like to do some things for me, like my mother did with her art and stargazing."

Disappointment weighed on Salm's heart. "I thought we were closer to being together and out from under the wings of our respective families. For me to sail on my own, soon, even a smaller craft..." That idea grated at his gut. "Anything larger than the 420s." Any boat of his would be *much* bigger. "And my folks would still want you to train in sailing alongside them."

"I can do that. Not full time, but once I'm settled, for a week or so at a time. Is that a compromise you're willing to make?"

"And after a year of sorting?"

"After a year, I will give you an answer."

That wasn't what he'd expected her to say. "You will know your mind in a year?"

"I—" She didn't look at him. "Who's to say if a year will be enough time? But I won't ask more of you. I will give you an answer, whether I know my mind or not. If you require an answer now, it must be no. You decide."

Blast it all, she was giving him an ultimatum. His jaw worked, but no words were forming in his brain, and luckily none were spouting from his mouth.

"It doesn't mean I love you any less," she said. "I simply need to spend some time loving myself. Taking care of *my* needs. I still want to see you."

Did that mean just to say ahoy, or... "To continue on as we have?"

She swiped back her hair, and when her hand returned to grip the counter, her knuckles were white. "Would you be willing to have it be openly? I'd like to prebond and tell my family."

"But that implies a commitment. You're not ready to make a commitment."

"Prebonding is *not* a commitment. It's a trial."

He turned the sound that came out of his mouth into a cough. "Before even starting it, we've already taken that trial further than the rules allow."

She spun away and, arms crossed, paced the small salon before turning back to him. "You turn nineteenth year in a few weeks. In my district, we can bond when both are nineteenth year, with no parental permission needed."

Aye, October seventh wasn't long to wait. But the Isle of Giuthas rules required waiting until twentieth year for bonding, preceded by a year of prebonding. If he wished to work on the isle's Seas habitat, going against the Giuthas council wouldn't look good, not to mention Pop was an elder. However, prebonding in either district would prevent trouble if they were caught merging magic.

"Bonds are difficult to break, but not impossible," she said quietly. "If you don't want your parents to be angry, I'm willing to bond."

Salm threw his hands in the air again. "You're impossible. You won't agree to live on a ship, but you suggest bonding with me so we can sleep together and not make my mother mad?"

Luna's face made it clear that she was upset. "You're right. I'm not thinking straight. That's a terrible plan. I'm just going to get your hopes up."

"Let's—" *Am I really suggesting this?* "Let's think on this a mite, lass. We have several weeks, regardless." He busied himself with poking a fish fillet. It was done.

Luna had turned on the burner under a frypan with butter in it. She kept her head down—clearly still simmering—and whipped the eggs once more, vigorously.

He put a lid over the fish. He couldn't take it if she thought getting their own ship was off the table... *Nay, I canna ask her again.* Best to talk to Manta before he blurted something he regretted. "I'll just, uh, go to the bakery for more bread while you cook those," he said.

Her gaze on her eggs, Luna gave a small nod.

He waited a beat, but she didn't look up. *What did I say wrong this time?* He left.

Manta was baking, of course, for Fest and easy to find alone.

"I canna stand it." Salm strode to the end of the bakery's commercial kitchen, then back again. "Luna helped me with the dolphins and Pop's ship chores. She seemed perfectly happy to sail with Ty and Coral, but persists in her plan to rent a room."

Manta handed him a storage container and pointed to cookies on a cooling rack. "Well, if she canna find one on my list of older people, then what about younger families that need a hand with their children?"

Salm stopped. "I did nae say the search was fruitless. She's rented a flat above Keenan's. I will not have her living above Dockside. Or taking care of children."

With a frown, Manta crossed her arms. "I really do not wish to let my new attic room, if that's what you're getting at."

"I'm not." He swung around, knocking into a counter and

losing part of the molasses cookie he'd picked up but hadn't eaten. He pointed a finger and magicked it to the refuse bin.

"I don't suppose I need to remind you that it's not up to you where she lives or what she does."

"No," Salm snapped. "I—" Blast it all, why did Manta always have to be right?

"Our docks aren't the worst place in the world to live, and Luna's a smart woman. You two would still need to work out which enclave your energy tithing would go to."

Every wizard had to contribute a portion of their generated energy to the shielding of their home enclave. Since he and Luna were from different enclaves, this had to be decided before they applied for a bonding license.

"Perhaps this can be a transition," Manta said.

"While I go insane," he muttered. "Fine, I'll stay out of that. But do I keep seeing her if she refuses to sail?"

"Do you *want* to keep seeing her?"

Of course he did. But not every few weeks. Every day. Every *night.*

Manta rolled her eyes when he didn't answer.

"Is it too much to ask to sleep with the woman I love?" His sister opened her mouth, but he blurted, "'Tis nae just that. I want to share my life with her—a life sailing, which she seems to hate."

"Surely she doesn't hate all of it? She sails and lives on the coast, too. Does she want to move elsewhere?"

"I reckon 'tis the idea of her home being a ship rather than a house and port being Giuthas versus Tern Bay. She suggests we live together and that I get a smaller boat that I can handle on my own."

Manta blinked. "There's an idea. Brilliant, in fact. I told you she's smart."

How would he command respect from the fisherfolk if he sailed up in a dinghy? Salm huffed. "I want a double-masted."

"Worse than you want to sleep with the woman you love? With the witch who calms your magic so that you're a bloke who's actually reasonable enough to live with? I've found you easier to get along with the last month, though I canna say I want to live with you again." His sister put up a finger when he opened his mouth. "Answer me this: Is she willing to learn to sail with Ma and Pop?"

Somehow, this had to be a trick question. "Aye, but what good will that do—"

"She's willing. Talk to Pop. Sort how the assignments might change. Coral is old enough to take more responsibility. If Luna is willing to compromise and learn the sailing, then you have to be willing to compromise on her priorities."

Salm pointed a finger at Manta. "Don't you think I can't see what you're doing. You're telling me I'm the one at fault here."

She threw a towel at him. "You came to me for help. Do you want it or not?"

"I want a ship. One like Ma and Pop's."

"Don't be self—" She pressed her lips closed and flicked her fingers to retrieve the towel. Manta wiped her counter for a moment. "I can't advise you. As much as I wish the best for the two of you, perhaps you'd best prepare to let go of your plans with Luna."

With the bread under his arm, Salm walked back through the dark to the ship, Manta's damned non-advice grating at his nerves. But it had made him think. Pop and Uncle Ray had already established that the Seas had enough work for four craft. Uncle Ray put to port in an enclave farther south, while Salm's sister Wind monitored their northern boundaries and harbored in a port up there. It shouldn't be out of the question for Salm to ask if he could put to port here instead of on the Isle of Giuthas. He'd just never considered moving from his home enclave. But for Luna, he would ask if Pop was willing to revise the rounds.

"Hullo," he called softly as he came down the companionway ladder.

No answer.

Belowdecks smelled of scallions and butter and eggs, but no lamps were lit. He hesitated, then started for her cabin. An apology would make him feel better at least. Though he'd never tell Manta she was right, it *was* Luna's decision to live above Dockside.

She wasn't in her cabin. When he backtracked to the ship's salon, he saw her tool bag was gone. Had she been summoned for an emergency repair? He tried calling her through their thought-speak channel.

Nothing…like it was shut down. He checked her cabin once more. Her laundry bag was also gone. The frypan for the eggs was empty and cleaned.

Where was she?

16

ACTUALLY ON HER OWN

Surely Luna hadn't gone to—

Salm charged up the companionway ladder, wings unfurling before his legs even emerged from the hatch. His feet never touched the deck. He expertly ducked the boom and lines, then swerved up to miss the forest of masts, the lights of Dockside Diner in his sights.

He had half a mind just to fly around the building and check in the windows, but he descended at the front. He reached for the latch as he craned to look inside for a fluff of white curls.

"Hoy, lad," a gruff voice called. "Flying in town is nae allowed!"

"Salm of the Seas," a witch admonished, "you know better. Have you been at the ale with your parents gone?"

Curses. He threw a glance over his shoulder. "Uh, nay. Wasn't thinking. Sorry." Another look into the diner assured him Luna wasn't seated at the counter or huddled in a booth. He stuffed his fists into his pockets and mumbled, "Sorry," again to the couple he didn't know and strode toward town.

Now that he thought on it, hadn't Luna said her rental started *next week*? She had no reason to be at Dockside versus anywhere else in town. He'd acted harebrained, exactly as Manta had accused him. Luna would be horrified and, even more so, embarrassed if he approached her like this.

He would be, too. This wasn't how a grown man behaved.

Still, he walked every deckwalk just on the chance he'd spot her. He flew up over the point, but couldn't bring himself to approach closer than a hundred feet of the keeper's yard. His search of the moors lasted far longer than it should have—she wouldn't foolishly be out there in the cold like he was.

When he flipped on a light in the dark salon, his gaze landed on the fishing boat numbers he'd collected. Salm groaned. He still had to write up his week's inspection reports for Pop, or he'd never get off probation.

As soon as Salm had left, Luna cooked the eggs and carried the hot pan to the table. While they cooled enough to eat, she tore a blank page from the back of her notebook. She would not allow Salm of the Seas to tell her what to do any more than she had allowed Papa to. Of course, Papa wouldn't like that she was about to reveal the family's private business, but coming to stay aboard *The Peaceful Seas* had done just that. Far better that she actually tell someone the truth than allow her family to fly apart.

Before second thoughts could stop her, she penned a letter to her uncle Rigel. She didn't mention drinking precisely, just wrote *issues have arisen*, and asked if he could come to help at the Autumnal Equinox Festival and perhaps consider staying on afterward to help Papa.

She addressed and sealed the envelope. *It's for the best,* she told herself as she ate her eggs, cleaned the pan and gathered her things. She walked to the town's main level and slid the letter into the box in front of the town hall. It'd go out tomorrow, and in a few days she could look for an answer. In the meantime… She strode down the deckwalk and knocked on the door of a familiar gold house.

The next morning, Luna simply wanted to roll over and pull the pillow over her head. Had she slept at all? The spell she'd used to dampen the outside noises of a typical Tern Bay night hadn't made a difference with her mind racing. *And when Fest starts, the late-night revelers will only be worse.* Had she made another rash decision? It seemed lame that all her moves in the name of independence only landed her in the debt of another friend.

She opened her eyes. No shafts of light spilled past the edges of the shades in Lady Anemone's parlor. But as Luna removed the spell, a steady patter filled the void. Rain. Which meant—she pushed herself upright to find her watch—the dim light was cloud cover, not dawn. Indeed, it was midmorning already. She had clients waiting, and being tardy might dash her hopes for gaining more work. She changed clothes and stuffed her nightshirt—Salm's shirt, which she'd taken because Nebula hadn't thought to include her nightgown—under the pillow and pulled up the covers to make up the cot.

The simple act made her weary. How long would it be before she had her own things again? A bed with the sheets she and Mam had embroidered? Her pillow? Over the last few days of having to borrow everything, she'd come to realize how many belongings she'd left behind. Clothes, towels, a water glass… She grabbed her hairbrush, the toothbrush and paste she'd bought yesterday and peeked out the door to see if the bath was clear.

Lady Anemone's Fest roomers seemed to have gotten an early start. Thankfully, the house was empty during her morning routine, and when she let herself out, it was…into a hard rain.

She groped with strands of magic to muster up her slicker and wellies from the pegs by the back door of the lighthouse quarters. No luck. She blew out a breath and gave over a fair amount of energy for a spell to waterproof her trainers and work coveralls. With her tool bag in hand, she headed for One Good Bun, her curls lengthening with each raindrop that hit her head.

She waited in a horrific line to buy a scone for breakfast. Piper's face held a glazed-over look, and it wasn't until he returned with her order that he actually saw her.

"Luna? Go on in the back. Manta has your messages."

In the hot and noisy kitchen, Coral spotted her first and grinned. "Salm has been in here twice looking for you. Did you go home to the lighthouse?"

"Coral," Manta admonished, "that's nae your business." She flipped off her mixer and led the way to a separate room, which housed her office. Pulling a pin from the bulletin board, she handed over a stack of notes. "Salm's is on the top."

It was folded, so Luna decided not to read it there. She flipped through the others—ten of them. "This many calls? I'm so sorry to trouble you, Manta. I figured it'd be two or three a day. I owe you some time. Anything you need repaired?"

"Not during Fest, but afterward I'll certainly take you up on it. Salm actually answered the phone for three of those messages while he hung around this morning." Manta's forehead creased. "I hope what I said to him last night hasn't come between you. I'd hate to be the reason you've split."

Luna shook her head. "We haven't talked since he came for bread."

"And it's killing him. You, too, from your looks—"

Luna tried to smile but couldn't. She lifted the notes. "At least I'll be busy today. Thanks, Manta." She left by the back door and walked down a few buildings before stopping and unfolding Salm's note.

I'm sorry. I hope we can talk later.

Stay safe, Salm

Luna leaned against a sheltering wall and closed her eyes.

Aye, they could talk more...she *wanted* to talk more. She and Salm wanted similar things—independence and a life together on or near the sea—but his rushed schedule didn't match hers. Would he agree to her compromises to slow down?

Or what felt like compromises to her. Spells, she wasn't sure anymore.

Three hours and four jobs later, Luna hadn't stopped thinking about what she'd said to Salm about him doing this and that to make it possible for her to live in Tern Bay. She had gotten out from under Papa's control—which was what she'd wanted, wasn't it? So why did she feel like she needed to continue to live in Tern Bay? Her sisters would probably be fine with frequent visits.

Her gaze tracked to Kittiwake Point Lighthouse, wrapped in fog with only the flashing light visible, a solitary beacon on an isolated point. Often, folks asked if she got lonely up there. Yes and no.

Her sisters, birds, trips to town and, now, working for folks filled her need for socializing.

And Salm.

She hadn't been looking for a partner, but their chance encounters around town had changed to visits she'd looked forward to. If they split... Her vision blurred, and she quickly wiped her eyes. She couldn't walk through town crying, nor could she turn up at her next client's with red eyes.

Time for a break. Luckily, a number of vendors were selling food in the rain, because she couldn't keep returning to One Good Bun. She bought a gyro and was eating it under the covered porch of her next client when Ty Sterling came trotting up.

"Hey, glad I found you." He lifted his chin toward the house. "Coral remembered these folks are one of your work requests today, and they're also on my delivery route. Your sister called the bakery. Elder Bentha contacted your father about an injured bird someone has brought to South Dock. Nebula said your father is working and didn't want to come down if you were able to look at it. They have it under the pavilion."

Luna rapped on the client's door, explained she had a wildlife errand and asked to leave her tools inside, then hurried along the deckwalk, Ty by her side.

"Mind if I tag along?" he asked.

She didn't, but... "You might not be able to get close, depending on how upset the bird is."

As they neared the pavilion, she groaned. A huge crowd had formed, and above them fluttered a frantic bird. "Spells, that's clearly the bird's mate. What are they thinking letting this commotion build?"

Luna pushed her way through the crowd under the shelter. Elder Bentha stood beside a stranger with a dazed cormorant in his arms and a teary little girl pressed to his leg.

"Ma'am?" Luna said to Elder Bentha. "This isn't good for the birds. Can you disperse these people?"

Instead, the elder blocked her. "Your father is on his way?"

"He's operating the lighthouse."

Elder Bentha didn't move, her expression hard—an echo of yesterday's.

You've got to be kidding me. "It's foggy," Luna said. "He canna leave right now, and I was closer. And with the birds"—she pointed upward—"this upset, we should clear the crowd."

Instead of answering, Elder Bentha turned and addressed the crowd. "Please? The cormorants need quiet. Rest assured, we have folks on the way to assist."

Inwardly, Luna rolled her eyes. Hadn't *she* just arrived? Extending her magic, Luna cupped the bird's head. Fright and confusion. It shook with that and the cold.

"It flew into our craft's windshield in the fog," the man who held the bird said. "When it fell to the deck, my daughter scooped it up and brought it in. It's breathing, but keeps falling asleep. Not good, right?"

"Losing consciousness. She needs warmth and some quick energy, like from—"

"I said we'll wait for your father." Elder Bentha lifted Luna's hand from the bird and roughly inserted herself between Luna and the animal.

Ty moved to stand beside her, for which Luna was grateful, but he was more of an outsider since he came from an enclave in the United States—or maybe she held that honor now?

"Nebula sent me the call, not my father," she said quietly. "He isn't on his way."

Elder Bentha raised a brow and glanced past her. "Call again," she said to someone.

Luna didn't look to see whom she was talking to. "How is it I canna do this today, when two weeks ago you turned over to me a bird that needed stitches when Mr. Grouse was nae available? Did I magically lose my wildlife skills when I left my father's house?" She crossed her arms. "Or has this something to do with my staying on a schooner with Salmon of the Seas?"

Elder Bentha flinched like she'd been slapped.

People shuffled around them, no one willing to say more while the bird sat limply in the man's arms. It was agonizing to watch her suffering continue.

"She said the bird needs food," the little girl said. "Are you going to let her take care of my bird?"

"A very good question."

Everyone turned at Lady Anemone's words.

She ran steely eyes over the townsfolk, the visitors and the tearful little girl. "Why have I been called when Luna is here?"

"You are a medical professional, an experienced healer." Elder Bentha gestured to the cormorant. "Please take over—"

"That bird does nae need me. It needs Luna right now."

"We learned in class," the little girl said, "'tis a mandate to care for the creatures in our natural systems."

"Exactly what I'm trying to do." Luna lifted her chin. "I am nineteenth year, an independent wizard, according to our rules, and doing nothing different than many adults in our enclave. Please allow me to use the skills bestowed upon me."

Within seconds, it was clear Elder Bentha wasn't going to back down. Luna called to Nebula, *Get Papa. The council won't let me treat the bird.*

It wasn't long before the cries of the cormorant's mate shifted to alarm, and an answering reassurance whistled back before Papa's figure appeared, his giant, blond wings blending with the fog. No one else noticed his arrival until he landed on the dock and strode up.

"What's this I hear?"

Elder Bentha drew to her full height and pointed. "Aquatic bird injured in the fog. Unconscious and needs—"

"Nay," snapped Papa. "What's this about you refusing to allow my daughter to treat wildlife? I shall be bringing this before the Windborne Wildlife Board." He pivoted to Luna. "What needs doing here?"

Elder Bentha backed up, but the look she shot Luna said the older lady wasn't done speaking.

Lady Anemone stepped between them to block Elder Bentha. "There will come a time when Jonah canna leave the beacon," she ranted. "And when Mr. Grouse is not available for consulting. Will we allow our wildlife to die?" The healer turned and paced down the dock, throwing over her shoulder, "This town is getting too citified for my liking. Perhaps 'tis time for *me* to move."

Luna looked up at that, then quickly ducked her head as Elder Bentha's gaze met hers. *Of course this will all be retold to be my fault.*

Someone pressed a baitfish into her hand.

She handed it back. "A warm glucose solution would be better. A teaspoon of plain sugar dissolved in a half cup of water. Could someone get warm towels? Everyone else should go away so her mate can land and reassure her."

Everything she asked for appeared, and people moved back. They didn't leave, which she also blamed on Elder Bentha. The elder had created a spectacle for this afternoon's entertainment.

Above her, Papa grumbled about leaving the foggy point in the hands of a teenager when he wasn't truly needed here, but he coaxed the mate down while Luna warmed the bird outside and in with wrappings of towels and dribbles of the warm sugar water into her bill.

It was all she could do to keep her focus on the cormorant fluttering in and out of consciousness. Once Papa convinced the mate to join her, the female came alert. At his nuzzling, she swallowed more liquid and maintained her cognizance.

After a few minutes, Papa checked her and grunted. "Let's get them home and quiet." He swaddled the male, and Luna did the same with the female, and around the towels they added bands of energy that bound the bundles to their chests for flight.

Ty, who was still there, laughed. "I was going to ask how you'd manage in this wind." He handed her the fish wrapped in paper. "Thanks for the lessons. Not sure I'd be as confident without the ability to communicate with them."

Her surprise must have shown.

"I could tell by the way you each concentrated and by what Coral has told me about folks here working with wildlife."

On Giuthas, he meant, not here. Tern Bay *had* become more citified. "We need to go," she said. "Thanks for your help."

"Can I say goodbye?" the little girl asked, and while she gave the female a last pet, Luna reassured the girl's father that they could visit the bird during the tours.

They fought their way home through the rain and wind that was far worse once they rose above the protection of the cliff.

Her wings ached by the time they stumbled into the yard, completely soaked.

"Here," Stella called from the shed doorway. She had a kennel ready for the two birds, a heating pad under one end and baitfish floating in a pan of seawater. After the birds had eaten a fish each and were settled, Papa gave Stella instructions, while Luna collected her dripping curls and wrung them out, then magically heated and dried her shirt and trousers, spending the last of her energy.

"Check the female every half hour for the next two hours," Papa said, "then after every hour if she's continued to eat. At dusk, I'll reassess her."

Nebula had run out for a quick check from the lighthouse. "What about Luna?" she protested. "I bet she slept last night when I was on duty."

Papa glared. "Luna does nae live here anymore. And she has a full schedule of repairs to complete during Fest, or so I am told." He stormed out of the infirmary.

Nebula's eyes were wide, her mouth gaping as Luna's had been for a second. "Well, doesn't that beat all after you deserted us?"

Luna shot her a glare, then ducked out after him. She caught up with him in the yard.

"Thanks, Papa."

He didn't stop walking, so she hurried to keep up.

"And thanks for standing up for me to Elder Bentha." He and Elder Bentha weren't friends, so that hadn't been difficult for him.

Papa grunted. "The bloody idiot. I wasn't bluffing about reporting her to the Windborne Wildlife Board. Grouse will support you, too, regardless of your poor choices."

Luna stopped, and he kept on walking. Did Papa mean moving out? Getting caught staying on Salm's ship? Or that she'd chosen to stick with Salm?

Or maybe all of the above?

Loving Salm wasn't a poor choice. Living with him might be hard, but it wouldn't be wrong. But she wouldn't win that argument with Papa. He wouldn't like any lad she fancied. She followed him into the quarters. He was filling a glass at the sink. His sagging shoulders popped up when he realized she was behind him. By the Orb, he was exhausted. She'd been so furious and then busy helping the bird down on the dock that she hadn't noticed the bags beneath his eyes.

"Nebula gave me your note saying you want to talk to me."

He drank half the water and refilled the glass before turning. "We'll need help the day of the tours. I'm willing to pay you for your time to wrangle these visitors."

Really? Nebula must have put him up to it. "Thank you. I could use the work."

"Fine. Arrive by nine to greet folks by ten. I expect you to stay until the tours conclude at six, or whenever we manage to get folks to move on," he said in a businesslike manner.

She nodded. "Have you given more thought to my suggestion to contact Uncle Rigel? Or to hire an apprentice? Someone who can work two nights a week would give you a decent break."

He snorted and started up the stairs.

She followed. "I'm serious, Papa. You and Nebs can't do it all and take care of Stella, too."

"And whose fault is that?"

"Not mine," she retorted. "I told you I wanted more time with Salm. I've become an adult, and you have to let me live my own life, which doesn't revolve around caretaking my younger sister when she has a father."

Papa picked up his pace. "So yer sister is the one to suffer when you selfishly leave without easing the change for her?"

"Mother's death wasn't a change anyone eased for me."

Papa stopped, and Luna did, too.

Bullsharks. Had she gone too far? Nay, it was the truth. "Being in her studio—that's the first time I've felt happy while remembering her. Please, Papa, can't we talk about her and the good times we shared?"

His shoulders sagged. "With you and Nebula pitted against me, I have no choice."

"Aye, you have a choice, Papa. You always have a choice. Just like I'm making choices for myself. It might help us to have somewhere to go to remember Mam. She and her magic were amazing. She brought you to a keeper's life. And you used to love it."

"I still do," he said vehemently.

"Maybe I made a mistake opening the room and looking at her things without asking you, but it wasn't locked." Her voice dropped. "I so wanted to see them again. Just because I'm nineteenth year doesn't mean I still won't make mistakes—like any other adult in this enclave. May I hold up Elder Bentha—one of our elected leaders—as an example?"

Papa's lips twitched, and he turned away.

Luna's heart softened. "Let's talk to Mr. Grouse before we report her. Both for my sake and for hers. Elder Bentha doesn't know what to do about a lass like me—"

"Neither do I," Papa muttered.

Tears painfully filled her eyes. "I'm sorry."

He turned on the landing, frowning down at her. "So am I." Then he descended and wrapped her awkwardly in a one-armed hug.

She hugged him back.

"I'm proud of your accomplishments, lass. The rest..." He shrugged.

"Could you start over and try to get to know Salm?"

Papa sighed. "Give me until after Fest to think on it."

17

TACKING

"You've progressed beyond sailing the harbor," Salm told Ty when he arrived at the dock for his lesson. "What do you think?" He gestured to the waters outside the breakwater.

The morning's fog had burned off, and they'd hit a lull in the rain, but the constant wind still set the waves into choppy lines. His student ought to be able to make a decision if sailing was safe for him in these conditions.

"I'm so done with the harbor." Ty glanced north, then south. "Where should we go?"

Good question, but Salm didn't want to make the decision for him. "You decide."

Ty pivoted into and out of the wind, continuing to watch the waves. "Okay, we'll tack southwest against the wind for a test of a mile. I'll let the prevailing wind push us back and hope you haven't set me up for a drowning, you bilge rat."

Salm laughed. "I can't *not* be a rat in someone's craft. But mind you, I'm not suggesting we try this in the Sunfish."

"Spells, no," Ty answered, which was what Salm wanted to hear.

He'd already arranged to borrow Luna's family's larger 420

sailboat for this lesson. Not only was the *Midnight Marauder* heavier for today's waves, but it was the standard racing craft Ty would need to sail in the regatta.

They set out, not speaking while Ty concentrated on shifting the jib sheet and tiller in his zigzagged fight upwind. Outside the shelter of the harbor, they tilted to the gunwales, and only Salm's quick shift to the upper side saved them from bailing. Both were soaked, and Salm ribbed Ty about it. Then Ty caught on, as he usually did, to the increased wind and sea currents. Once they passed Kittiwake Point, he gradually made his line and tiller adjustments quicker, keeping the boat on as even a keel as Salm could have.

With less monitoring necessary, Salm watched the point recede. Gulls circled the sea cliffs, but no larger figure showed up among them. He'd had his eye to it as much as he could today, but hadn't spotted Luna. Where else could she have gone? He couldn't go around asking folks if she'd moved in with them.

Blast it. As soon as this lesson ended, he'd… Fine, there was nothing for it but to go up to Kittiwake Point and ask. He'd just petition the Blessed Orb to let him run into Nebula or Stella before he encountered Keeper Jonah.

Salm shook himself. "Hoy, matey, you're doin' well," he told Ty. "Workin' up from scallywag to old salt. Don't see why some of the townsfolk won't give you a chance."

"I'm trying." Ty rolled his eyes. "Helps to see that it isn't just me, the newcomer, that the local folks rail against. Poor Luna had a time of it earlier."

"You saw Luna?"

The question burst from him—and Ty's grin confirmed how ridiculously eager he must sound.

Salm scowled. "Had a bit of a spat. Wish to make up, but canna if I dinnae know where she is."

"She took two cormorants home with her father, if that's any help." Ty told him about a confrontation with Tern Bay's head elder and Lady Anemone running interference. "The healer is on my route and always prodding for information, but if that means she'd stand up for me like she did for Luna, I guess I'll put up with it."

"Don't know if she'd do it for me, but glad to hear she's got Luna under her wing. The lass needs a friend after the trouble I've brought her."

Ty gave a knowing nod. "Talk of the town. Since my lessons with you have also attracted attention, folks guess we're friends and have even lowered themselves to ask me about you."

They laughed over that one.

"I've been there," Ty said, "hiding a relationship from my family when both my parents taught at the academy we attended." He gestured toward the harbor. "I can't imagine trying it here. Why don't you prebond?"

Salm hesitated to tell anyone more when Luna was already so furious. Ty might be a newcomer...but after days of sailing together, they'd become friends. "She won't come aboard the ship."

"Is that a firm requirement in your family?"

Salm kicked at the hull. "I haven't considered asking for an exception. Manta and Piper did it. We all knew Manta wanted a bakery, so Ma and Pop gave them a down payment for the building instead of a schooner like they did for Wind. 'Tis part of our earnings for working with the family. I—" He closed his eyes, trying to imagine a life onshore. He couldn't. "Sailing is my life. Plus, only Coral and I are able to speak with dolphins. The two enclaves need us to carry on their care. It's not like Uncle Ray and his partner, Bert, are gonna have kids. Except for some second cousins over in Ireland, we're the only ones of our generation."

"Luna speaks to birds. How is that any less significant?"

Salm frowned. "It's not. But different. The local enclaves

depend on us and the dolphins to continue managing the fisheries."

"Have you tried using the birds to help with the fisheries? They eat fish the same as dolphins."

"The smelt," Salm said thoughtfully. "The seabirds follow schools of them. And they have a different view of them. Aerial." Salm cupped a hand to his chin to stroke his—damn it all, he was growing a beard again, hang what Keeper Jonah thought.

"Who is this Mr. Grouse that Elder Bentha wanted to wait for?" Ty asked.

Salm explained the bird expert's position and had to agree with what Ty was suggesting. "If anyone knows if birds could help with our work, he would." He could talk to Luna to learn if this might be possible. And he'd ask her that if she had her own role with birds aboard their ship—one that he helped with— would that fulfill her need for her own work?

The harbor buoys bobbed ahead. "Ahoy," Salm said. "You aren't taking this craft to port yet. Head northeast, and let's see you fight your way back."

Ty glanced in the direction Salm indicated, and his eyes widened. "Against the wind and around the breakwater rock?"

"You want to be in this race or not?"

After they docked, Salm went to One Good Bun to report to Coral on Ty's progress in preparing for the regatta—anything to keep his mind off Luna.

Aye, right.

At the bakery, Manta mentioned she had another message for Luna that she hadn't picked up. He copied it. He hadn't seen her while walking through town. Maybe Luna had moved back home. Delivering her messages would be a second excuse to be up on Kittiwake Point, the first being to complete the white-washing he'd promised to do.

Salm landed in the keeper's yard like he belonged there—not too hard since it was empty—but at the door, he hesitated to knock. Nay, waking Jonah Ness would be a poor choice. The buckets of whitewash and their stirring sticks were still tucked under the splotched canvas at the kitchen door. A brush sat inside one bucket, whitewash three-quarters of the way up the handle. That and the new coat of white only halfway up each of the ground-floor shutters—and the spattered stone walls—confirmed that Stella had started this job.

Clouds filled the sky, but right now it wasn't raining. They didn't have many days left before the first tour day to do this. His reach a good two feet higher than Stella's, Salm easily finished the doors and lower shutters. He eyed the second-floor windows. The bedrooms.

He didn't dare. Keeper Jonah and the rest of the family were likely in them. Though Luna's room... He bit his lip. Nay.

He retrieved the ladder from the tool shed and carried everything around to the oceanside column of the lighthouse. The round stone structure had five lookout windows with shutters, plus doors at the top and the bottom and the trim around the domed roof. Fortunately, the railings on the widow's walk were brass and already polished.

That made the old paint look worse. Grabbing the bucket handle in one hand and the brush in the other, Salm flew up to paint the roof trim.

It was a good plan, because he had his feet on the ladder a few hours later when he heard the back door slam.

Someone was awake—and singing.

He grinned. Thank the Orb, the door paint was dry, because Stella wasn't likely to notice the upper part was now white. The chickens clucked louder than before. He stroked the brush over the top edge of this shutter's boards, finished, climbed down and moved the ladder to the other side.

Funny, she'd stopped singing.

He scanned the ground. No one was about. He looked up in time to see a bird flying directly at him. He threw up an arm—

The peck caught his forearm with enough force that he slipped one direction, and the ladder went the other. He grabbed for the sill, unfurling his wings and automatically dropping weight to buoy himself.

The window rattled above him— and Stella poked out her head.

"Oh, it's you," she exclaimed in an overloud whisper, then hissed, "Rissa! Stop!"

"Great fiery Orb," Salm muttered. "You sicced Rissa on me?"

"Well," she said sweetly, "I did nae know who it was and dinnae wish to wake Papa. He's been in the most awful humor." She held out a hand, pursed her lips and whistled to the bird.

Salm fluttered back. The gull alighted on Stella, keeping his small black eyes trained on Salm.

"Well, thank the Blessed Orb for that good sense." He grimaced at Stella while fingering the hole in his shirt.

She winced. "Sorry about that. He won't do it again, will you, Rissa?" she cooed.

Salm shook his head and swooped down, fetched the ladder upright again. The hanging bucket of whitewash had slopped over the wall. He magically dashed water over the stones, but paint still ghosted them.

"Spells, I'll have to take a scrub brush to that." He magicked an old brush from the schooner, settled on a rung and began scrubbing. "You didn't want to wake Luna either?" he asked in a casual way.

She sighed. "Luna isn't here."

Blast it.

"What are you doing here without her?" Stella asked as he worked.

"Painting. I said I'd do it."

"Except for the doors, Papa said we could do without." She leaned out the window and studied the cottage's lower level. "But it looks much better."

"Good. You want your best foot forward and all that."

"Luna would think that, too. I understand that you didn't take her away, but I still wish she'd come see us. Like for dinner once a week, as Molly's older brother does with his partner."

Nice idea, but… "Isn't your pap still mad at her?" And didn't Jonah hate him?

"He told Luna to bring the cormorants here. So he's talking to her. Papa never stays mad for long."

At his daughters, but probably not the case for Salm. He magically doused the stones again and rechecked for white spots. Gone. He tossed the scrub brush down and magicked up the dropped paintbrush. He had to pick a few leaves off. Stella looked on guiltily, but didn't comment.

"So where is Luna staying?" he asked.

"You don't know?" Stella frowned. Then she disappeared.

Huh. She either didn't know or wasn't telling. He finished at that window, moved the ladder to the next and by the time he climbed up, that window was open and two cookies sat on a napkin on the sill.

Ah, a peace offering. He ate them.

After he'd finished half of that shutter, Stella reappeared with a folded paper. "Could you give this to Luna for me?"

"Ha. Then those cookies were a bribe?"

The little girl looked chagrined. "You may not know where she's living, but I figured you'll see her in town sooner than I will. Please?"

He put the paper in the pocket of his breeches and patted it.

"Of course." It would be an excellent excuse to track down Luna.

"My friend Molly says you can run away to Gretna Green to get married."

Salm looked up. "What is that—oh, some human place?"

Stella nodded. "Molly says that all the eloping lovers in her sister's novels do. Is it far?"

"No idea. But it doesn't matter. Windborne have our own licensing offices, like at The Moors, because our bonding agreements cover more magical issues that human agreements don't."

A knocking sound came from far off inside. The smile slid from Stella's face. "Uh-oh." She left, scampering down the spiral stairs and disappearing from sight, her scuffs fading as the sound of heavy footfalls increased.

Magic tingled over Salm's back, his wings ready to carry him off. He squelched it.

"Good morn—evening, Papa," she said. "I'm going to feed the birds."

"Who were you talking to?"

"Rissa?" she squeaked, the lie evident.

"Luna has *not* returned."

Whoa, that sure sounded like he wasn't in favor of the idea either. And Jonah wasn't waiting for an answer. Footsteps pounded firmly on stone steps.

Salm hurriedly brushed whitewash up the shutter's outer board, his body as far from the window opening as possible, his gaze fixed on the job. But his ears didn't miss the abrupt grating of boot soles coming to a halt. Or, from the corner of his eye, Jonah filling the window.

"I thought I told you never to come here again."

"I said I'd complete this work," Salm managed in a steady voice. "I keep my word." He dared a glance at Luna's father.

Jonah's bushy brows smashed together, his moustache went

lopsided with his twisting lips, and every inch of his exposed skin turned red.

Salm dipped his brush in the bucket again and kept painting. "To everyone?"

Where was he going with that? Had to be some reference to Luna. He nodded.

"Then I am still waiting for you and my daughter to talk to me about a mysterious subject that I have no doubt I will refuse to agree to."

"But—" *She's nineteenth!* Hoy, that was not the thing to say. "Aye, sir. After Fest be all right?"

"I will nae give my permission for you to continue embarrassing us. Either you prebond or stop these clandestine visits. I will nae have her be the talk of the tavern or folks blaming her actions on the lack of a mother's direction. Her ability to care for birds is excellent, and her skills at her trade are expanding nicely, but association with you is jeopardizing her name with the elders and townsfolk. If more tales spread"—he waved a finger—"I canna stop them."

Really, he was worried only about what people thought and said?

Like you are, not having a large boat?

This would be so easy to agree to and get on her father's good side. Easier for him. Not for Luna.

Salm lowered the brush. "I can't do that, sir. I can't tell Luna what to do." He swallowed. "Any more than you can. Sir. She's her own person. Her life and decisions are hers to make."

"I see there is no talking to you either." Jonah leaned out the window, and Salm backed away as much as he could on a ladder.

Jonah looked right and left, then scowled at him. "Dinnae rush and make a sloppy show of us."

"Nay, sir."

"And for spell's sake, dinnae grow a beard until you can do a decent job of it." Jonah stomped off.

18

SEEING A WAY CLEAR

As Salm put away the ladder in the shed, Nebula carried in another crate. He insisted on taking her load and, because Ty's suggestion was poking at him, asked for a peek at the birds.

Nebula scrunched her nose. "We're due to clean their cages, if you…"

"I'll help," he said quickly. "And you can tell me how they're doing." He might get more information from Nebula than Luna at this point.

"Are you asking so you can get in good with Luna?"

He grinned at her. "How do you know I'm not interested on my own?"

She frowned. "We *always* have birds. You've never asked before."

"First time for everything. Unless, of course, you're turning down my help."

With a roll of her eyes, she led the way.

The bird shed held their supplies and a variety of cages—a dozen, but only three were occupied.

"Ever have them all full?"

"Once," Nebula said, and her story gave an avian version of the sort of injuries they ran across with sea animals—an assortment of cuts and fractures, as well as the hooks, fishing line, nets and human plastics they dealt with, even in their shielded waters.

"Aye, 'tis become worse the last decade, enough that even I remember the rare excitement of spotting a turtle that wasn't swimming right." He scooped the soiled sand from a cage's tray while Nebula measured salt for the freshwater for the birds in another. "Now that's all too common. Or is it that the Windborne are outside more and more tuned in to wildlife in trouble?"

"Oh, no!" Nebula exclaimed. "If you think we're going to expand like Mr. Grouse wants us to, then think again."

Salm eyed her. That sounded like a frequent protest. "Eh? I've not heard this."

She huffed. "That's probably because Giuthas is too isolated. I personally think we ought to be teaching these other enclaves to handle their own wildlife problems instead of them carting them to us."

"Like an apprenticeship, but in their own enclaves?"

"Neee-buh-la," Stella wailed at the doorway. "Papa has dumped more things outside the door for us to haul." She hefted her box and glared at them. "He says if that scruffy lad is still here to ask him to carry them. Would you, Salm?"

"Scruffy?"

Nebula elbowed him. "Hey, you've moved up a step. I won't tell you what he called you yesterday."

Stella hooted. Playfully, Salm batted at her, then ducked beyond her reach and jogged for the quarters with Stella chasing him. Any progress with Keeper Jonah was good, though he sorely wanted to tell their father that he certainly hadn't looked scruffy the night he and Luna were supposed to have spoken with him.

After the threshold was cleared, Stella disappeared into the quarters to prepare a meal, while he and Nebula blew the yard clean of leaves by magically redirecting the wind, a skill that came in handy for sailors. The lighthouse was lit when Salm left near dusk. He didn't see Jonah again, but maybe that was for the best until he thought through his new ideas and ran them by Luna.

Music rose up to meet Salm as he flew down from Kittiwake Point. The cove was a veritable beacon, with lights on inside the businesses, strings of colored lights lining the vendor tents and mast tops alike. Boats of all sizes jammed the harbor, and the deckwalks swarmed with people enjoying the night. Well, they ought to—rain was in the air, and tomorrow a storm was due in. Likely, many had traveled today to avoid the weather. The folks he passed walking in from the southern end were nearly all visitors.

Why was Jonah worried? Gossip about him and Luna would be forgotten amid this activity. Next week, when things quieted again, would be a different matter.

Now to find Luna to give over Stella's note. Salm headed for the bakery, weaving among people and scanning the crowd in case she was still about. He'd check if she'd dropped by and if Manta knew where he might find her now.

Inside One Good Bun, customers had his sister occupied.

Seen Luna? he asked impatiently.

Nay. Manta tilted her head to the back. *She has messages.*

He copied over two new ones—not taking them in case he couldn't find Luna—and returned to the front just as Luna walked in behind more customers.

The knees of her coveralls were stained brown, and a streak of rust crossed one arm. He stopped in front of her.

"Oh," she said. "Um, hello."

Spells, was she actually avoiding him? He searched her face, noting her weary eyes, smudged cheek and frizzed hair. No, she was exhausted. He held out the papers. "Your messages. I made duplicates in case I ran into you."

She reached for them, the tool bag slipping off her shoulder.

He caught it. "Let me." The darned thing weighed a ton.

She took the notes. "Thank you." Her nails were dirty, and she'd cut her wrist somewhere along the way. Spells, that streak on her clothes was dried blood. Frustration on her behalf boiled inside him.

You canna do a thing to help or say a word. This is what trade work involves.

Another bakery patron queued up in the doorway, peering around Luna to check the line, so Salm pulled her aside. His magic thrilled at the touch—and hers did, too.

He dropped her arm at the same time she stepped away. "Finished here?" he croaked. She nodded, and he ushered her outside, throwing the strap of her tool bag over his own shoulder. They paused awkwardly, then turned in unison toward North Dock.

She's not headed there, you dreamer. He bit down on asking where she was going. "A lot of business today?" he asked lightly.

"More than I would have dreamed of hoping for."

"Still getting questions about us?"

Frowning, she stepped out of the flow of the passersby and stopped to look at him.

Blast. A smart lad would have said something about the birds, Stella...*anything else.*

Luna covered a yawn. "I've put off all but the townsfolk's most urgent repairs to focus on the visitors' repairs, and most folks have accepted that as reasonable. 'Tis Fest, so they want to be outdoors as well."

"Checking for more gossip," he couldn't help muttering.

She gave a short laugh. "How did you spend your day?"

He was silent for a time, rubbing his neck. This would either please her or anger her. Under Luna's current mood, he wasn't sure which. "I finished the whitewashing at your place," he finally admitted.

Her mouth rounded in a silent gasp. "Did Papa see you?"

Salm grinned. "Might have missed me if Stella hadn't traipsed up and down chatting with me out the windows." He pulled her note from his pocket. "She sent you this."

Luna flipped it over, started to break the seal, then stopped. She put it in her pocket. "Papa let you finish?"

"Not without a lecture, but aye, he did."

"You weren't supposed to go back, so a lecture is light."

He grinned. "I suppose so."

She side-glanced at him. "By the Orb, you're splendid, Salm, doing all that for us. Did Nebs say anything about the birds?"

"Aye, the shag's stitches look good, but since he feels better, it's very difficult to get the pills into him. It takes both Nebs and Stella. The cormorant is recovering nicely. They'd like you to see her before they release the pair."

"Papa can check her over."

"Who did he learn his bird care skills from?"

"His mother."

Her answer was clipped, and the deckwalk was busy with people walking past them. This was not the place for that conversation. Yet he couldn't resist asking, "Will you be calling in Mr. Grouse? I'd like to see him work more. I'm rarely on Giuthas when he is."

She cocked her head in question and put out her hand for her tool bag, "I'll let you know."

He gave it over and tapped her elbow, all he dared to touch. "Where are you staying?"

"Don't try to convince me to return to—"

"I'm not." He raised his free hand. "Just wanted to know where I can reach you. And your sisters plan to visit again tomorrow."

"They can't." She pressed her lips into a thin line. "Thanks for your note. I'm sorry, too, but not ready to talk yet. I'm too tired to be reasonable." She turned on her heel and disappeared into the crowd.

Salm took a step. He stopped. She did look exhausted, so it wouldn't go well to press anything now.

"She's not leaving town," said Coral at his side.

He startled, then rearranged his face to glare down at his younger sister.

She shrugged. "Manta sent me out to make sure you didn't do anything stupid. Following her would be stupid, if you don't know that already."

He couldn't be mad at either Manta or Coral. He'd gotten himself into this with Luna.

"Have you heard the news?" Coral asked. "Tern Bay has closed the enclave's borders until they ensure no surprise rips lie along the routes folks take to sail into town."

He cocked a brow. Giuthas wizards dealt with rips on a daily basis. The small island community had lost members over the years, and now their reduced energy production couldn't hold the isle's shielding. Most of the rips—breaks in energy—were on land, between the habitats. The council knew several were on the ocean, but those were harder to spot. And repair.

"I have an errand I'd like your help with." She waved him toward the bakery. "Maybe it'll answer where our missing dolphin pod is. Come have a bite of dinner while we talk about it."

Salm glanced in the direction Luna had taken before following Coral. *Curiosity be damned, she's not leaving town.*

Luna navigated past Lady Anemone's card-playing friends watching the Fest revelers on her front porch with the same excuse of being tired. No one challenged her, which made her feel worse.

After a shower and dressing for bed, she opened Stella's letter.

To my dearest deserting sister,

How are you? I am fine, as is Nebula and our dear father.

Luna snorted at the opening pleasantries that she herself had instructed Stella to use when writing thank-you notes. Then the next lines brought tears to her eyes.

So is Rissa, the shag and the cormorant pair and another kittiwake recently brought to us.

Not that you have asked about us or them! Why didn't you come wake me up when you brought the cormorants? I am furious with you. Papa says I am to be nice and do my work, but it is hardly fair that you have gone and left when we have so much work to do.

And then you don't wake me up to say hello.

Now the real Stella was writing.

I'm doing my regular chores: the birds and chickens, trimming the wicks, sweeping the kitchen, preparing breakfasts—aye, I prepare ALL THE BREAKFASTS since you have left us.

Add to that:

cleaned my room

cleaned the upstairs bath

dusted and swept the ENTIRE lighthouse stairwell

Dusted all I can reach in the living room. Did you know we have twenty-six float balls and forty-one fish, bird and turtle skulls? We did have forty-nine, but Papa made me toss out the more gruesome ones with their ligaments still attached. I have hidden them in the shed until you return to decide.

Anyway, I have done my share. Nebula has cleaned the kitchen and mudroom. And her room.

Thank you for sending Salm to whitewash, as I was not getting very far with it when no one would allow me to use a ladder or fly to finish. He says you didn't, but you must have. Who goes around doing work at other folks' cottages? He's nice. I don't care what Papa says, I think you should run off to Gretna Green and marry him.

Luna traced the human village name again. Where did Stella hear about that?

But come back home afterward to live.

No one tells me anything. Papa and Nebula stop talking when I come into the room, or even near it, so they must have it magicked to know. I can tell they are angry, even though they say they aren't. Papa says Salm is a no-good scallywag and I'm not to talk to him, so don't tell that I did.

Please send back a note with Salm telling me when you are coming home—or when you are marrying him. I don't want to miss your wedding.

I still have the ribbon you tied in my hair.

Luna rolled her eyes. That meant Stella hadn't brushed her hair.

I love you even if the others are mad at you.

Papa hadn't seemed that mad yesterday—or had she mistaken what she'd thought was his anger at Elder Bentha?

Please do not tell him I have sent this note with Salm, because he says we are not to encourage you to return. He says he will not allow you to.

Oh. Tears flooded Luna's eyes. That hurt.

And I rather wish you would, because the shag will not allow either Nebula or I to inspect his neck stitches. Papa says he'll do it, but he keeps forgetting.

Your loving sister. The youngest sister.

Stella

Lines of x's and o's filled out the page.

A pang of homesickness hit Luna. If she was home now, they'd have finished breakfast. She'd have brushed Stella's hair —or, more likely, told her to bathe. She'd have made sure the gruesome skulls were out—there had to be far more than eight. Stella had likely hidden her favorites. More thoughts of home and family hit her. She rose, the urge to fly up to the lighthouse grabbing her...if only Papa hadn't told her again not to come back.

She sat down again and reread the note. News from home left her wanting to see Mam's drawings, but she'd forgotten to bring the map case from the schooner.

Well... Salm wouldn't block her from picking up her drawings, and the schooner was a five-minute walk away. She tucked Stella's note under her pillow, climbed into her dirty coveralls again and, after a wave to the card players, strode into the night.

Not many people were out now that it'd started raining. Her hair was wet by the time she arrived at North Dock, but thankfully the waterproofing on her coveralls had held. At *The Peaceful Seas'* mooring, the ship was dark. Salm must not be aboard. No matter. She knew where the case was and could grab it with just a light of magic on her fingers.

She paused at the bottom of the gangway to flush her hand, and a motion along the boom caught her eye.

Someone knelt on top of the Seas' stored mainsail...and was jabbing their arm down.

Oh, this isn't good. Shock pushing away her weariness, Luna continued walking. She didn't want the person to see her standing there.

She opened her channel and called, *Salm?* as she tried to better see what they were doing. *Where are you?*

He answered immediately. *Out at the isle, tracking our missing dolphins. Can I talk to you later?*

Later would be too late. *Aye,* she said quickly and called Nebs instead. Her sister was in the kitchen. *Excellent. Call the town elders and report vandalism happening right now at the Seas' schooner.*

Blessed Orb, this isn't a joke, is it?

Not hardly. Hurry, please. Luna paced in the shadows of a boat several moorings away.

I've called, Nebs said, and as Luna watched, a wizard materialized at the end of the Seas' gangway. Then disappeared.

A flash of magic lit up the mast and boom. A shriek cut off midcry.

What's happening? Nebs asked.

I think they caught the person—oh. Someone ran down the gangway, turned and came straight for Luna.

"Stop!" a man shouted. She recognized Keenan's voice.

The vandal kept running. The shadowed form of wings grew over their shoulders. They began to flap, looking back over their shoulder.

They plan to fly away! Luna hesitated. The vandal came closer, feet lifting. *I can't let them.* She tackled the wizard like she had the shag, grabbing their legs. The two of them lifted—

"Get off me," the person—a witch—screamed and began to kick.

Luna held tighter, dragging her heels. Abruptly, the witch dropped with all her weight into Luna's arms. They tumbled to the dock, Luna landing on top with the wind knocked out of her, but the witch was rocking and swearing.

"Don't move," Keenan shouted from very close, his energy blinding her.

Running footsteps pounded closer, several people shouting. The witch was pulled upright. Then hands grasped Luna's elbows and helped her roll over.

"Are you all right?" Keenan squatted beside her. "I saw her take off, but was lowering the other vandal and couldn't get a clear shot to stun her."

That explained why they'd fallen all of a sudden. "I'm...fine."

"None of it hit you?" He waved his glowing hands, checking, then shook his head. "Your sister placed the call, but we'll consider it came from you. I need you to come along to the town hall to give your story, while we book Maeve and Pauly for trespassing and damages." He rolled his eyes. "The last thing their poor ma will believe, but I caught them in the act of cutting a sail, so there's no doubt this time." He lifted his chin to the schooner, where a wizard was inspecting the mainsail, and several others were talking to Maeve and Pauly, both with their hands behind their backs and surrounded by a glow of restraining magic. Keenan's, Luna guessed.

"I'm glad you were able to come so quickly," she said in a shaky voice.

He helped her to her feet and escorted her to the town hall, where she explained why she'd been headed for *The Peaceful Seas*. Manta arrived, and the story had to be retold before old Sir Porbeagle accompanied them back to the ship and verified that the map case was indeed where Luna said it was. Manta gave permission for Luna to take it, and then Manta set a magical alarm on the ship.

"Though I doubt it's needed now," she muttered to Luna. "I'll catch Salm up when he gets back, unless you'd like to?"

"You do it," Luna agreed. "You'll need to handle this with the enclave anyway, and I'll talk to Salm tomorrow."

Manta hugged her. "He'll like that. You know this isn't usual? We've never had anyone attack us personally, and I don't want you to think you'd be in danger—"

"I don't," Luna said quickly. "Salm explained why they hate him."

Manta didn't look convinced, but said good night and thanked her for alerting the council.

Back in Lady Anemone's parlor, Luna was more than ready for bed. "Five minutes, ha," she mumbled. Nothing was simple these days. Carefully, she unrolled Mam's drawings, put Salm's maps away and crawled under her covers. The scene on the paper she held was as dark as the night of its reality. Faint converging lines depicted the lighthouse in the center, but the cliffs were lost to scribbles, the waves just a suggestion.

A drop of silver magic welled up under one of Luna's fingernails. She touched it to the paper, and the static scene came alive. The moon sparkled on the sea, and the waves crashed against the cliff. High tide covered the rocky shoal. The beacon circled—its repetitive flash comforting—and she watched the waves until she could feel them pounding the rock. The scent of the sea seemed to fill her...

Of course, the sound of the waves and their salty tang were more present inside this house at sea level than at Kittiwake Point three hundred feet up. Luna could no longer keep her eyes open, so she propped the drawing under the lampshade to hold it upright, snuggled sideways with her pillow and fell asleep.

In the morning, fog obscured the drawing. Outside, she kept glancing to the lighthouse throughout the morning's trips. Papa kept it operating in the fog. But was he monitoring it, or was Nebula? They always split a storm's twenty-four-hour operations into three shifts, and now she wasn't there.

The beacon stopped flashing at midday when the fog lifted. Not many people were out, and even fewer remained when it began raining. That was inlanders for you, trying to escape the weather. She shook her head. The fishing boats were still working, the birds still flying and...was that a sail going up?

Salm was taking Ty out in this? Why, they could... "Spells," she muttered. "I'm as concerned about him as if we were together."

What did that mean? Oh. In her heart, they were together. But in real life, *practical* life...

Bullsharks, what do I really *want?*

19

ROUGH WATERS

A magical tickling brushed Salm's mind. *Luna?* He looked around. The fluff of white curls was unmistakable, but she was walking on, not looking toward the sea. Or him.

But he could've sworn she had been.

He shrugged off the feeling that she was upset that he couldn't talk when she'd called last night. If he'd known it was an emergency, he would have been there for her as soon as possible. Or did she disapprove that he was going sailing in the high winds? "'Tis only an hour's run to get a taste of the forthcoming storm."

"That's fine," Ty answered from his place at the tiller. "I trust your judgment."

Salm hadn't meant to say the words aloud. He gave a nod without looking up and finished tying off the line. If Luna would spend more time sailing with him, she wouldn't have doubts about his judgment either...*argh!*

Here I go again. He had to shake this eddying worry that they wouldn't come to an agreement. The break with Luna had battered his ship when he should be singing about his and Coral's success of finding their missing dolphins last night. He couldn't wait to share the news with Luna and that the elders had decided that Maeve and Pauly would have to do work for him to compensate for their stupid stunt.

But you need to be patient, mate, keep your head here, on your tasks. If he kept in the council's good graces and did all his work—including conducting his scheduled fishing boat inspections and their blasted written reports—Pop would be pleased. And perhaps then he wouldn't have to keep doing these reports for months.

Salm slid into his seat along the hull. "Ready when you are."

The sailing lesson went well. Ty didn't bring up Luna, and neither did he. By the end of Ty's fair handling in the rough waters, Salm had an idea, but one he could do nothing with until he spoke with his father. He delivered a standing order of the bakery's buns, then fulfilled a couple more requests Manta had from folks who didn't want to go out in the driving rain. He didn't blame them. He would have grumbled himself if it hadn't given him an excellent excuse to be running through town looking for Luna.

"You missed her," Manta said when he returned.

"Is she upset about the vandalism? Did you tell her I'd be back?"

"No and yes," Manta said. "A repair call from Pete Smith came in and another from Elder Bentha while she was here, so I handed over the phone. She left immediately."

Salm shifted to go...but he had no plans. His entire week *had* been planned around Luna. *Except now I have a slashed mainsail to repair.*

That, however, wasn't a chore to tackle in the rain. During a lull this morning, he'd unrolled the sail to assess how much work it'd be to repair—*hours!*—and angrily started a list of his most loathsome chores, like barnacle scraping. The elders had ruled Maeve and Pauly would remain in jail or under enclave surveillance until they'd repaid the time in triplicate in work for the Seas. After, they'd be permanently banned from Tern Bay.

Now, he didn't want the reminder that he'd be seeing more of them *or* that Luna had left the ship. "I'm going to shower and change," he told Manta. "I can come back if you need more help."

Manta dipped a measuring cup into her bin of sugar. "I'll not turn it down. Can you be back by five?"

Their cousin Pete's house was on the way to North Dock, so Salm took that deckwalk toward *The Peaceful*. He scanned the front windows. No sign of people or activity, but it was a corner place, and his feet led him around the side.

A broken gutter splashed water onto the deck of a cart shed's upper level. The room beyond it was dark. So was the shed. His gaze tracked over the rain-blown garden to the house. A figure watched him from under a back porch covering—Pete Smith—frowning and his arms crossed.

Damn, caught snooping. "Ahoy, cousin," he called. "Luna's a friend of mine. I understand she's to repair something for you. Is she about?"

"Nay, didn't expect her in this weather, but I wanted a slot on her list." Pete nodded toward the gutter. "I'll confirm with her tonight when I see her at Anemone's."

Ah. So that's where she was rooming. A weight lifted from his shoulders, Salm gave him a two-finger salute. "Thanks, sir."

Of course, he couldn't just turn up over there asking for her, but Lady Anemone thought him a charming lad, or so she always said with a laugh. She wouldn't kick him out if he came calling. Better yet, her home was visited by elderly card players, not the lonely fishermen who frequented Keenan's diner.

Surrounded by the rattling shutters in the town hall, Luna ran her fingers over a new kittiwake Elder Bentha had called about. The head of the council claimed she'd called Luna about the disoriented gull that'd been brought in because Luna was closer, being in town now. But she knew the real reason was Elder Bentha didn't want Papa's complaints going to the Windborne Wildlife Board.

"Nothing broken," Luna announced. "Just a first-year's poor judgment in this wind. He's exhausted." She held out another baitfish and magically urged him to eat. The disheveled kittiwake gobbled it down. She'd straighten his windblown feathers later if she needed to. "He'll be fine after this meal and a rest. He can be released in the morning."

"They haven't all flown?" asked one of the clerks.

"Half the fledglings are still about. Likely, this storm will encourage them to get moving." Rissa, too. Would she see him again before they left? At least she knew she had a chance to, thanks to Stella's note. That thought pulled at her heart as much as Stella's letter had.

"Then you'll see to him tonight," Elder Bentha said. She didn't ask.

That's what they usually did. Luna couldn't fly up to the point, not in these high winds, and after yesterday, Papa didn't need another rescue bird to care for, or the reminder that he was mad at Elder Bentha. But neither would Luna reveal that to the town elder, who would love nothing more than a chance to poke at her family.

Feeling vaguely like she shouldn't, Luna nodded. Fifteen minutes later, she *knew* it hadn't been a good idea.

"A kitten I'd understand, but a bird?" complained Lady Anemone.

"I promise, all he'll do is sleep."

"And at dawn?" Lady Anemone crossed her arms. "I won't have my slee—my guests' sleep disturbed."

"I'll be awake at his first coo and take him outside. To the cliffs," she amended at the healer's continued frown. "Look, he's asleep now." She unwrapped the towel from his head.

Lady Anemone stared down her nose. "With magic."

Figured she could tell. "Because he needs his rest to recover, and I had to carry him back—"

"Instead of up to your infirmary."

"It's too windy to fly." Luna bit the inside of her cheek, waiting for Lady Anemone to argue with that.

"Still at odds with your father, I bet." The healer harrumphed. "See that you keep him quiet. And keep my upholstery and rugs safe."

The front door burst open, letting in Mr. Smith and the howling wind until he slammed it closed again. "Ah, Luna, just the lass I'd like to talk to... But what have you here?"

Luna held up the kittiwake, and Mr. Smith nodded appreciatively.

"Pete," Lady Anemone said sharply, "don't encourage her. I can't have this with the other guests. This is a one-time exception because of the weather. It'd be difficult for her to fly the thing to the point."

Luna stepped toward the back parlor. Better to make her escape while Lady Anemone was still agreeing. "I got your message and have you on my list, sir. First sunny day? I must get the gull settled. Thank you, Lady Anemone. Good evening."

Behind the closed door, she slid her tool bag off her shoulder and looked around for a place to put the bird. She didn't have a kennel...not even a box. "Spells," she muttered. She couldn't get herself kicked out of Lady Anemone's house.

With a sigh, she magicked open her tool bag, set the bird into it to hold the towel secure around him, then dug through her laundry. With a change of clothes set aside, she molded the rest into a nest shape within the lightweight laundry bag and settled the bird and towel into her clothing.

His breathing and heartbeat were steady. She shed her coveralls while watching him. The bird remained held in sleep under her magic, but to leave him while Lady Anemone was on alert was a risk. Luna pulled the bag up around him and cinched the drawstring to a mere inch opening. 'Twas breathable enough.

Then she ran to the bathroom.

When she returned, her stomach growled. Ugh. Even if she could go out, it'd be a wet trip all the way to the grocers or Keenan's. No vendors were open in this rain. She dug through her bag's outer pocket and removed her day's leftovers—half of a pasty, a roll and two cookies Manta had given her when she'd bought two rolls. No cheese, no fruit and, worse, no eggs. Even hard-boiled ones would have been good. She ate what she had, drank the water she'd brought from the bathroom and then refilled the glass. The other players and guests had arrived for the card game, judging by the laughter in the front room. Joining them wasn't an option now, and besides, this was a chance to catch up on her sleep, even if it wasn't dark yet.

After putting up a magical noise damper, Luna picked up her laundry bag and crawled into bed. After a bit of adjustment, she had the bird nestled at her belly and slid her hand along his back. She removed her magic. The kittiwake remained asleep. Good. That was better for him, and if he became distressed for any reason, she'd feel it. Hopefully, before Lady Anemone did. She closed her eyes, thinking she wouldn't sleep...

Manta hadn't needed him for long, so Salm borrowed her phone and called Mr. Grouse to inquire about seabird fishing habits. The connection to his home on Giuthas was terrible.

"Do any of the local seabirds track schooling fish?" Salm repeated.

"Can barely hear...wind...the storm is hitting," shouted Mr.

Grouse. "Sorry…later…must stay available for emergencies." He hung up.

Salm hung up, too. He'd also wanted to ask about their trainability, but, really, Luna could answer either question.

When we're talking again. He'd have to make that happen. "Manta? What do you know about this storm?"

"Four cups," she said to herself, then answered, "What? People are staying in. I hope these extras go fast in the morning."

Salm hesitated at the door. The near gale winds were about thirty knots and gusting up to gale, sending the pelting rain sideways. Visibility was a hundred feet. *I've been a mite too slack in caring for the ship.* Too many activities on shore. He'd get better weather information on *The Peaceful*, so he ran to it. The afternoon skies had looked like the usual storms, but often the shielding of Windborne enclaves altered what they saw versus what was coming…and Tern Bay's southern barrier was only a few miles out. This enclave had a weather wizard like the Isle of Giuthas, but that was for the land. No one tried to manage the weather over the sea.

After clearing the deck, Salm flipped on the boat's solar-charged batteries and within minutes was studying the graphs and data coming through the weather devices. Huddled over the newest fancy radio that HIT, or Human Information Technology, had installed last year, he listened to the humans' nautical forecast for the storm coming up from the south, then called his grandfather over on the isle.

Their radio connection was better, and Granpop was more determined than Mr. Grouse to talk and run Salm through a weather check.

"Aye, I have both anchors down and every line secure," Salm answered. "Nothing loose on deck."

"Additional bumpers?"

He hadn't, but… "I'll get them out."

"That'll do for winds gusting to forty-five, fifty knots, particularly within the protection of the harbor breakwaters." Granpop had news on the rest of the family ships, too. Salm's sister Wind had anchored at their northern fisheries boundary in the lee of a headland, and Uncle Ray had sailed northwest of Giuthas to put the landmass between his ship and the storm. Both were safe to ride it out. "Before you ask, that schooner you have your eye on is well protected in Hidden Cove."

Salm rubbed his jaw, then dropped his hand and squeezed the radio button again. "If I wanted something smaller, say, a sloop or a cutter, would Humphries still be the place to go?"

"Aye."

There was a pause, and because of the static, Salm thought they'd been cut off.

"Trouble with your lass?" Granpop asked.

Blessed Orb, now he wished he hadn't opened his big mouth. "Not sure she is *my* lass yet. And...I want to give her some options."

He could imagine Granpop's nod, but all he said was, "Glad you checked in, lad."

Salm turned off the electricity and dressed in his slicker and rain pants. He put out the additional bumpers. The nearby sailors, doing the same, hailed him, and Salm shared his findings.

"Terrible night to be out," one said. "Couldn't have been more opportune for the council to close the enclave for those rips to be sought out."

"Let's just hope no one's been left sitting on the sea instead of tucked into a harbor." Salm tossed a final wave and went below. He fixed his dinner and Skipper's, cleaned up and then donned all his rain gear again to give the pup one last walk for the evening.

"Should have done this sooner, li'l mate," he told the dog, and they headed up the companionway ladder. Judging by the waves beating at the hull, they'd be lucky to get down the gangway.

A bird shrieked, cutting into Luna's dream of watching a storm from the lighthouse. Not Rissa from her dream, but this kittiwake in her laundry. His chest swelled against her hand, preparing another breath and cry—

"*Shh,*" she hissed. She failed to stop him, but his cry was lost to a wicked howl breaking through her magical noise barrier. She withdrew the energy, and the full thundering of rain pummeling the windows, house siding, town deckwalks and everything else blasted her eardrums. No one in this house could have heard her bird. Comforting him automatically, she scrambled to sit up and lifted the shade.

A murky blackness lay beyond the window. Lightning flashed, momentarily scattering sparkles through the raindrops beating the glass. Darkness fell again...unsettlingly so. The lighthouse should have—

Could she even see the lighthouse from this angle?

She shoved her legs from under her covers. The front door would give a better view—oh. Mam's drawings.

She cast about for the map case she'd stored under her cot. The bird squawked. She lit her fingertips aglow and found the case. Unzipping it, withdrawing the papers and unrolling the maps took forever, but less than a minute passed before she had one drawing activated, its lines blurrily depicting the all-too-real rain.

The thick clouds boiled as they swept across the paper, but the lighthouse beacon didn't flash.

URGENT FLIGHT

apa? Nebula? Stella?

None of them answered. Where was her family? What was wrong? Had another part of the turntable failed?

"No," Luna moaned. "Not on a night like this." She flung open her door and bolted down the hall to the front room.

The card players pivoted toward her, their chatter falling off.

Lady Anemone got to her feet. "Luna, dear, whatever is wrong?"

"The lighthouse..." Oh, Papa would permanently disown her if it was a family matter, but the safety of the enclave went beyond family troubles. "'Tis dark."

That brought everyone else to their feet. Lady Anemone was already dashing toward her kitchen—and presumably her phone —as Sir Porbeagle shouted, "Alert the council!"

"Surely no craft is sailing in this," Mr. Smith said. "Most probably haven't gotten the word that we opened our borders again."

"Someone has to light the beacon!" cried an old lady whom Luna couldn't place.

Exactly. Luna's head cleared. *I canna wait for any of this to sort out.* She rounded from the townsfolk and strode for the door, Papa, her sisters—

Wham, wham. Someone pounded on the door, and it flew open.

Salm tripped over the threshold. His gaze found hers. "The beacon," they said in unison, and Salm shoved a mass of stiff, bright yellow fabric at her, trailing water over the foyer. He snatched back one part of the rain suit. "Magic on the trousers."

It was an order, but she didn't care. Salm knew what to do. "Thank you," she gasped, swirling energy to dissolve and draw the rain trousers over her while continuing to try to reach her family. He held open the slicker, and she folded into it. The latches found their ways together, while the hood flipped up and drew closed. He grabbed her hand and pulled her out the door.

They ran along the deckwalk. Briefly, she closed her eyes against the pelting rain. Salm was here, his hand warm in hers, and the feeling of being anchored passed through her. She didn't need to face this alone. They had to hurry. She unfurled her wings, opened her channels to him and sent, *We'll fly. The rules are suspended for emergencies.*

Salm's wings emerged, and they lifted off together. She made a beeline for the point, like always, but Salm pulled her seaward.

Safer away from the buildings.

Wings beating impossibly hard, they fought against the headwind, barely making it over the line of waves crashing onto the beach.

Luna? came a shaky voice. The muddled next line might have been, *Are you home?*

Stella.

The wind broadsided them and blew them upward. Salm gave a mighty wingbeat and pulled her with him. *Ride it!*

Up, up above South Dock they soared, then the gust shoved them back above Fintail's and died in the shelter of Kittiwake

Point's cliffs. Beating hard, they flew seaward again. Luna caught her breath and called to Stella, *Where's Papa?*

I don't know, Stella whined. *I'm scared to leave bed. Come home, please!*

Find Papa. Find him now! Salm's hand jerked in hers, and she realized she'd yelled it to him as well. *Or Nebs. Something is wrong. The lighthouse is dark.*

Noooo. Stella began crying. *What's happened to Papa?*

That's what—

Luna's magic caught, and she couldn't talk through it, the rain and the wind. Salm pulled her, keeping her with him. She flushed magic over her feathers to shed the water and flapped harder, head down, straight into the wind. Papa never let them fly when it was like this, but clearly Salm had experience doing it.

Luna?

I'm here. Papa has likely cut me off. Please find him.

Her little sister's moans were lost to another gust that canted Luna backward.

Salm hauled her upright.

We have to get in the lee of the cliff, then go up, she told him, then repeated to Stella, *Find Papa.* Stella didn't answer.

Had she not heard?

Go find you father, Salm boomed.

Is Salm with you? Stella asked.

They must be sharing magic. *Aye, and you best be out of that bed when I get home.*

Between gusts, they beat their wings in full, hard strokes. Agonizing minutes later, they came alongside the cliff below the keeper's quarters.

A little higher, she said. *I've done it before. If we approach at the right height, the winds will carry us over, not into it.*

I hope that holds in today's current, he muttered.

Just watch out when we come up over the top.

The gulls huddled, nearly pushing each other off the narrow ledges in their efforts to crush against one another. Luna pulled Salm toward the uppermost rocks and alongside them.

Maybe she was mistaken. *'Tis worse than I've ever tried to fly in. We should land and climb up over the top.*

Crawl up, you mean.

Aye, she shot back. She approached a crevasse in the rock. It offered more protection, but was too narrow for them to enter together. *We have to let go,* she called and, much as she hated to, loosened her grip on Salm's steady hand.

You first.

With a hard beat of wings, Luna threw herself into the gap. The wind and rain ceased. Rock loomed before her. She lit her fingers with magic, reached for a ledge and, at the last second, saw a shrub clinging near the top. She lunged and grabbed a branch. Her knee slammed the cliff—

Ouch. She faltered, then her foot found a ledge. Stable, she drew a breath. *Salm?*

Here.

He'd landed below her and farther out. As he eased closer, she used her glowing fingers to find handholds in the roots and branches above her. Climbing the dozen feet with a fluttering of wings was easier than flying had been. Luna pushed her way up and over the cliff edge onto her belly. The wind whipped at her slicker as she pivoted to help Salm, but he was already scrambling over.

Still breathing hard, they dematerialized their wings, shoved themselves upright and ran. The gusts lashed at them, sending them into a zigzagged path that doubled the distance to the stone wall surrounding the grounds. A magical boost over it, and the structure protected them from the worst of it. At the quarters, Salm wrenched open the door and ushered her inside. He trotted beside her to the lighthouse staircase. "Hate to say it, but you need to light the beacon before looking for your father."

I know, she replied, unable to speak aloud.

They pounded up the stairs. Papa wasn't at the top. The wick was trimmed, the kerosene filled. She grabbed up the lighter, opened the valve and lit the wick. The beacon flared to life. She released the brake. The clockwork gears turned smoothly on the track, rotating the light upon the turntable.

Flash. Pause. Flash. The beams pierced the clouds, illuminating the sea cliffs and rolling ocean in sweeping arcs of light.

"Where could your father be?" Salm asked. "Or Nebula, for that matter? Lighting the beacon took but a moment."

It did. It was routine for anyone in her family. What had happened? Instead of moving toward the stairs, she made other habitual checks in the lighting procedure. Lastly, her gaze automatically went to the sea...

Something dark rocked on the storm-high waves. Beside her, Salm rubbed the wet from his eyelashes and looked, too. Aye, a black shadow wavered behind the sheets of rain the wind tossed toward them. Between the gusts, it took shape.

A boat?

WORSE NEWS

"**B**lessed Orb, no!" Salm shoved his way through the door onto the widow's walk. Keelboat. Thirty-feet or thereabouts. Who in their fishing fleet—

Luna called after him, "Tell me that's not a boat!"

He didn't want to believe it, but he knew that silhouette, as any mariner would. Luna joined him, grabbing his shoulder and pointing as he raised his own arm to do the same.

"'Tis," he yelled. "Where are the shoals?" He knew the location from below, but not from above.

She spun and aimed her finger northwesterly. As the beacon flashed, she said, "Off the corner of the wall. They're headed for it."

Keenan had that type of boat. Why was he out? He was as experienced as anyone, but in this weather... Fear for the sailor roared in Salm's ears. It could easily be his sister Wind, or Coral, or even him down there.

The second beam flashed, revealing several figures entering the keeper's quarters below.

Adrenaline surged through him. "Help has arrived."

They ducked inside. Stella stood at the top of the stairwell. Wide-eyed, she flung herself at Luna.

Luna hugged her, then squatted and held her sister's face. "Where is Nebula?"

"S-searching for Papa."

"You have to tend to the beacon. We have an emergency on the sea. Understand?"

Salm took in Stella's nod as well as footsteps pounding on the stairs. He charged to the railing—

"Ho," called a man from below. "Everything all right here?"

"A thirty-foot keelboat is headed for the shoals," Salm bellowed down the stairwell. "Might be Keenan's. Send anyone who sails down to help me. We've got to get it turned out to sea." He darted back outside. Thank the Orb, things were falling into place so he could get to Keenan. His wings unfurled, and he flapped to rise, then dove over the railing.

"Salm, don't!" Luna yelled after him, her words echoing.

Wind slammed him. He narrowly missed smashing into the lighthouse. He fell dangerously, caught himself and leveled.

How the hell—

A hand grabbed his wrist, and Luna pulled him out of the wind into a pocket behind the curving stone.

Bullsharks, Salm, would you listen to me for once? It would have been safer to take the stairs.

They dropped down the leeward side of the lighthouse. When they landed, he quickly kissed her. *I love you.*

You're not getting yourself killed without me. She didn't let go of his arm. *We have to go back to where we came up.*

They flew-ran across the yard. "Boat headed for the shoals!" Luna yelled at a man. "Send the call to launch the rescue boats. Phone in the kitchen."

"Any sailor should join us," Salm added.

The wizards began shouting instructions. Salm and Luna didn't wait.

They jumped the wall again and ran for the cliff. He never would have found the crevasse without Luna.

Climbing down the quiet, protected space, she told him, *Other boats won't arrive quick enough.*

What other ideas do you—

Dolphins, they sent in unison.

How close are they? she asked.

He stopped, hanging on to the roots, his panting audible. His ornery blue magic wouldn't cooperate. It jumped and scattered, weakened from fighting the wind. He tried again and this time located the dolphins. *Come.*

Each pod swirled together, ready, waiting—

He couldn't form up the image, and the frustration broke his bond with them.

At his shoulder, Luna's breaths came in quick spurts, too. Their gazes met. He shook his head. "They aren't far. The cove north of North Dock. I'll try again."

She put her hand over his, and her silver magic flowed to him. "I'm low. Do you need much?"

He grinned back at her. "It ought to be enough." Both her magic and having her here calmed him. He concentrated and sent his magic out to find the dolphins again.

See-low responded instantly, and Ni-lee, farther away, was seconds behind.

Come. Salm sent the image of South Dock followed by the shoals below the point. Then one of a sailboat. *Out to sea,* he told them. *Push it out to sea.*

He waited until the pods began to swim, then opened his eyes and sighed. "They're coming. Ready to go?"

"Are *you* ready?" she answered. "We should hug the cliff going down, then skim the waves to avoid the worst of the wind."

"Like we did to rescue the shag."

Her mouth formed a tired grin. "Exactly."

"Luna, that's crazy. How will you know where the rock is in the dark?"

"I can tell by the cooing of the birds." She pointed to her temple. "It's a rising and falling hum." She took his hand, and her magic swirled to him.

He tamped down on his excitement at having it again and passed her a supply of his energy. They merged. The hum came from outside and below the crevasse.

"'Tis not so different from your dolphin communications. Arch your wings. We'll take it slow."

He squeezed her hand. "I'm ready."

They dropped out of the crevasse. *Slow* still seemed like a plunge in the dark, but with Luna's slender fingers tight in his, he stayed the course. Her magic filled the unknown void of black rock with a hum that she kept to a steady decibel through adjustments of her wings.

Level out, she sent and pulled up.

The bird hum cut off, and they soared over the crashing waves, the splash mixing with rain, the wind driving them back. Hand in hand, they fought against it. The sailboat loomed ahead, and dolphin squeaks grew louder in their magic.

Hoy, I need to get to the boat before they start pushing it or Keenan— or whoever—will think it's Davy Jones himself.

The boat tilted, the boom swinging free, sails flapping. No one was visible on the deck.

Blessed Orb, this was the stuff of Salm's nightmares. Had the lines broken loose, or had someone gone overboard? Was Keenan sailing solo? It was a small boat, so that was possible. That'd be a better situation than a man overboard.

They'd learn soon enough, but not without another fight. *Too risky to land on the starboard with that loose boom. We have to get around to port to approach the deckhouse safely.*

Several minutes passed as they struggled to circle the pitching boat, then avoid being blown into the rigging. They fell onto the stern. He yanked Luna to her feet and pulled her over the pitching deck with a firm grip, nearly losing his own footing as she lurched because she didn't have sea legs.

Spells, we have no life jackets. It felt naked, and he feared for Luna. This would surely convince her to be a landlubber forever. However, a glance revealed her folded wings shone with magic, ready to take her airborne. *Brilliant idea.*

He tucked her under his arm, and they stumbled toward the deckhouse. Through the rain-splashed windows, Salm could make out the figure of a man in a life jacket bent over the wheel, clearly fighting to strong-arm it to the port. He was losing the battle without a crewmate.

Salm wrenched open the door and shouted, "Ahoy, did you lose a man?"

An ashen-faced boy of about eighth year turned, his arm clenched around one of the man's legs—a man whose bulkier physique established he wasn't the lanky Keenan.

"Daddy?" the lad said in a proper British accent. "Angels have come to rescue us."

By the Orb, these sailors weren't wizards.

LIFESAVING LIES

L una managed to pull in her wings. Heedless, Salm shoved forward, his wings still visible—

Ohhh! She darted out a hand and washed an invisibility spell over his feathers. The captain turned, and Salm careened into him as he grabbed two handles of the wheel.

The captain blinked and shook his head. Or he might have seen—they all struggled to keep their footing. He stared, and dread wound through Luna.

Bullsharks. He'd seen.

Mouth agape, the human captain threw a look outside, then at them again. "Where did you come from? How the—get on a life jacket, you idiot."

"Please, I need one, too!" Luna blurted. Anything to change the subject, and maybe Salm was thinking the same, because he repeated urgently, "Did you lose anyone?"

The boy tugged his father's clothes. "But he's an angel. Angels don't need—"

"Emmett," the man barked, his gaze on the blurry view out the deckhouse window. "Life jackets."

Rain and wind battering the deckhouse filled a beat. Then

the boy leaned back and flipped up a padded seat, revealing a storage locker.

Luna grabbed a life jacket and slung it around her neck. She got another for Salm, but he'd curled his body over the helm, his elbows jutting at angles as he strained to turn the wheel.

He planted his feet wide and turned to face the man. "Did. You. Lose. Anyone?" Salm ground out.

Blessed Orb, she'd been so worried that they'd exposed themselves that she hadn't realized the man hadn't answered.

"No, just me 'n my boy," the captain gasped. "Line snapped when we passed through a freak storm that literally shoved us to the shore."

Luna met Salm's gaze. *A rip,* they shot at each other. *Literally* was correct. Thank the Orb, they had worse things to worry about than angels.

She lifted the life jacket over Salm's head.

The boat pitched sideways, and Luna slammed into his side. He caught her, and blue magic zinged between them, securing his straps and hers, making the life jacket as snug as his arm. Then he rejoined the struggling captain at the wheel and hauled it around again.

"I'm gonna drop your sail," Salm told the man. "I train dolphins and have called them to help. They'll push your craft away from this shoal. Keep your rudder steering port until Luna tells you to straighten."

"You can't go out there," the man snapped. "You'll be swept away. I need you here, adding your strength to mine."

Spells, Salm, you canna do this alone.

Nay, I canna. While I cut loose their sail, I need you to direct the dolphins with this image. He sent his magic over.

An image appeared in their merged energy—the submerged hull moving away from the rocks over and over in a repeated movie. As she watched, several dolphins swam into the scene.

Their melodic squeaks trailed beneath the rain pounding on the deckhouse windows.

There. With words and images, Salm directed them alongside the boat, to the stern's port side. *Push.* He pointed past the boat's captain and thought-spoke, *Send those that arrive next to the—*

Aye. Dolphins on starboard bow and port stern. I'm not that terrible a sailor. Go.

He did, to the captain's curses. Within their merged magic, she felt his magic clinging to the mast to support his hand-over-hand climb, his folded wings energized to catch a fall. *As long as he doesn't knock himself unconscious, Salm is safe.*

The pod's mothers and young'uns arrived. *There,* she sent the six to the starboard. Behind them swam another group. *There,* she relayed the image. *There.* A stubborn one wasn't following her direction. She was forcing the image to him again when the sail dropped over the deckhouse.

The wheel jerked in the captain's hands. He swore and ranted, "That idiot cut my rigging!"

Salm? She grabbed the wheel with the man.

I'm fine.

"He's—'tis fine," she grunted. "Get that rudder steering to port."

"Can't see a damned thing," he railed, but he helped her push the helm around and hold it.

The boat moved gradually. The dolphins pushed. It might have been her imagination, but the boat didn't pitch so horribly.

Push. Push. Push.

Salm's chant sounded over the dolphin squeals. They began echoing him, and Luna sucked a breath at the image coming through her magic: Salm hanging to the boat's gunwale, his head a foot from the breaking waves as he yelled to the dolphins, aloud and magically.

She couldn't watch.

But she did echo Salm's encouragement to the dolphins in the rear even after she pulled from the merge. Their squeals quickly matched with those in the front, and the sound became a drumming through her channels, pumping her magic and her heartbeat to a frenzied level.

The wind didn't let up. They couldn't see out. The man was angry and his little boy scared. Her arms were aching, her body abuzz with Salm's magic. He was excited, thrilled, not a worried nerve about him.

She would be having a serious talk with the lad about putting himself in danger like this. She could nae stand it.

'Tis working, he called to her.

"Thank the Blessed Orb."

"What did you say?" the little boy asked.

"Um...a, uh, thanks."

Relief warred with fear, and finally she gave in to curiosity. Sinking into the merge again, her view became Salm's view. The wind whipped at her hair, salt coated her tongue, water soaked her skin, the cold stabbed her bones and numb fingers locked on the gunwale. When Salm glanced up, she peered through his narrowed eyes at the retreating shadowy cliff of Kittiwake Point.

Straighten the boat, Salm called, and a beat later she repeated, "Straighten the boat." The captain didn't comply, so she repeated the request and then tried to shove the wheel.

The man wouldn't let her turn it. "How can you know?"

"The dolphins. Don't you feel them pushing the hull?" Luna wrestled against him, but he elbowed her aside.

"I have no idea what's pushing this craft, but if it's some sort of devil-worship spell you're casting, you'll regret it the minute we set foot on land."

Luna! Salm yelped.

She couldn't let the captain hamper their progress. She nudged her elbow to his and let loose her magic. The captain collapsed to the floor, and Luna grabbed the rotating wheel with hands that still shone silver.

"Daddy!" screamed the boy.

How far around had the boat gone? It was all she could do to hold the helm alone. "He's fainted," she yelled to the crying child. "Help me hold the wheel before we all die."

Sniffling, the boy grabbed the rim, and together they kept it in the direction she hoped was straight.

Farther port, Salm called between beats of his chant.

"Turn it port," she ground out to the boy, but they couldn't move it.

Salm, I need your help.

Luna, he shrieked, *this is a bloody emergency. Hang it if he sees, use my magic to shove the blasted wheel.* His chants to the dolphins resumed.

Oh Blessed Orb, I've never…but… With a side-glance to the boy, she flushed a palmful of magic, coated the wheel and shoved.

The boy gasped.

"Ouch," she said theatrically. "That lightning is hot."

The boat turned from the shoals. It crept offshore, and Salm tried to judge their progress. They gained no discernable distance for what seemed like ages while he pounded out the leading beat. When the second dolphin pod arrived, the boat shifted. The flashing light of Kittiwake Point fell behind them. Their speed increased, a little at first, then more. Less wind? Calmer waters?

His sensibilities were tangled with Luna's—her putting the man under the sleep-torpor she used on her birds, her keeping the boy calm and her blindly piloting a larger sailboat, a first-time feat. Between their deep merge and his magical directing of thirty-some dolphins, Salm had practically left his physical body and was operating on pure energy. It took a blurry figure flying within a foot of his face before he shook himself out of it.

"Let go of the gunwale," the wizard yelled, the words sounding like they'd been repeated. "We have control of the boat." He pointed, and Salm looked over his shoulder. Multiple shades of red, orange, blue, green and brown magic wove over the hull, controlled by five wizards on the starboard alone. They had stopped short of his position, waiting to take over.

The man landed on the deck and stretched an arm to give Salm a hand up. It was Keenan grinning down at him, his long hair escaping his slicker hood. "Have a warmed blanket waiting for you. Whose boat is—"

"Human owner," he gasped. "Be careful."

Keenan's eyes widened. "In our waters—"

"Aye. Because of a rip."

Keenan sprang off the deck, flapping furiously upward and shouting to the nearest wizard, "Leave that sail! Humans! Get the hell off the deck."

Within a minute, he was back. "Take care of your dolphins first. Then we'll need your word on the next steps."

"Luna's word," Salm clarified. "She's captaining the boat right now." *Luna, did you hear?* he asked.

I heard. Bring one of those blankets for the boy. Wrapped in it, he'll fall asleep easily.

Salm relayed that and then spent several minutes ensuring the dolphins had strength enough to continue pushing the boat with the wizards along the hull magically stabilizing and guiding it. Keenan had to help uncurl Salm's frozen fingers with a warming spell and help him to the deck.

"Carmen has Luna's directions," Keenan told him as they wrapped him in the promised warm blanket and guided him to the lee of the deckhouse. "She also has this model sailboat. We're fetching someone for memory work."

Salm barely knew Carmen, a Tern Bay witch, who was his

parents' age, and because she didn't fish, their paths didn't cross. "Good," he grunted. *Have you heard from Nebula?* he asked Luna.

She can't find... Her voice broke.

He turned to Keenan. "I'll instruct the dolphins to continue propelling the boat to our northern boundary, but Luna and I need to find her father immediately."

Luna was wrapped in a warmed blanket only long enough to down a re-energizing tonic, then she relinquished it to take Salm's warm hand as they lifted off. She let Salm guide their flight while she grilled Nebula on the search for Papa.

You searched every room in the house?

Aye.

Under the beds? In the closets?

Aye, snapped Nebula. *The baths, basement, the chicken house, infirmary, shed, the yard.*

The entire yard, all sides?

Outside the wall, too, Nebula shrieked. *In case he fell over it some-how. Luna, he is nowhere to be found! Kelly went to check the tavern and then send an alert over town. His mam came up and Frannie's mam, too. They rechecked everyplace we'd already checked. We are drenched to the skin, but at least no one can tell I've been crying. Except Kelly.*

And me, Stella put in with an exaggerated sniff. *I've been crying more. Whatever will we do with no Mam and no Papa and Luna aban-doning us?*

Oh Blessed Orb, no one is abandoning you. Hush now and let me think.

Salm squeezed her hand sympathetically. The wind had blown them close enough that she should be able to see the yard, except for the low clouds. But she'd flown over the point so many times that it was visible in her imagination. To satisfy her own mind, they'd have to search again. Systematically. The lighthouse, the cottage, the shed—oh.

What? Salm asked.

Mother's studio. They won't have searched it, not with the lock in place.

But if it is locked—

Papa still could have gone in and magicked the lock into place. That daybed was suspiciously dust-free, now that I think on it.

23

THINGS SOMEONE HAD TO SAY

Holding her breath, Luna eased open the door at the top of the shed staircase and held her lit fingers high. Their glow outlined a figure on the studio's bed…snoring softly.

Her breath released, and Salm grasped her shoulder. She leaned into him for a moment. "He's alive."

They entered quietly, and Salm stepped past her to pick up a bottle on the table. He swirled the inch of amber liquid in the bottom. "It's not empty at least," he whispered. "I'd not heard tales that Jonah was a drinker."

And now everyone will know our family business. But worse, it hurt to admit this to Salm.

"Up until midsummer, I'd have said only in the tavern and only on nights I was monitoring the lighthouse." Luna crossed her arms. "Then one morning after his shift, I caught him with whiskey. To sleep, he said." She sighed. "I didn't see the bottle again, and it never kept him from his duties, but I've smelled it on him after a nap."

"What happened midsummer?" Salm asked. "Something make him anxious?"

Aye, she'd told Papa she was seeing more of Salm. Luna felt her shoulders creeping up to her ears, goose bumps rising—

"Hoy, there," Salm said softly. "What—"

She shook her head, unable to look at him, but Salm took her into his arms and tilted her chin up. "Us?" he asked. "But I've done everything I can think of to get in his good graces, and *he's let me*. You, Luna my love, are the perfect daughter. It canna be what you're thinking. Ask him." Salm added a firm nod.

After a moment, she went to the bedside and knelt, Salm a comfort hovering behind her.

"Papa?" Luna gently shook his shoulder. "Papa, wake up."

Her father opened his eyes, glanced toward the window and bolted upright. "The beacon—"

"I lit it. But a boat nearly wrecked below."

His skin paling, Papa searched her face, but he knew as well as she did that this was something none of them would ever joke about. He pressed a hand to his eyes.

"In all fairness, it sounds like it passed through a rip and got dumped quite close to shore. But if the beacon had been operating, the captain would have acted sooner to avoid the rocks. It was bloody dangerous for them and for Salm and me to be down there. We only just managed to get it turned away in time!" His face crumpled, but she wasn't going to let him off, not after the last harrowing hour. "We could have died in that storm. Those sailors could have died. Or any of the dozen wizards from town who came to our aid. Because you're drinking. Why?"

Slowly, he shook his head, lips trembling before he clamped them tight and lowered his hand. "I-I canna keep up. I'm growing older. You girls are growing up. I should be doing and telling you much more than I manage, things that Celeste would have done. You'd seem to be getting on, then something always changes the rules. Female undergarments, female... functions. And then...*lads*. Which I know well too much about from my own younger years. I wanted to have that talk with you, but Anemone let me know that she had done it in Celeste's place."

Outrage flooded Luna. "That should have been private."

Papa patted her shoulder. "She merely informed me that you had your birds and bees straight. Probably for the best. I could never be frank about those issues with a lass. Not like Celeste. I..." Papa hung his head. "I miss her so much."

Luna drew a breath. He'd spoken of Mam more in these seconds than he had in years. "I do, too," she said carefully.

Papa glanced at her. "Your mother always knew how to care for you lasses. For the quarters and livestock. I learned from her. When she passed... She would have taken all the guesswork out of raising lasses and dealing with lads coming around."

Luna patted his shoulder this time. "You've done fine, Papa."

He grimaced. "Maybe with the seabirds—"

"And us!"

He nodded. "You're good daughters, but the house...and this cursed tour. Celeste would have had this tour business in hand, or at least freed me to address only it. Honestly, the thing was a thorn in my side until you lasses stepped in." He lifted his gaze over Luna's shoulder and cleared his throat. "And Salm, here."

We would have started earlier if only he'd let us know. Hands fisting, Luna groaned. "Is that when you brought the whiskey home? When they started badgering you about a tour?"

He wouldn't meet her gaze. "Aye." He jerked his chin toward the bottle, then Salm. "Pour it out, if you would?"

Salm took the bottle to the patio and did.

"Papa, I've said it before, and this time you have to listen: You need to hire help."

"I—" The stubborn look formed, then fell away. "Not you, I suppose."

Luna rocked back onto her heels. Had he just offered her a *paid* position? Never had he... She glanced toward Salm. He didn't react in any way—wise of him. She thought fast. "I accept your offer of employment *temporarily*, while Salm and I work out our plans. For two nights a week, back-to-back." She leaned closer. "And only if you are actively seeking an apprentice and interviewing applicants. Otherwise, I walk."

Papa's eyes narrowed, and Luna held his gaze. He glanced to Salm. His frown increased momentarily, and within her energy, Luna could feel Salm struggling to keep still. Papa looked back to her. "Agreed."

Luna offered her hand. Papa hesitated, then clasped it in his large one and shook it.

"I suppose there are explanations to be made." He swung his feet to the floor.

While his gaze lingered on Mam's telescopes, Luna got to her feet. He'd taken the worst of it better than she'd expected.

"You realize this employment will be possible only if they keep me on as the lighthouse keeper. I take full blame for what happened tonight." He rose and started for the door.

Luna followed. "Aye, I know that," she said quietly. "There's something else you should know: The boat was captained by a human."

Papa spun around. "How under the Orb did that get into our waters?"

"Rip, sir." Salm stepped up behind her. "Not sure if it's on the Giuthas-Tern Bay border, but both councils have been alerted."

Papa's surprise dissolved into a weary, pained frown. "I shall still take the blame for the beacon, if they're arguing that, but these rips are solely due to Giuthas' restrictions and loss of power. The situation in your home enclave begs me to ask after a worry that weighs on my heart: Why are you so keen to take my daughter away to this broken enclave?"

Luna's gaze shot to Salm. *Please, drop this for now. Papa has agreed to get help, and he still has to face the elders with the truth.*

"I'm not, sir. I mean, yes, her living with us would help, sir, but tha's not the reason. We do nae need to make our home on Giuthas." He darted a glance at her, but didn't heed the shake of her head.

Her heart sank.

Salm squared his shoulders. Luna didn't like it, but for weeks now he'd heeded her decision that "now isn't a good time" to talk to her father. In Salm's humble opinion, Jonah Ness needed to know where Salm—and his daughter—stood. "In fact, I doubt we would make our home on Giuthas, much as the isle needs people to."

Luna put a hand on his arm, the pinch of her fingers echoed by one in her energy.

He pivoted to face both father and daughter. "Luna is carving out a good business here. Or, if she desires, I suspect she could take her bird care skills to the neighboring coastal towns. I'd be willing to help and would love to consult with you and Mr. Grouse on whether seabirds might fill some role in helping the Windborne." He fully met Luna's wide-eyed gaze. "I can get a smaller boat that allows me to sail alone or with you, or with an apprentice, like my father sometimes talks of. When he returns, I'll be speaking with him about shifting my tasks to make my homeport Tern Bay." He turned to her father again. "Where we will live is the topic of nearly all our discussions, sir, and I'm willing to see where the winds take us, because I love her, sir."

"Salm? I do nae think this is the time to—"

"Then when?" Salm asked Luna. "He has to know I love you. If he does nae, why does he and the whole town think I have you living on our ship when you are nae and whisper of us making love without The Moors paperwork signed and sealed with an inked blessing, not one the Golden Orb has any hand in. Let's put this ridiculous line of gossip to rest so you can go about your jobs and care for your birds with no bloody interference. So I can know which boat to purchase, and we can live together without garnering frowns when we walk past your critical townsfolk."

Luna covered her mouth. *Did you have to say those things aloud?*

Jonah stared at Salm, and he was sure the man was going to order them out.

"Luna has discussed all this with you?" Jonah heaved a sigh. "And you are willing to change the course of your work and where you live, your life, to meet her desires?"

Salm took Luna's hand, brought it to his lips and kissed her fingers. "That's up to Luna, sir. But I hope she agrees to bond with me."

Jonah pursed his lips, before finally saying, "Then, indeed, I believe you are what fishermen call *a keeper.*"

Salm blinked. That was the last thing he'd expected to hear. From Jonah Ness, it sounded like a raving testimonial, yet Luna hadn't said a thing.

Her father turned and descended the steps. Once he was out of sight, Salm dared to look over at Luna. "Will you? I promise we'll work something out."

Luna had questions—so many questions—about how Salm had decided he could settle for a smaller boat. Aside from the single thought, *Perhaps we can do this,* her emotions were so ratcheted up she couldn't form the words.

"We...I..." She looked toward her father's retreating back. "I canna let him face the elders alone."

Salm nodded, and they ran after Papa to the keeper's quarters. A crowd of folks blocked the doorway. Elder Bentha was among them and, of course, was itching to confront them. Luna clenched her hands. What more would she have to endure today?

Lady Anemone pushed past Bentha and came out to meet them. "Everything all right here? I was called to come, though no specific ailment—"

"No ailment." Papa waved them inside. "No injury, except to my dignity."

Stella shrieked and threw herself at Papa, which caused Nebula to come running down the stairs and do the same. Papa reassured them to much crying and complaining. Salm was busy shaking the hands of those who had turned out, and Luna began to shiver from cold and…everything. She wanted to go upstairs to change, but not with this many folks in their house.

Nebula's hands flashed silver, and she pushed Mam's sweater into Luna's hands with a grin. "I found it during my search."

Luna hugged her and magicked on her sweater.

"Let's get to the bottom of this," Elder Bentha demanded, her frown focused on Papa. "Anemone alerted me, and I put in a call to Giuthas. Their security wizards alerted their elders." She gestured to the gray-haired wizards Salm had greeted—the tall, stern Sir Humus and the steadfast Mr. Grouse. "Explain why," Elder Bentha continued, "we were left unlit, which put a boat in danger."

Papa held out his hands. "I'm sorry for my failure to light the beacon and for endangering the craft. I…" He glanced at Luna and swallowed. "I take complete blame. I had a drink, whiskey, this afternoon. That caused me to nap longer than I should have."

The room went silent. Everyone stared at him.

Luna shuffled closer to him. So did Lady Anemone, who, along with Mr. Grouse, blocked Elder Bentha.

"Have you been drinking on workdays for long?" the healer asked carefully.

Papa's stiff shoulders relaxed a bit. "Nay. Started this summer. Truth be told, the combination of preparing for these tours and the reality of my oldest lass leaving the nest has me missing my beloved Celeste more than words can say."

"Of course this is a sad reminder," Lady Anemone said softly. "The last lighthouse tours saw both you and Celeste welcoming visitors."

"But 'tis nae a reason to turn to drinking," Papa said sadly. "I neglected to think on *asking* for help, or that Luna's courting wouldn't take her away, but would *bring in* another wizard to assist."

Mr. Grouse blinked furiously. "With winds like these, no craft, let alone a human one sailing unknown waters, could have avoided the shore, flashing beacon or no."

"But that doesn't excuse the fact that our warning beacon was left unlit," Elder Bentha blustered behind him.

"Entirely my fault," Papa repeated. "Under Lady Anemone's counsel, I will stop drinking. I shall begin a search for additional help and in the meantime will take actual nights off while Luna maintains the lighthouse."

Sir Humus raised his hand, forcing Elder Bentha to remain quiet. "I can't speak for the mishap of the lighthouse not being lit, but the Isle of Giuthas takes blame, too. Our energy shortage has caused the rips, and we sent our monitoring vessels to safer locations."

"Or no one should be blamed," Mr. Grouse insisted, making Luna like him more than ever. "It's the dammed weather, a natural occurrence that usurps our tiny beings' efforts to defy it."

"Obviously!" Lady Anemone hurled her hands upward. "I should like for our Tern Bay enclave to assist in closing these ocean rips with a loan of energy. That is in all our interests. Can we put that to a vote at the emergency council meeting you've called, Bentha?"

Why was an emergency council meeting called? Luna swallowed as the answer came to her. If Elder Bentha had called it, it was to remove Papa as lighthouse keeper. If they didn't believe he'd stop drinking, then Papa was out.

Lady Anemone leaned toward the head of the council. "Maybe you should have accepted his refusal to open the lighthouse for tours this weekend, *Bentha*. Those preparations could nae have been easy to fit in for a single father who works full time *every night of the week*." She gestured to the tidy living room. "Yet he has done it. On top of many wildlife calls this week." Lady Anemone suddenly shot her gaze to Luna. She opened her mouth and then closed it.

Spells, no. Would the kittiwake still be in her laundry bag?

Mr. Grouse looked around. "Your place has a shine to it that my bachelor quarters could nae achieve in a fortnight of work."

"Thanks," Papa muttered. "The credit for getting her ship-shape goes to my lasses. Salm here proved a regular hand as well."

"Bentha?" Lady Anemone persisted. "These Giuthas elders have come all this way. We can adjourn with them to the town hall to await the other elders, have the vote about our assistance and possibly send them back to their enclave with good news. That leaves these young people to recover from their heroic rescue of that wayward boat."

Under the others' gazes, Elder Bentha pressed her lips tight and nodded.

Luna reached behind her and wove her fingers into Salm's. She could talk to him once their quarters emptied out.

Sir Humus had stepped toward Papa when Elder Bentha said, "You best come to the meeting as well, Jonah."

Luna's heart lurched.

Papa nodded. "I need to check on things upstairs. Nebula?"

She and Stella trailed him up the staircase, while Lady Anemone intercepted Elder Bentha and Sir Humus.

Mr. Grouse lingered at the door, slipping a tiny pair of pliers in and out of his pocket. "Probably a terrible time to ask," he said, "but while I'm here, how are the seabirds?"

Luna cast a glance to Salm, who'd been here more recently than she had. "I haven't seen them in days, but Salm relayed that both are healing nicely. Shall we run out?"

In the bird shed, Mr. Grouse pronounced both the shag's and the cormorants' progress good, though he wanted to wait until the course of medication was done to remove the shag's stitches. They'd moved to the door, but Salm was blocking it, his head tilted in question, his gaze steadily meeting hers.

It was her call to ask, he was saying without speaking a word.

Salm had opened the discussion with Papa, and now he was leaving the choices up to her: continue to do repairs for people in Tern Bay, or sail with the Seas working on the fisheries or on her own bird interests. Or a combination of these... Maybe she could do both from a boat—repairs for people *and* wildlife calls.

"Mr. Grouse, if you have a moment, could you answer a few questions about other coastal enclaves and if they might need help with their wild birds? And if"—she glanced at Salm —"seabirds might be trained to track schools of fish?"

Mr. Grouse laughed. "I believe several species have perfected that skill already. You just need to find a way to encourage them to share the information. As for the first, I've always said I'd take you on as an apprentice."

They discussed the commitment of sailing to places Mr. Grouse sent them—and applying for a peregrinator transport device for emergency travel—with Salm asking more about the various ports.

"You are serious, then." Mr. Grouse enthusiastically tapped his pliers against his palm. "I worked for years at convincing Beri to apprentice for me and never thought to poke you for an interest in seabirds, Salm of the Seas."

Salm grinned. "Birds have grown on me, the same as Luna has."

Mr. Grouse blinked fast and seriously. "Going into the more remote enclaves means a smaller boat that can hug the coastline."

"Already looking into my options for that craft." Salm tilted his head toward Luna. "The critical question is, would this be something we could make a living at?"

"Sadly, no. The majority of wildlife positions, both in the human and Windborne worlds, are volunteer."

Salm groaned, but Luna asked, "What about odd jobs? Do these remoter areas have a need for someone handy?"

With a cautious smile forming, Salm met her gaze.

Mr. Grouse bobbed his head. "Once they know and trust you, they'd save up jobs for when you came on rounds. Caring for their birds would make a strong start. Certainly, you'd garner more repairs amongst multiple enclaves than you'd find in one town alone."

Luna looked at Salm. "That'd work?"

"If you took Jonah's job temporarily, and I keep working for the isle, and we build it up."

But to make a livelihood of it could take…years. Weariness settled over Luna. If they wanted to live together anytime soon, it'd be simpler for her to become a part of the Seas fisheries.

Salm tried to catch her gaze, his eyes hopeful, but she couldn't…just couldn't. She walked out of the shed ahead of the others. *If I do that, it's like I'm giving up the progress I've made with Papa and the townsfolk. And Salm.*

This was going to be harder than she'd thought.

24

DELAYS AND DETAILS

After that last look of Luna's, Salm was having a hard time paying attention to the discussions still taking place after they slid inside the door of the keeper's quarters. He wanted to get her alone so they could talk more—

"Salm of the Seas!" Elder Bentha hailed him from a group of elders. "And Luna Ness. We have a problem."

"A situation," Keenan said, stepping from among the group.

If Keenan was here… "What happened with the boat? Are the dolphins—"

"The craft is at our northern border with wizards from the Department of Magical Regulation on board, but the memory work isn't taking with the human captain."

This is nae making me feel better. "That's possible?" Trained DMR officers stepped in whenever the Windborne were exposed to the larger human populations. One of their fake ports—a dock and a few shanty buildings—sat just north of Tern Bay. The Seas routinely checked it for DMR.

"Anemone agrees with DMR that it's those preservatives and additives these humans ingest. Too high of a level and they prevent our natural magic from working. They've got him unconscious again, but we'll need the two of you to put on a performance at DMR's closest stopgap site." Keenan gestured to the living room sofa. "Have a seat. We need to review what you told him during the rescue."

The little boy had seen their wings. Salm had said he trained dolphins. "He was bloody angry I cut his rigging," Salm said.

"We'll get the supplies to replace it and smooth your way for when he wakes in the morning," Keenan said. "One of DMR's team has already told the man he hit his head. The kid saw him faint. But they say it'll be more realistic if you two return. It might take most of tomorrow to pull off before we can send this man on his way."

Luna shook her head. "Tomorrow is Saturday. I'm giving lighthouse tours starting at ten. I need to be here to help my father."

"You're rather unforgettable," Keenan said. "Your hair, that is. They need you, Luna Ness. Easier than magicking up someone else to look like you."

"I can handle the tours without you," Jonah said. They hadn't seen him come down the stairs.

"I'd rather be here," Luna said firmly, and when Jonah protested again, she rose and clasped his arm. "It's the first time without Mam here. I can't let you run the lighthouse tonight, get three hours of sleep at the most, then face folks alone. Well, Nebs and Stella will be here, but you ken my meaning? Our family must do this together." This she directed at Keenan and Elder Bentha behind him.

Oh. Salm stood up. He was beside Luna before he'd even thought about it. She was standing up to the elders, and he would support her decision. "Trust Luna to know what's best for her family." Yet DMR still needed local wizards to fill these roles, and in this case, that meant folks who knew sailing…

"I have an idea," Salm said. "Have Luna make one appearance tonight, then let her return to Tern Bay so she can be at the lighthouse in the morning. I'm free to stay at the stopgap port, and Maeve and Pauly owe me work time. They can help me install the new rigging tomorrow instead of Luna." It let the sisters off with an easier job than Salm would have had them do, but if it helped Luna, so be it.

Keenan shot a look at Elder Bentha.

She shook her head. "I doubt either of those lasses will be willing or convincing as part of your crew."

"If I talk to Captain Penny, they'll be convincing," Salm said. "Without her daughters free to work any job, they're losing a good part of their livelihood."

Elder Bentha huffed. "Give it a try. They're another thorn in my side right now."

"Let's do this," Keenan said. "The lasses are being held at town hall, which is where the DMR team is meeting us to transport you to the stopgap port."

Thank the Orb. Now Salm just had to use the no-nonsense attitude that Pop had counseled him in—on Captain Penny.

As folks got out their peregrinators, Lady Anemone elbowed her way over to Luna. "That bird is still alone in my parlor."

Pressing her lips closed, Luna locked gazes with Lady Anemone.

"I, er, will look in on him," Lady Anemone said.

Luna lifted her finger. "Could you bring him to me, please?"

Great Orb, the last thing they needed was a kittiwake to care for tonight. But Salm kept his mouth shut.

At the town hall, a DMR officer, young and dressed in a modern overcoat, met them. William definitely dinnae fit in with the locals, and his accent was British. On the other hand, Maeve and Pauly did, slouched and sullen in their cell in their thick sweaters and old dungarees smelling of fish.

Salm got the use of an empty office to meet with Captain

Penny. How long until she arrived? William said they'd wait to finalize things until she'd talked to her lasses, and now everyone—he and Luna, the Tern Bay and Giuthas elders and a few DMR people gathered in the larger meeting room—was fidgeting. Especially him. His gaze met Luna's. He'd had no chance to learn how she felt about his outburst to Jonah. *We need to talk.*

She dropped her gaze to her bag, and she adjusted the ties. *I'll give myself away trying to thought-speak with this many people around.*

He hadn't meant thought-speaking. Nay, this was a conversation to have in quiet with direct looks, hugs and—hopefully—more. *Come with me into the office—*

Captain Penny arrived, and everyone looked at Salm.

He ushered *her* into the office, telling himself, *Get your head to business, mate.*

"Don't tell me you've drummed up another charge against my lasses," Captain Penny spouted as soon as the door closed. "I've proof where they've been the last two days."

Had he expected her to be anything but confrontational? Crossing his arms, Salm steeled himself. He wasn't going to give an inch. Not if the alternative forced Luna to miss helping her father.

"And I've been assessing the damage," Salm returned in an even voice he hoped was a copy of Pop's. "Maeve and Pauly sliced our folded mainsail in eight places, going through four layers. Thirty-two holes." In the bottom layer, there were only blade pricks in the material, but she didn't need to know that. "I'll be patching for days to repair the vandalism to a sail costing ten thousand pounds. Unless you'd like to replace it?"

"You know I can't," she spat, but her face had paled. "Not even before I lost my crew."

"I didn't do anything wrong in citing your lasses for taking berried hens. Yet what they've done to my family's ability to work is mean-spirited and equally as harmful to our fisheries if we can't be on the water."

She grimaced. "They're sittin' and thinkin' through what they did. They have the jail time coming, but I also can't raise the credits to bail them out."

"Aye, it'll be a while before they earn any credits. I've been working up a list of compensation chores." He handed over the list. "Or, if they want out sooner, I have need of a couple of sailors to help the Department of Magical Regulation put on a performance for a human intervention." He told her about the rescue of the boat earlier. "This is happening tonight, now, and they have to be convincing. If they perform as a model crew, I'll consider the debt to the Seas paid, and they can go on to other paying jobs. If they sink things for me and the DMR team, then they answer to DMR *after* our chores."

Captain Penny eyed him, then eyed the list. "Leave it to me," she snapped.

Fifteen minutes later, Captain Penny, Maeve and Pauly were shown into the meeting room. Maeve shot dagger-eyes at him, and Salm's gut sank. But as the DMR officers took over explaining their roles, her expression cleared. It wasn't long before they were split into groups to be magically transported out to the stopgap port.

Luna squeezed his hand. *You know them better than I do. Are they going to do this properly?*

Salm glanced at Maeve and Pauly, both trudging to their DMR escort's side with downcast eyes, their fists shoved in pockets. Probably thought-speaking, coming up with some new plan. He'd trusted them too readily before to trust them again… Salm blew out his breath. How they acted was out of his hands now, but he could buoy up Luna. *I'm gonna walk the plank here and say, aye, we've got a chance at a smooth run.*

COMPLICATIONS OF A HUMAN SORT

Using a peregrinator transport device, William pereported Salm and Luna to the stopgap port. They raced out of the blowing rain and into one of the shanty buildings...that wasn't at all a shanty on the inside. After the clothing and makeup artists were done, he and Luna looked like they'd just come from the storm again, complete with human clothing—no wing slits in their slickers!—and the boat's life jackets that they'd borrowed.

"I've never seen you so bedraggled. Not even an hour ago," Luna tried to joke, but her voice held an edge, and her movements were jerky as she tugged at the knit cap they'd given him to hide his radio earpiece. Luna's device had disappeared under her wet, limp curls. Briefly, he cupped his hand over hers, wanting so badly to kiss her...or simply talk freely. They hadn't a moment alone, and now DMR officers were listening in on their every word.

"We'll allow the man, Captain Allen, to wake for the docking," William said, "and see that his boat is safe, but you must encourage him to remain aboard. He'll still feel drowsy, so we hope he'll agree. Salm, Luna, you each have your story straight?"

When they nodded, the DMR officers began speaking into their headsets. Seconds later, William said, "We're clear to send you to the boat." He ushered them out the door and pereported them through the dark to the boat a mile out.

Salm grasped Luna's arm, knowing she wouldn't have proper sea legs. The waves beat the hull, but the deck wasn't pitching wildly for how hard the wind was blowing. Why—oh. His dolphins were still propelling it—

"Blessed Orb, the poor animals. I have to see to them immediately." He opened his magical connection to them, hearing Luna explain what he'd meant to William. *See-low? All here? Work hard?*

The pod's leader sent back a stream of information. Before he could sort it, Luna interrupted, "Salm? William says their people have also pushed the ship with magic. The pod should be fine."

That made sense with See-low's assertion that this was the lightest ship they'd ever played with. Still, Salm took a minute to answer See-low and seek out the wizards on either end of the boat that the dolphin eagerly described as having *floating magic.* In the deckhouse, Captain Allen lay on the floor, and the little boy was curled on the bench seat, both wrapped in blankets. A grizzled old sailor—no, Salm corrected himself, a DMR wizard who *appeared* to be a sailor from a rescue boat—sat between them with a hand extended to each, magic glowing at his fingertips.

The person piloting the helm turned, the silver-gray curls escaping from her slicker hood a fair match to Luna's white ones.

"Carmen," Salm whispered. "Thanks for filling in."

"Glad I could," she whispered back. "It's been most interesting. Since the humans never saw me, they told me Luna Ness is going to take over, which I found hard to believe." She nodded to Luna. "No offense."

"None taken," Luna answered. "I'm here because I'm rather unforgettable in appearance."

Carmen chuckled quietly. "That you are."

And, ironically, this has led everyone to know me by name now, Luna sent him.

They swapped places, and William ushered Carmen out.

"I've got these two drowsy," the older sailor said in a hushed voice. "As soon as William gives the go-ahead, I'll release them from their sleep. Before I can put them under again, they'll need to be sitting so they don't fall."

Salm joined Luna at the helm while they closed the distance to the port. Within minutes, William's voice sounded through Salm's earpiece. "The lights in the port are visible, so we ought to begin. Salm? Luna?"

"Aye," they answered in unison.

The sailor got up and, with a nod, withdrew his magic. He left, then Salm and Luna were alone with the humans.

Think it'll be long? Luna sent him.

The boy is stirring already. Salm moved to the doorway as Emmett rubbed his eyes.

Don't leave me yet! Luna swung around, her eyes wide. *I'm getting nervous.*

Ha, Salm laughed. *This kid won't push you like Stella does.*

Luna shot him a smile.

"Hey!" Emmett pushed himself up to a sitting position. "Where's my dad?"

"Sleeping off his head bump," Luna answered. "How do you feel?"

"Tired still."

Luna laughed, and Salm could hear her relaxing. "Me, too. It's the middle of the night."

"Do angels sleep?" Emmett asked.

"I expect," Luna answered, the edge back in her voice. "I've never met one, though."

Good, Salm tried to reassure her, but just as quickly the kid shot back, "But you *are* one!"

"Emmett, that's enough," said the man.

"Sir?" Luna said. "You took a nasty bump when you fainted. How are you feeling?"

"Where the hell are we?" he snapped in return.

Oh Blessed Orb. Salm was supposed to let Luna handle this part, but this man's attitude was out of line.

"The coast of Scotland," Luna answered, as they'd been instructed.

"Scotland! I sailed out of Newcastle, Northern Ireland, this morning, headed for Liverpool," he ranted.

Then their boat had been on course straight through waters surrounding the Isle of Giuthas. Usually, a spell somewhat like a pereport would take over when a human craft hit their shielded waters and would convey it to the opposite side—a point in the open sea, *not* near the sea cliffs. Flights! That meant the magical diversion had failed. Giuthas had a worse problem if their spells were defaulting.

"Sir, I can show you the location on your navigation charts," Luna said.

"*Captain* Allen," he muttered.

"Don't know what to tell you, Captain," Salm chimed in. "Seems like you ran afoul of some heavy weather."

Captain Allen grumbled something, and the boy quietly asserted again that Salm and Luna were angels.

"Sorry to disappoint you, young man," Luna said. "But I'm only a local lass that happened to be on call for this nasty weather. After what you went through—the sea tossing your boat, wind, rain and lightning, I bet you were so grateful for our help that you wanted to believe angels had arrived. I don't have wings now, so could that be right?"

Emmett peered at her back, frowning, but he nodded.

Thank the Orb they had switched to slit-free slickers.

"I had another rescue before yours. Could you help by holding him?" Indicating that Salm take the helm, Luna picked up her laundry bag. He hadn't realized she'd brought it aboard. She showed Emmett how to pet the sleeping kittiwake's head and settled the bag onto his lap, leaving the boy completely distracted.

Captain Allen got to his feet and, ignoring Luna's suggestion that he sit, held to the wall to come stand beside Salm. "How'd you move my boat to this cove without sails?"

"My dolphins hauled you from the shoals, but I got to you from a rescue boat." Ha, the man blinked. He hadn't thought of that yet. "That boat joined us as soon as it was safe and is giving us a tow."

"I don't believe it."

"Luna, you want to dock us?" Salm opened the door and waved for Captain Allen to follow. "Come see for yourself."

The boy clambered to come, too, so Salm set the kittiwake's bag in the corner while the lad's father checked his life jacket. The boat had bumped to a stop by the time they got up on deck. The weather-beaten dock and a handful of buildings lay in shadows, except for one light on at a building with a sign that read *Fishing Supplies*. The only other boat—a fishing boat DMR had pressed into service to act as a rescue boat—was docked beside them. Maeve was helping the grizzled old sailor who'd been on their boat earlier to tilt up an outboard motor. On the dock, Pauly had finished removing the towline and waved to Salm, her slicker flapping in the wind. He threw her Captain Allen's mooring line, and she made it fast to a piling.

Once Captain Allen and Emmett joined him at the stern railing, Salm leaned over and gave a whistle that was lost to the wind. He followed it up with a real call. *See-low? Head count. Stern.*

Dolphin heads began appearing, big and small, and once they spotted him, they rose and danced.

The boy squealed in delight, and Salm called, "Great job!" out loud as well as through his magic.

"Harrumph! That's done with treats," the captain shouted over the wind.

"Indeed," a woman shouted back. Maeve, standing on the deck of the rescue boat.

Salm's heart sank. He'd heard that crowing tone before— right after she'd cast him overboard. Their gazes met, and Maeve grinned. He couldn't read her intent.

She hoisted a bucket, dipped in her hand and drew out a fish.

Oh Blessed Orb. What was she about?

"Sorry," William said over the earpiece. "That's the baitfish you requested, but I'm not sure what she's planning. Go with it."

Right, go with something Maeve said.

Maeve strode over her bobbing deck until she came even with them. "We certainly do reward them for a job well done," she said in a mocking Scottish brogue. "Or, city sailor, would you rather we bribe them to haul your sorry arse back out to sea?" With one hand, she dangled a seven-inch herring—far larger than the fish they ever fed their animals—over the side, while her other hand pointed to the side of Captain Allen's boat. The dolphins began squealing in excitement, and she raised her brows.

Blast. Was this a dare? *See-low! Take the pod to my boat, noses to the hull!*

The dolphins rushed to do as he ordered, pushing water into the boat, too. The deck rocked, and laughing, the boy fell into his father. Captain Allen careened against the rail and slid down onto his back.

He lay staring upward, so Salm gave him a hand up, only to have the man once more in his face.

Captain Allen pointed to the mast and, eyes bulging, shouted, "You cut my rigging! You owe me—"

"I'll replace it," Salm said quickly. "We've got the supplies in the boathouse for exactly these emergencies. You'll be good to go by midmorning tomorrow."

A rush of wind hit them. Captain Allen staggered, and in Salm's earpiece, William said, "Time to get them below."

Right, that gust wasn't by chance. "Hold tight," Salm said with exaggerated concern and grasped Captain Allen's arm, trying to direct him to the companionway.

But Captain Allen held his ground. The human had better sea legs than Salm had realized—if dolphins hadn't been slamming the hull. After sending his son below, Captain Allen began asking about the rescue boat and how they'd managed to tow his boat.

"Get off with any excuse you can," William said through the earpiece.

Luna had already debarked and, holding her laundry bag, was on the dock speaking with Pauly. It looked like they were saying goodbye. Indeed, Luna waved and then bent her head and walked down the dock.

I'm supposed to go, she sent him.

Well, he wasn't going to get Captain Allen below without an argument. "I've my own boat and dolphins to settle for the night," Salm said. "You'll sleep the rest of the night aboard your craft, I ken?"

At Captain Allen's blank look, Salm climbed the railing.

"See you in the morning," he called up from the dock, and because Captain Allen continued to watch him, he went aboard the rescue boat and got the bucket of fish from Maeve.

She looked a little sheepish. "I dinnae dare feed them without your permission."

Then why had she acted like…

"The great louse!" she exclaimed. "'Twould have been easier

to leave him stranded. Grumbling and not lifting a hand to help, on his own boat, too!"

Salm rubbed his forehead, not daring to speak or even look at her. In some way, Maeve must think she was supporting him, but it hadn't come off well. They fed his dolphins their oversize treats, shut things down for the night and went below. Then... they waited. Maeve and Pauly sprawled on the bunks they'd be using for the night, but Salm paced the tiny salon.

Had Luna gone to the shanty again? Or another one of the houses to make it look like she lived somewhere more decent? She'd done such a great job with the lad. Reviewing the entire performance, he swelled with pride—they made a brilliant team.

Finally, finally, William said, "They are both asleep!"

By the time Salm returned to the shanty, someone had returned Luna to Tern Bay, and the DMR's congratulations didn't make up for missing his chance to talk to her again.

FALLING INTO PLACE

With Maeve and Pauly cheerfully—and colorfully—pitching in to help, Salm's morning's work of replacing the rigging went smoothly.

The human captain surveyed their work, and at his grunt that they took for approval, they collected their equipment and debarked. William had instructed them to hurry things along, which Salm wholeheartedly agreed with. While Maeve carried their tools to the adjacent boat, Salm called, "You set to sail?"

Captain Allen's response was to winch up the anchor, so Pauly untied the boat's rope from the pier and threw it aboard, then they both bent to shove the hull.

Above them, Captain Allen leaned over the bow. "I still don't understand how I sailed this far off course," he growled. "There's something fishy going on in this backwater cove."

Orb take it—really? Captain Allen had never offered his thanks for their replacement of the rigging—free of charge—and now he was returning to this complaint? It took every ounce of Salm's control to evenly answer, "We're regular folks trying to help a fellow sailor."

Captain Allen snorted. "I've never had any boat repair go this smoothly. I'm a hundred miles off course. My kid insists you're angels. I blacked out for no reason. And this"—he waved toward the rundown buildings—"isn't a dolphin research facility. Marine wildlife are regulated. I'll be back to check this out."

Argh, what was he supposed to say to that? He couldn't invite humans back to a place that humans weren't supposed to be able to access.

"Wish him well," William said in his earpiece.

"Have a good trip," Pauly piped up. "We're off to pull in some dinner." She rolled her eyes at Salm as she turned on her heel and marched toward the fishing boat.

Aye, done. Giving a wave, Salm strode to the boat as well and jumped aboard seconds before Pauly cast it off.

Maeve smirked as he joined her to haul up the sheets. "You're being too nice again," she told him.

"And you were…efficient. Thanks for doing this on short notice."

She sniffed. "Your lass seems a decent sort, and 'twas far more entertaining than scraping your barnacles."

Salm laughed. Maybe he'd talk to Pop about putting in a word for the sisters. They were good workers in the right circumstances.

Salm and the sisters sailed out on the borrowed fishing boat and turned north. Captain Allen steered his boat south toward his original destination, Liverpool—which meant he'd once again pass through the Windborne waters held by Tern Bay and Giuthas. DMR was ready with extra magic to pereport the boat past the wizard town and had directed Salm to sail beyond the next headland so he wouldn't be in the humans' view when this happened.

They anchored offshore and waited. And waited.

When William finally pereported onto their boat, he looked glum. "Our shielding magic carried him beyond the enclave as smooth as we could have wished. But he stopped the boat. He knew something had changed, despite our seamless imaging of the coast. We had lookouts hidden on the shore who saw him comparing the terrain to a map."

Salm whipped off his cap and threw it to the deck. "Then he intends to make good on that threat."

William nodded. "We expect him to return. You've all done what you could, but this is one stubborn human. The problem runs deeper."

Heart sinking, Salm didn't have to ask. With the Isle of Giuthas' current shielding weaknesses, it was at risk, as was Tern Bay because of its close association. The DMR would meet with their councils for an assessment.

By midmorning, Salm had seen the dolphins back to the cove north of Tern Bay. Circling their frolicking forms one last time, he flew higher and ascended over Tern Bay's colorful houses dotting the cliffs above the crescent-shaped harbor. The moor spread out on one side of him, the sea to the other. On the horizon, the mountains rose on the Isle of Giuthas. His gut wrenched. This was home. These hidden pieces of land, this glorious stretch of sea with its rich life. He couldn't imagine not living here.

At the keeper's quarters, he found Luna admitting a queue of folks and pulled her into the kitchen against her protests.

"Captain Allen knows something is wrong here," he blurted and told her what had happened.

Her grip on his hand tightened, while her gaze shot to the window overlooking the coast to the south. "What will we do?"

"I..." He searched her face. He'd been ready to tell her that he had to get a boat—*any* boat—and be out on that water every day so he could watch for human boats. That waiting a year for her to decide... But Luna had remembered what he hadn't. "I'm glad you asked what *we* can do. I want to do this with you."

The front door opened. A man stuck his head in and spotted Luna. "Is it our turn yet?"

Salm wanted to talk about *them*, but Luna put him in charge of supervising the admission of the visitors. When she turned to go, he clasped her elbow, holding her just inside the front door. Their gazes met, but too many interested parties stood around them.

He had to risk thought-speaking. *Please. We need to talk.*

She looked everywhere but at him. *I have a break coming at noon.*

For an hour, he kept busy and his mind off of her. Then the door opened from the inside, and Nebula emerged. She poked him. "You're needed in the bird shed," she said, then stage-whispered, "Don't mess things up!"

He hustled over, careful to close the door behind him.

Luna straightened from inspecting one of the cages. "Even before we learned Captain Allen posed a threat, you were navigating us together by telling Papa everything! Salm, what were you thinking?"

He wrapped an arm around her waist and pulled her against him. "That I love you. That our magic is something I never want to be without. That I canna let you go." His lips met hers, and he ran his fingers up into her hair.

She pushed him back before he'd fully explored the kiss. "You're willing to get a smaller boat?"

"I'm willing to compromise if you are."

"I-I am. I want to come aboard *The Peaceful* with your family. I canna see how I've managed to grow up on the coast and have not applied my magic to sailing."

Salm put up a finger. "Pop won't teach you that right off."

"Will he let us share a cabin?" she asked teasingly and kissed his finger.

Hoy, did she mean... "Only if we bond. Are you saying—"

"I want to sort a few details with you!"

"Luna!" he cried in exasperation. "'Tis always the details! Do you love me or not?"

She opened the shag's cage and deftly removed the water dish without the bird escaping. She dumped and refilled it before saying, "I love you. You know I do. But—"

He rolled his eyes. Would she ever agree with no attachments behind it?

"—I have nae had this fight with my father for nothing. Or the fight with you."

"Or the fight with me," he agreed. "You canna let that die a quiet death in the ocean depths."

She side-glanced at him. "Are you laughing at me?"

"I'm trying not to. Won't the end result be the same, that you love me and we will work out a way to be together?"

She added salt to the water and stirred it. "You joke when I want seriousness. You sometimes…embarrass me."

"Like when this week?" he prompted.

She pursed her lips. "No incidents come to mind. You are getting better at discretion," she admitted.

"And I have come around about my boat. That is *huge* for a lifelong sailor."

Slowly, she smiled. "Aye, that is. You're putting my work before yours, but I can hardly believe you will stick to that."

He shrugged. "If I want to be with you, then I will. It's not a trick. Besides, our enclaves will need lookouts, which can be done while we sail for any reason. That we can work well together and merge magic is more wind in our sails."

Luna returned the dish to the cage, then grabbed a towel and wrapped the shag's head to capture him and inspect his stitches.

What could he say to convince her when they'd both already declared their love? "Lass, you are trying my patience despite me promising myself I could wait *forever*."

She met his gaze. "I don't want to wait forever. I've made progress by getting Papa to admit he needs help, but he doesn't have it yet, and a *promise* to stop drinking is difficult to keep if he still has the same burdens."

Aye, all of her problems didn't reside with him. "You have to keep an eye on him."

"I could still start training on *The Peaceful* if it was days at a time. Then I could keep working two days a week and make regular check-ins. If things seem to go awry..." She shrugged. "Is that a compromise you can agree to?"

Well, now seemed as good a time as any to admit he was under watch himself. "I, uh, have a bit of a probation myself. Pop will be monitoring my work until December, the end of this lobster season." He explained how he'd been blustered into not doing his complete inspections by a couple of crews, including Maeve and Pauly.

Luna rolled her eyes. "Then why the push to get me to agree?"

Salm rubbed his neck. "Your agreement to come onto *The Peaceful* for my parents' sailing training stood in the way, and...I wanted you on board. I miss you, Luna."

Her frown melted into a shake of her head. "I miss you, too. And after this week together..." She gave a sharp nod. "Then somehow we get my father settled so we can be."

"Bonded?"

Luna poked his chest. "You have a one-track mind."

Salm lifted his arms in a false gesture of helplessness. "I'm a fellow."

She wrapped her free arm around his waist and leaned against him. "Aye, I want to bond with you, but I still can't promise when."

"Finally," Salm breathed and captured her lips. As he kissed her soundly, the shag began to squawk within his towel.

As the day after the storm turned nice, the visitor numbers at the lighthouse swelled into a considerable line after new arrivals called back to friends in town to tell them that Salm of the Seas, the rescuer who'd used dolphins to save the doomed human boat, was there. He could have charged buckets of baitfish as entrance fees and given dolphin demonstrations. He'd just suggested an evening demonstration on North Dock to his line of tour-goers when Jonah exited through the kitchen door and walked over.

He nodded pleasantly to the visitors, but jerked his chin to Salm and led the way around the side of the quarters.

"Be back in a minute, folks," he said and followed Jonah. What now? Had he misread the keeper's attitude yesterday when he'd spoken with Luna and others present?

"Your father been sailing long?" Jonah asked.

"His whole life. My ma, too."

"That schooner ever inspected?"

Ah, this was about safety. "Per code that HIT keeps in alignment with human standards." When Jonah looked at him blankly, Salm added, "Every six months. All our Seas' crafts. It's an aboveboard fleet. My sh-boat will match those standards as well. I assure you, Luna will be as safe as anyone can be."

Jonah nodded. "You see to it, lad, or you drown with her." Jonah clapped him on the arm. "I will see to it."

"Aye, sir. I won't let anything happen to her." He swallowed. "If she agrees."

"I ken, *if* Luna agrees. Can you do nothing to hurry that lass along so I don't have to listen to these questions about her?"

"Sir? I think she put that in your hands. Hiring folks."

Jonah sighed and magicked two handwritten papers into his hand. "I've sent Stella to find the tape we misplaced during the cleaning. Can you place these at the door and in the stairwell so everyone can read them?"

He handed Salm the papers that read: *Seeking Lighthouse Keeper's apprentice. Inquire with Jonah.*

Salm grinned. "Aye, sir!"

At four, when the tours were to end, Salm cut off the line

and began turning folks away. "Tomorrow! Be here bright and early!" He caught Stella to guard the door while he circulated around the yard and asked folks to leave so the keepers could eat and prepare for the evening. One man sat out along the wall, watching a wizard leap off the cliff with arched wings and soar until the kid—teenager?—was blown back upon the point.

"Ahoy," Salm called and gave the man the closing information.

He smiled. "I'm here to see Luna. Wanted to wait for things to clear out. Could you tell her Rigel and River are here?"

The wizard was clearly a traveler, now that Salm took a moment to study him. The middle-aged, white-haired wizard wore a brown wool jacket over a cream waistcoat and wool trousers. An old canvas rucksack and a duffel bag sat near his feet. Curious, Salm reported—thought-speaking—to Luna.

She answered with a squeal. *Where?* In minutes, she was flinging herself at the man. "Uncle Rigel! I canna believe you came!"

"How are ye, lass?" he asked and pulled her into a hug. "I'm verra glad you wrote and even happier to see you up here. Didn't want to alert your father until I was sure you had a chance to tell him."

"I haven't, but I think he'll be happy to see you now." She turned a brilliant smile on Salm. "Could you—"

"I'm nae being anyone's errand boy without information."

"Salm, this is my mother's brother, Rigel, and that's my cousin, River. Rigel, this is Salm."

"Salm?" Her uncle let the question hang.

Salm looked at Luna.

She sighed, but smiled. "Salm of the Seas, my beau and maybe more, if you are here to help Papa."

Rigel held out his hand, and Salm shook it. "Pleased to meet you, Salm, Luna's beau."

When the visitors had cleared from the point, Luna asked, "Ready to talk to Papa?" with more bravado than she felt.

River paced along beside her, while her uncle and Salm chatted behind them. It had been the solstice since they'd exchanged news with Uncle Rigel and a year since they'd been inland to visit her mother's brother, but he looked the same.

Papa had come to the door to say goodbye to the last of the visitors who'd been at the top of the lighthouse when she'd run down to meet Rigel. With them out the back gate and on the path to town, no one else would be around to witness it if Papa blew up. Still, she twisted her hands together. It'd been brazen of her to ask their relatives to come stay at their home without Papa's knowledge.

Papa turned, his gaze passing right over River, who Luna wouldn't have recognized either in her mishmash of clothing—shorts over wool leggings and a striped sweater under a man's suit jacket decorated with an assortment of pins. But Papa's eyes widened when they landed on Rigel. Nebula and Stella had come to the doorway and were figuring it out as well.

"Rigel!" Papa hurried the few steps and extended his hand, then wrapped his brother-in-law in a hug. "This is a surprise. Has Fest brought you to the coast?"

"Papa?" Luna interjected. "I wrote to Uncle Rigel and asked if he'd consider coming to help us. Last summer, he said that he missed the stargazing he and Mam did as children with their keeper family. I figured since he'd reduced his business, he might have time to spend helping to keep the lighthouse."

Papa stilled, then turned a thunderstruck gaze upon her.

Luna met his look, all too aware that her chin had lifted. She hadn't planned to challenge him, and Papa had been coming around, but she hadn't known that days ago, when she'd sent the letter. Tense moments ticked by. Luna held her ground, even as Stella muttered, "Uh-oh."

Papa finally drew a breath and pivoted back to Uncle Rigel, extending his hand again. "Welcome. My lass has taken to arranging my affairs without my permission, but the quarters are clean and the guest room ready. We shall be happy to host you for Fest, and I suspect we can come to an arrangement over a pint—er, a good meal."

Uncle Rigel gave a slow nod. "The arrangements must include River, too. The lass and I have been 'round and 'round about her academy plans. She wishes to have a year off from studies. I wish for that year to be more than flying with friends and napping."

"Dad—"

"Have I mentioned that Luna's room is also available?" Papa interrupted. "Permanently, it seems."

Oh? A small stab of hurt coursed through her, but then Salm nudged the small of her back and trailed his hand down her arm. He wove his fingers into hers. *'Tis what you want.*

Uncle Rigel gestured toward Tern Bay. "I want River to take a look at your town. Perhaps a fishing town would offer new opportunities."

"Dad!" River snapped.

He winked at Jonah. "Sounds like we single fathers have some catching up to do."

"Do you like to fish?" Nebula asked River. "You don't look dressed for it."

True. Their cousin must be about seventeenth year now, but her city clothing style didn't fit outdoor pursuits. Or their enclave.

"Totally." River tapped one of her pins—a jumping bass—and gestured to her lapel, where several colorful fly-fishing lures hung on a swivel. "I love it. I fish every day in streams. Never tried in the ocean."

"How about birds? Do you like birds?" Nebula waved toward the gulls overhead.

Cousin River followed her gaze and wrinkled her nose. "Do they have enough meat on them?"

"What?" Stella asked, while Nebula spouted an insulted, "As *wildlife*, not food!"

"Never thought about it."

Stella sniffed. "You'll have to if you're staying with us. The keepers of Kittiwake Point are the wildlife rescue people."

Cousin River grinned. "I might be able to get into that, if it can extend to frogs. Frogs are my favorite animal." She tapped a second pin of a climbing frog with crystals on its back.

Stella wrinkled her nose. "People might think we're witches if we start keeping frogs, too."

"But we are," River answered with a roll of her eyes.

After a lot of catching up with her mother's relatives and a dinner-breakfast of eggs and potatoes, Luna finally excused herself and Salm. They flew down the cliffside to Tern Bay, the wind a mere breeze compared to yesterday.

Salm squeezed her fingers. *Come stay on the schooner with me tonight. My parents will be back tomorrow, so this might be the last time we can be together for weeks.*

But…in two weeks you'll be nineteenth year and won't need their permission to bond in our Scottish District.

Aye, but even with your uncle installed to help, I'm preparing for you to think of some other last-minute detail tha' prevents us from going to The Moors.

He was right. Papa wanted her to work until he could refresh Uncle Rigel in the upkeep and repair of their beacon's mechanics. Salm didn't like Keenan's studio as a place to live, and now she didn't even have home to fall back on. Not that she wanted that option anyway. She sighed. This was part of being her own person.

Look, Salm said. *I respect that you don't want to live on board* The Peaceful *full time. In a week, your uncle will have settled in. Tern Bay will have settled down. You said you'd start part-time sailing training. If we do well, in the spring my parents might be persuaded to let me get a sloop or a cutter and sail alongside them when you're able to. We'd have our own living space and berth that you could come and go from. Is it too strange to suggest that we go to The Moors and bond, but don't plan to live together right away?*

She side-glanced at him. *Aye.* As he stared in her direction, she licked her lips. *We must have* some *plan for after bonding. I still have a deposit on the studio at Keenan's. You don't like it, so I can look for another flat to rent after Fest. Just…this week and next are paid, and I don't wish to look during Fest. For tonight, I need my toothbrush and night things and—*

Salm spun her by the hand and kissed her in midair. They were both breathless when they broke apart—from flapping to stay airborne as much as from the kiss. She couldn't stop a grin from matching Salm's as they landed on the beach and then strolled along the deckwalk, Salm's arm around her shoulders. People stared, at least the ones who knew them. Others just smiled back.

At Lady Anemone's, she stopped him from pulling her into his arms again. "It'll be faster if you let me run in!"

With a last quick kiss, Salm let her go inside.

"Luna." Lady Anemone waved from the front room. "Come say hello to Pete. He has been waiting to share his bad news and his good news."

She groaned inwardly. What did Mr. Smith's news have to do with—oh! "The gutter repair you asked me to do. Of course I have it on the list. Can it wait until after Fest? I'm helping with tours up at the lighthouse. And Salm is waiting."

"We won't keep you long," Mr. Smith said. "There's more to

the repair that you may wish to share with him. Those young renters I had were rowdy enough that several of my neighbors complained. When I went over to tell them it couldn't continue, I discovered the place in a shambles."

Arms crossed, Lady Anemone leaned forward in a conspiratorial manner. "Completely trashed, as you young people would say."

"Indeed, trash everywhere, screen door hanging by a hinge, gutter off like they'd used it to swing from, and the roof slates don't look right. I've pressed for damages, and they are out. I'm in need of someone to clean the place and repair things, if you might be available?"

Luna nodded. So might she be able to—

"He also needs a stable renter," added Lady Anemone.

Mr. Smith lifted his hand that wasn't in the sling. "I had thought to just close the place up. I'm getting too old to deal with this nonsense. Anemone mentioned your bed here is quite temporary, and you said you'd like to rent the place."

"He's being kind. I insisted he offer it to you."

Blessed Orb, this might work out after all. Luna shot a grateful smile to Lady Anemone for understanding. But... She took a breath. "I am interested in renting it, but you have to know it's not just me. Salm of the Seas and I are...together." She couldn't announce a thing like bonding without telling their families first.

"I might have heard something about that going around town. The Seas are my cousins, which figured into this offer."

He eyed her, and Luna struggled to keep quiet.

"Not sure how handy he is with repairs," Mr. Smith continued. "Any work you do on the place that leads to a discount in rent, you'll have to work out with him yourself."

Luna grinned. "Aye, sir, we can manage that. And likely I won't be in residence full time, though I'd like to let the flat full time. I have an invitation from the Seas to spend time on their schooner learning to sail. 'Tis time I take them up on it."

Mr. Smith held out a key. "Then the place is yours."

She took it, turning the warm brass over in her fingers. *I can finally call a place my own.* "I can move in whenever I like?"

Lady Anemone laughed, and Mr. Smith joined in. "Whenever you have it clean enough to suit you," he said. "You did take the job to clean it as well."

She collected her few things into her laundry bag—the kittiwake had joined the other birds in their kennels this morning—and stuffed her coveralls into the top of her tool bag. Out front, she handed one bag to Salm.

He frowned. "I thought you were just staying the night."

"If you don't mind, I have to drop these off first."

"Sure. Where?"

She held up the key between them. "Our new flat at Mr. Smith's."

For the second time in ten minutes, their kiss left them breathless.

LETTING GO

Once the Autumnal Equinox Festival had ended and the successful lighthouse tours were over, Luna kept busy and held her breath. The first part wasn't difficult—Mr. Smith hadn't exaggerated the damage to his flat. While she cleaned and made repairs, Salm pitted his negotiation skills against traditional Windborne policies.

Salm spoke to his parents and convinced them that the Isle of Giuthas' year of prebonding didn't suit their hard-won and immediate plans. In a fortnight, he'd be free to go to the Scottish District office at The Moors of East Galloway on his own. The Seas agreed they'd rather welcome Luna into their family free and clear of public comment, as did Jonah Ness. For Windborne, applying for a bonding license was no more glamorous than filling out paperwork, but everyone wanted to witness them doing it.

Still, neither was twentieth year, which left them in a sticky situation with the council of Salm's home enclave. Salm met with the elders and proposed their energy tithing go to the isle. Then, they waited for a reply.

Nebs, Stella and River, as well as Manta and Piper, helped

Luna and Salm paint the flat at Mr. Smith's. It looked lovely, though it was spare with the few included furnishings. The last afternoon, when Papa came to collect Stella, he brought the Dobsonian telescope.

"It's just gathering dust," he said as Luna hugged him. "And the skies down here can be fairly decent, too. Or perhaps you'll want to track a ship on the horizon." He winked. "I was thinking, 'tis much easier to clean the quarters with less furniture in it. Have you use for a dresser or a cat-fur-covered armchair?"

Stella screeched, but Papa chuckled. "Maybe a few fish skulls? We've plenty to choose from. Nay? Then how about a lovely desk and chair to keep track of your business at?"

A laugh died in Luna's throat. "Are-are you offering me Mam's desk?"

Papa nodded. "Celeste would have loved to see you use it."

Choking back tears, Luna hugged him again.

When Salm and Piper returned with the gifted furniture and household things, Salm had a message from his father: Since the Isle of Giuthas enclave sorely needed additional energy to make repairs, the elders accepted their offer...as long as the couple became Giuthas residents.

Luna rolled her eyes. "Did no one know that we will keep a flat in Tern Bay?"

Salm tucked a curl behind her ear. "Our work with the habitat and wildlife is seen as more important. Plus, it doesn't hurt that we just rescued a boat from smashing against the shore," he said smugly, "and are needed to meet the DMR's requirements for concealing our enclaves from humans."

"Or that your father's work brings in a major portion of the isle's food."

"*My—our* work," Salm retorted.

Accepting the residency was the easiest plan. They sealed the decision with another kiss, an extra-long one to also compensate for Luna spending that night at the lighthouse. She said it was to pack her things, but really it was to spend time with her sisters. They shared Nebs' room, staying up late doing each other's hair and reading childhood books that had surfaced during the cleaning. River was dragged in, too, and they found that, despite the odd clothes, their cousin hadn't changed all that much. She still loved *The Tale of Mr. Jeremy Fisher*, a story that interestingly combined both frogs and fishing.

The next morning, the quarters' kitchen bustled with the sisters dancing around each other to make deviled eggs, potatoes and salad for a family brunch. The house smelled heavenly with the baked salmon that Salm had caught himself.

Voices in the yard sent Luna to the front door, and she sighed contentedly. These visitors were family. Hers and Salm's...soon to be both of theirs. Not all of them could make it, but Stella was getting her wish: She would see her sister bonded at a remote Scottish village, though it wasn't Gretna Green.

Salm joined Luna, giving her a quick one-armed hug before striding across the yard to take a basket of rolls from his mother.

Stella pushed past, but Luna caught her. "Go wake Papa and Uncle Rigel, please."

Salm's mother, Mer, kissed her cheek, then Manta pulled her into a tight hug, and Piper filed up, carrying a large tray upon which was a cake.

"Oh, Manta, for us?" Luna gasped at the beautiful decorations, including icing shells, dolphins and seabirds. "You've outdone yourself!"

"This day has finally come. We're prepared to celebrate!" she exclaimed.

Papa and Sir Dolph shook hands. Skipper raced around the yard, chasing Stella until Papa called her into the wildlife shed. Seconds later, Stella came running across the yard.

"Papa says with the fair weather and low tide, the rescue

birds should be released. I have dibs on letting Charlie go! Nebs, River! Come help!"

Papa snuggled each of the four birds in a towel and tucked them into flight satchels. He, Luna, Nebs and Stella clipped on the satchels' leather harnesses and gathered everyone to fly to the base of the cliff.

"Why aren't we releasing them from up here?" asked River, gesturing like she was throwing a ball.

Papa laughed. "Tossing them into the wind is the glamorous way most people would like to see it done," he said. "But the poor shag has been sitting too many days. Though he can stretch his wings in our kennel, 'tis nae the same as using them. His muscles might not be strong enough to battle our winds."

Down in a quiet cove at the back of the headland, Papa took out the European shag.

"The first injured bird I ever caught," Salm said as they watched.

"That's right." Luna put a hand on his arm. "You should have the honor of releasing him. Stella—"

"No, let the lass." Salm ran a hand over the trace of a new beard on his jaw. "But do you think I can say goodbye?"

They each took a turn smoothing the iridescent green feathers, then Papa put the shag into Stella's hands, his beak facing away from her face, and prepared to remove the towel. "When I let go, you set him at the edge of the sea and promptly back away. You don't want your nose bitten like Salm's finger."

The smile slid from Stella's face. "I, uh, Papa?"

"A little heavy for you?"

Stella pushed the shag back at him. "Aye. Salm should do it. He caught Charlie."

Luna laughed. "Careful, Salm. I don't want your nose looking bitten when we go to The Moors office!"

Salm held the bird at arm's length and did exactly as he was told, gently placing the bird on the damp sand where he could adjust to his surroundings. After a minute, the shag flew-walked into the surf and paddled out beyond the low waves where he bobbed as he rested.

A little farther down the beach, Stella released another kittiwake they'd had for a week—the one Luna had cared for the night of the storm had gone a few days ago—and Nebs and River released the pair of cormorants together. As everyone watched the birds float and preen their feathers, a flock of kittiwakes rose from the cliff face.

They circled the cove several times, collecting more gulls on each round.

"Looks like they're ready to migrate," Luna said.

Then one gull broke from the group and angled directly for them. Luna put out her hands and caught Rissa. "Oh, baby," she whispered, tears already flowing down her cheeks. "Is this goodbye?"

The gull rubbed his head against her neck, and she held him tight, stroking his silky back feathers. Then she lifted him, kissed the crown of his head, said, "Come back when you can," and tossed him upward.

As Salm's arm wrapped her shoulders, Rissa circled them, gave a sharp cry and flapped up to join the others. They watched the flock head westward until their motion melded with the horizon's clouds.

"Your bird is off on new adventures," Salm said softly.

Luna wiped her tears and smiled at him. "It's time for me to do the same."

ABOUT THE AUTHOR

Before kids, Laurel Wanrow studied and worked as a naturalist —someone who leads wildflower walks and answers calls about the snake that wandered into your garage. During a stint of homeschooling, she turned her writing skills to fiction to share her love of the land, magical characters and fantastical settings.

She's the author of *The Luminated Threads* series, a Victorian historical fantasy mixing witches, shapeshifters and a sweet romance in a secret corner of England, and *The Windborne*, a nature-focused YA fantasy series set in our world.

When not living in her fantasy worlds, Laurel camps, hunts fossils, and argues with her husband and two new adult kids over whose turn it is to clean house. Though they live on the East Coast, a cherished family cabin in the Colorado Rockies holds Laurel's heart.

Visit her website at www.laurelwanrow.com.

facebook.com/laurelwanrowauthor

twitter.com/laurelwanrow

instagram.com/laurelwanrowauthor

bookbub.com/authors/laurel-wanrow

pinterest.com/laurelwanrow

www.ingramcontent.com/pod-product-compliance
Lightning Source LLC
Chambersburg PA
CBHW030653190726
48286CB00008B/2798